Follow You DOWN

book #1 of farfalla

ted persinger

Follow You Down
Book I of *Farfalla*

Published by Ted Persinger

2014 Edition

ISBN 13: 978-0-9862521-0-5
ISBN 10: 0986252107

Editing: Lisa Aurello

Formatting: Mayhem Cover Creations

Cover Design: Melissa Ringuette

Disclaimer :
This is a dark, erotic romance, and is intended for mature audiences. This novel is a work of fiction, and contains strong sexual situations, explored in graphic detail. Read at your own risk.

DEDICATION

I dedicate this novel to two amazing women to whom I owe so much:
Aleatha Romig, whose kindness, caring, and mentoring show that she is
much more than just an amazing writer, but she is definitely that, and
Cassandra Dixon-Houston, who set me on the path of writing, cares
about what I have to say, and inspires me every day.
Ladies, thanks are not enough, but they are all I have.

TABLE OF CONTENTS

Foreword...
Part I: Abstraction..
1..
2..
3..
4..
5..
6..
Part II: Lepidoptera...
7..
8..
9..
10..
11..
12..
13..
14..
15..
Part III: Transfiguration......................................
16..
17..
18..
19..
20..
21..
22..
23..
24..
25..
26..

Part IV: Chrysalis……………………………..…

27…………………………………………………..

28…………………………………………………..

29…………………………………………………..

30……………………………………………..………

31…………………………………………………..

Part V: Imago…………………………………

32………………………………………………..…

33…………………………………………..………

34…………………………………………………

35…………………………………………………..

FOREWORD

So why an erotic romance? A dark one at that? From a bi-racial female's point of view? How did I get here?

Well, two things came together for me to write this, my second novel. First, I was talking to a friend about my first novel, *The One Way*. She asked me if Danny Shields, the protagonist, was auto-biographical. I hadn't thought of it directly, though I knew as I had written that I had inserted a lot of things that were unique to my life, even though Danny was actually inspired by a couple of people I knew in Bangkok. Still, it had me thinking about whether I would always be doomed to write as myself, and all my characters would end up looking like me.

I'd heard that painters and sculptors always put a bit of themselves in each person they paint. Some have pointed out similar features of the *Mona Lisa*'s demure smiling face and Leonardo's own countenance. The noses are the same. The mouths are the same. She is Leonardo in a dress, some would argue. He therefore painted his own image, and simply feminized himself. In that sense, would I always be looking at my own mug as I stared into the *faces* of my characters? Would all my characters just be me in other clothes? Am I Rockwell looking into a mirror and painting the mirror?

My second inspiration was a waiting room, where I sat for an appointment. On the table next to me was a cheesy, worn romance novel, complete with a bodice-ripping cover. You know the type: tanned Fabio in pirate costume with rippling abs, and the delicate flower looking constipated as she runs her delicate hands across his manly muscles. I was bored, so I flipped through a few pages. It was horrible. Simply horrible. I had one of those, *I should write one of these!* moments, even though I don't remember ever really reading a single romance novel. Arrogant? Perhaps. Okay…definitely!

So I set about to do two things: write in a genre in which I had no knowledge or experience, and write a character who was as far from me as I could make. It was a writing assignment I never thought I would do anything with. I would just write as exercise to develop my chops. I'd write about fifty pages, toss it, and be done with it.

The romance part took me thinking a bit, though. The point of romance novels, after all, is the struggle for the relationship. The *lovers* have to be ripped apart by some insurmountable obstacle or immovable force. They have to fight to be together. So, then, how to make a man and a woman *struggle*? Well, being me, I had to take an unconventional approach. In the classic romance, it's life circumstances that often force the two lovers apart. Wars. Evil-doers. Family ties. Consider Romeo and Juliet being torn apart by rival families; *Two households, both alike in dignity*…it had all been done before. I didn't want to write just another Fabio-covered romance. I wanted something different. But how?

Well, what about the characters themselves? What if it was their own flaws that put the obstacles in their way? What if it was they themselves creating the struggle? What if these were character traits they could not change? It started with creating my protagonist and her lover.

For the lead character, I decided to make this person the opposite of me. I'm a male, so I wrote as a female. I'm a single-race, so I made her bi-racial. I'm from California, so I made her from New York. I waited until later in life to write, but young Rachel gets to it rather quickly. Everything about her had to be somehow different or opposite from me. Yet, I found myself writing with some commonalities, some that I just didn't notice at the time. For example, I made her a teacher, which is a profession I have held. I put her in the 1970s, which is the era I grew up in (though I put her a few years earlier, as I wanted to explore that decade more). I made her a writer, and, well…working on that.

But what started as a simple writing exercise has changed into something unique, I think. My plan to stop about fifty pages in went away. I couldn't wait to find out what my characters did next. The more I wrote about Rachel and her friends, the more I wanted to know and understand.

And now I do love Miss Rachel. She's my new favorite character. She is so many things I am not, yet I identify with her struggle. As much as I tried to make her the Opposite Ted, she very much reflects me. She struggles with her identity. She is torn between a need for normalcy and a desire to explore. She wants the house with the white picket fence, but finds herself roaming the darker side of life. Yet, she's also immensely different. I guess it's similar to seeing a photo negative of yourself. You see the familiar outline, but all the shades are different.

So, then, I guess I am staring at another semi-autobiographical character. Maybe, after all, we're all doomed to model our creative works after ourselves, or at least some aspect of our lives. I guess I will always *write where I live*, as the old axiom says. While my novel is definitely not a da Vinci, it's the best art I can create, and it comes from the heart.

And I feel that I am getting better as a writer. I'm working on a follow up to *The One Way*, and I feel so much better equipped to take on the challenges of writing. That is, I'm a better writer than I was just a year ago. I hope you'll agree.

Thank you for taking this journey with me, and I do hope you enjoy it. Find me online and tell me what you think!

Ted Persinger

December 20, 2014

Part I : Abstraction

"We have to continually be jumping off cliffs and developing
our wings on the way down."
~Kurt Vonnegut

I'm old now, but I was young once.

To this very day, I remember the first time I saw him. It sounds corny, of course, to say my heart skipped a beat. But it did. Several. I do believe in love at first sight…it has happened to me a few times in my life. But this was the first, and the first is always special. He set my soul on fire instantly. I would've done anything he wanted…and I guess I did.

Rachel Walker, I'd like you to meet David Wright. I still tremble when I remember those words. That day changed me forever.

I was in my third year teaching sweet little fifth graders at IS10, now Horace Greeley Intermediate. I was living in Queens with my father, still not making enough to live on my own in New York. It was 1979. Jimmy Carter was president. The economy was struggling and the future looked bleak. They called it stagflation. Having a job was an accomplishment that year, and I tried to keep that in mind. I had seen President Nixon resign while I was in college. Now, a recent graduate of Columbia, I was teaching in an economy that made many of us think the

US was soon to fail.

There weren't many options for young women in those days. Teachers, nurses, secretaries, and mothers…that's what most of us did. There weren't many role models in those days. My mother had only been a wife and mother, and little girls played with dolls, practicing to be mothers. But I knew I wasn't living up to my potential. My best friend at Columbia, Clarice, told me she was only in school working on her "MRS Degree." It worked: she met her husband, Mike, in our final year, and they already had a child and a mortgage together.

I had not met a husband. I felt that life held more for me, but I was also not as popular as Clarice. She was a pretty white girl from Albany. Even in New York, I was an oddity at this time. I am biracial: my black father met my white English mother at the end of World War II, while he was serving as a quartermaster in the Army in the Midlands of England. They moved to Queens in the early 50s, where my family was rejected.

Whites completely avoided us, and white men viewed my father with anger. He had, after all, stolen a poor white flower and tainted her with black seed. She was not only white, but also properly British. He was the worst of *them*—he didn't know his place and didn't stick to his kind.

But it was no better in the black community. My father was viewed as a traitor for not being with a black woman…like he wasn't black at all. Black women were angry that he had passed them by. Black men viewed him as not fully black, though many were curious about tasting the *forbidden fruit*. How could you trust a brother who didn't want a black woman? He wasn't one of them. He wouldn't back the black community in a pinch, they felt. At this time, many still spoke of revolution.

Can one person really change you forever? Or does that one person simply unlock what was inside you all along?

I was neither white nor black. My features belonged to neither side. How sad that there were sides that I didn't belong to. My skin was light, more Hispanic-looking than black. My nose was higher, and much closer to my mother's. My hair was thick, curly, and grew long down my back. I was painfully skinny growing up, not developing curves until I was nearly out of high school. I felt tall and gangly and awkward, and I was invisible to boys for most of secondary school.

Our section of Queens was mostly black, and black girls wanted nothing to do with me. The teasing was incessant. The comments were continuous. The cold shoulders were everywhere. I was called *yellah* and *lightey.* Girls can be very cruel to each other, and I felt lost. Despite being from two worlds I was accepted in neither. Adding to my alienation, I had lost my mother early; I had no role model to teach me things a woman needs to know. My father loved me and tried his best to help me grow, but he never knew the tears I shed. It took me years to learn many of the things young girls learn from their mothers.

Culturally, though, I had no choice in far too many ways. There was the "single drop of blood" rule: though I was half-white, I was black. Besides, my mother would've been my bridge into the white citizenry, and she left me before I could connect. Consequently, I was forced into the black community, though they didn't make me welcome.

We weren't African-Americans then. We were fighting to be called black, and still kindly asking people to stop calling us Negroes. Once when I was walking to school, a cute little boy called me a coon. I didn't even know what that meant, and had to ask my father. As much as he could, he had tried to shelter me from the ugliness of the world. I felt disconnected from the Black Power Movement. I didn't listen to Marvin Gaye or James Brown. I didn't pick my hair into an Afro, and anyway it wouldn't have stood up no matter how short. I was living in Queens, not in Selma, so I was definitely removed from the struggle and didn't feel it impacted my life. Yet when I looked at positions of power around the country, from CEOs to senators to book publishers, I saw only white faces. Did the world have a place for someone like me? I wasn't sure.

His eyes...his charcoal-black eyes...the eyes of a predator...

Feminism was also going through many changes at this time. We heard "Our Bodies, Ourselves." We were claiming the right to our own anatomy, which seems odd now but was critical then. Women had shrugged off the free love of the sixties...what would a woman gain from giving away her assets to any man who wanted them? We wanted choice over our reproduction, but we also craved traditional families. We wanted to be our unique selves, but were still tied to worrisome concepts of our gender. Could a woman lead a unique life and still be a mother and wife? Our feminine culture was evolving, but without my mother to help guide me, I often felt like a member of the audience instead of a participant.

With all the confusion and fighting in our country, I had retreated into books. When my mother died, they gave me solace, and became my truest and most reliable friends. I read everything. I lived in books! But I didn't just take in: I also wrote stories and poems, both informed by my distance and longing, my inclusion and exclusion from all that went on in the country. I colored my world with imagination...

...and fueled it with a drive to succeed. I worked hard in high school, harder than anybody I knew. Some girls viewed me with even more suspicion as a result. I was a sellout. "She's trying to be a white girl!" "She's an *Aunt* Tom!" I would hear them hiss as I walked by. If a black young man were interested in me, I would suffer the wrath of every black girl in the school. Even speaking to an interesting young man brought sharp glares and sneers from the girls in my class. I avoided that pain as much as I could, though not completely.

What is change, after all? We're not caterpillars metamorphosing into butterflies, are we? Our changes are less than that...small course corrections, right?

Those of us who were good in school banded together, and we rode out the storm of anger, spite, and distance as best we could. These few awkward, geeky girls gave me my only sense of belonging...my only circle of friends...my only feelings of self. We didn't play sports. We didn't go to parties. We didn't date the hot guys. We studied. Only other unloved, awkward girls were my friends, and we all shared the same solitude and exclusion together. We didn't go to proms (or even get asked). We didn't go to homecoming games. While others spent weekends at parties, we spent the weekends writing poetry, or studying together, and sometimes crying together. We lost our virginities unromantically, more to just get it out of the way. High school for us was Dickens' "worst of times."

And while we all worked hard, I worked harder...and excelled. I

4

was the top student in my high school, and earned a full scholarship to Columbia. My father cried when I received my acceptance letter. I had never seen him show much emotion at all. He hardly ever laughed—maybe a smile if he was in a good mood. He was a serious man from a serious generation. He had seen things that had made him as hard as iron. When I saw those tears, I finally realized how much my education meant to him. As their only child, I was the focus of all my parents' energy. When my mother died, I was all my father had in the world. I guess that's something I didn't realize until later.

My father had survived the Great Depression. Fought the Nazis. Battled prejudice at home and abroad. Built a small distribution business when nobody wanted to do business with a black man. When his wife died, he raised his only child and gave me everything he had, even if he didn't understand the things a young girl experiences growing up. He fought through every challenge in his life. He was my entire world.

His generation had a strength no generation has had since. He had never had the opportunity to attend college; he had worked since he was twelve, helping support his family. He had enlisted in the Army as soon as the war broke out, fighting for rights he wasn't allowed to enjoy himself. Nothing ever came easy to him, and he bore the physical and emotional scars to prove it.

I hadn't realized college meant that much to him…he had never told me…but his tears told me everything. Seeing my hero, my pillar of strength, break down and cry made me want to put everything into my education.

I had only memories of my mother. She had left her home country, and had few friends in Queens. She was quiet and kept to herself. Though she rarely spoke of it, I was astute enough to know she suffered rejection in her hometown of Birmingham. She had married, God forbid, a dark-skinned black man, at a time when men who looked like him were janitors and bus drivers. Most of her family back home wanted nothing to do with her, though I didn't find this out until much later, and it was a painful lesson. My memories of my mother were of a quiet, somewhat dour woman.

Does the butterfly remember its life as a caterpillar? Does it think, "That was me then, and this is me now"?

Before my mother died, my parents had shown me how to build a world in which you could live and find satisfaction without the acceptance or approval of your community. All they needed was each other…and me. Every holiday and life event we shared together…within the circle of the three of us. Our photo albums were filled with pictures of just us. We camped, hiked, and went for weekend drives…just the three of us. While I boiled in the hot waters of my problems, my parents modeled a steely resolve and drive to succeed, and an unblinking focus on our family unit. It would serve me well through my life, as rarely have I ever fit in in the traditional sense. Instead, I learned to be an island… and let the waves of judgment wash onto my shores, then wash back out.

I also learned to hold tight to my relationships, which wasn't always the best thing I could do.

Everything good in my life had flowed through my family, so I didn't dare let my father down. At Columbia, I worked harder than I ever thought I could. I read everything. I joined clubs and helped out with research. I edited and published the annual poetry magazine for the school. I was recognized by several professors, earned honors in all my work, and graduated *magna cum laude* from Columbia. Mine was one of just a few non-white faces on the platform that day. When I stood on that stage, I could see my father weeping and clapping and shouting for me. I would only see my father cry one more time in my life.

What would the butterfly tell caterpillars, if it could? Would it say, "Change is good, but there'll be some pain involved in it." Or would it simply flit away, and let each learn the hard lessons individually?

Whenever I heard my father speak of me, the first thing he told anybody who would listen was, "My baby girl is a *magna cum laude* graduate of Columbia." He would never mention that it was just English, or that it had only resulted in my being a teacher, as if I had graduated from a SUNY school. To him, I think, I was the embodiment of all he had worked and struggled for. He continued to believe in America because he could see his mixed-race daughter go to the same school as rich white people…and achieve there.

But *I* was frustrated.

I felt like I was meant to do something in life, but I didn't know what. I didn't have blonde hair and blue eyes, so I wouldn't get many chances in the bustling entertainment industry in the Big Apple. My lack of a business major kept me from much of the industry on the Eastern Seaboard. I didn't understand politics, and couldn't tell a senator from a councilman, so government was out. In fact, I had succeeded in garnering the least profitable degree at Columbia—English for God's sake! What was there to do with that degree? Teach and write, that's it.

And aren't all English teachers merely frustrated and unpublished writers? I know I was.

My true passion and love was poetry, though I also wrote short stories. I had written poems since middle school, and poetry was my voice. It allowed me to put my feelings into art. I could shout at the injustices of the world. I could scream at the ignorance and hate I saw. I could imagine a better world, and let my poetry show the path I felt we needed to follow. To a powerless girl, poetry was like a gleaming sword.

I had written enough to gain notice for my writing in Columbia's rigorous English program. Though I collected poems from the entire campus, nearly a third of the poems in our annual poetry collection were from me. I often used pseudonyms to disguise my work, so that others wouldn't think I edited and published this collection to lionize myself.

Do caterpillars look at butterflies with green-eyed envy? Do they shout out, "Someday I'm going to be one of you!"? Or are they oblivious to the change within them?

But by the time I had graduated, none of my work had made it off campus. I had received wonderful rejections from publishers and agents around New York, and even as far away as LA. They were kind and complimentary: "You have a strong, passionate voice..." or "You have the makings of a great poet..." or "Your work is so compelling!" but those compliments were always followed by, "Your work isn't what we're looking for right now."

I guess I took teaching as a temporary job, hoping I'd be published within the first year or so. Surely, I thought, I'd get noticed right away, sign a multi-book deal, and then I'd live in a balcony apartment in the San Remo and listen to the whisperings of my muse. With all the time off teachers get, I'd have lots of time to write. Teachers only work eight months out of the year, right? That would leave me four months to create. To battle with my heart and mind. To wrestle my spirit, and extract from her every word the gods would share.

Little did I know how exhausting teaching is.

Chasing around ten-year-olds takes everything you have. I would come home exhausted, barely able to reach my bed before collapsing. I'd spend my weekends lesson-planning and grading. Breaks were spent catching up gradebooks. Summer vacations were punctuated with faculty meetings, curriculum changes, pamphlets and information to parents, and perhaps a couple of weeks of downtime to recharge on the Jersey Shore. I felt I was lost for the first time in my life. Probably most twenty-four-year-olds feel that way to some degree. After having a clear path from birth through college graduation, I now found myself wondering who I was and what I would do. How would I write a great novel or poetry collection when I spent weekends grading the work of under-performing ten-year-olds? Is this all there was to life?

I was about to emerge a new woman. A butterfly? Well, compared to the caterpillar I had been I'd say yes. You be the judge. I'm not everybody's favorite butterfly, I imagine.

I was very happy when I received a party invitation from my favorite professor from Columbia. Dr. Frank taught Shakespeare and British literature. I took every class he offered. He was a beautiful man in every sense of that word. I had felt an oddity, and I knew he understood me. Very few men were openly gay in those days, even at Columbia. Most professors felt stiff and distant, formal like a tuxedo. Dr. Frank, though, was open and warm. He was a kindred spirit...he loved words, and his passion for them shone through his teaching. He was gentle and kind, and helped me take emotional chances in my writing and analysis. I loved him instantly, and we stayed close through the years. He was one of only a few people I trusted and loved.

Dr. Frank and his partner, Dr. Bill, also a professor at Columbia, held wonderful parties at their Upper West Side home. Though their apartment was small, stuffy, and had too many cats, they were always sure to invite the most interesting people to their soirees. Their network of friends included writers, photographers, musicians, and intellectuals. This was my third one, and I was so excited. Now that I was an alum, I had become even closer to Dr. Frank, and he was always quick with supportive words and praise for my work. He encouraged me to create, and scolded me when I wasn't writing, which was often these days.

At this party, I wished I had a novel or fresh poetry collection I could pitch, as there was always at least one literary agent at these events. Frank and Bill knew everybody in the big city. Alas, I hadn't written more than a few lines of verse since graduation. Plus, I was uncomfortably shy in social circles, and could rarely talk about my work. Instead, I usually clung to my gentle hosts, and when the evening was over I would feel more depressed than ever. How would I ever get a break if I couldn't earn that break when the opportunities presented themselves?

I was standing right next to Dr. Bill when *he* approached.

He was just a little taller than everybody else around. Shoulders a bit broader. While other men were dressed in sport coats and slacks, he was wearing a black turtleneck and jeans. A beatnik without the horrible goatee. Tanned. Gleaming smile. His movements were sleek...he had the gait of a cat...confident, balanced, cool. When I saw him, my eyes blocked out the rest of the world.

I'm sure every woman has been there. At some point in her life, every woman has seen a man that made others seem small and insignificant. I was dating someone off and on, but when I saw David, Darnell was the furthest thing from my mind. David had what I can only describe as a presence. He was like a sun among the planets...he burned brightly and beautifully, but staring at him too long could hurt. Others were drawn to his gravity, especially me. I was about to find that out right away, as he was moving toward me.

"Rachel Walker, I'd like you to meet David Wright. David is a travel writer, freelancing some, though I think you're under contract with *National Geographic,* right, David?" Dr. Bill was so relaxed, but I was clenched tight, looking up like a frightened rabbit. It felt like my tongue was glued to the top of my mouth.

"Yes. Hi, Rachel. Nice to meet you." Time slowed. His rough, warm hand took mine. His voice was deep and earthy. His eyes were dark...deeply dark and deeply set, like chips of coal set into a craggy mountain. He smelled of outdoors, like wind in a valley. His smile was like a flash of lightning across a desert sky. I had never seen a man so beautiful in my life.

"Hi...yes...nice to meet you." My cool veneer was shattered. I had practiced so hard to greet people, look them in the eye, smile confidently, and say my shtick. That was gone, and my eyes were looking away from his. I knew those eyes would see right through me. No façade would blind those eyes. I couldn't meet them with my own. All my pretense, obliterated.

"Frank tells me you've written some great short pieces and poems, and that your style is crisp."

"Thanks." *He heard about my writing? Dr. Frank told him?* I wanted to run...he knew about me, but I knew nothing about him. He was still holding my hand, and I could feel my palms getting sweaty. God, his hand was so warm...and rugged...gentle but strong. I finally pulled it away. I still could only peek up at him, and then look away. Broad shoulders, casting a shadow over me. Tousled black hair all over the place. He had a weather-beaten look, like he had just come in from the rain. He needed a shave.

But his eyes. They were the eyes of a hawk. Sharp. Watching. He could see everything with those eyes, including my awkwardness.

Dr. Bill continued, "How about your own book, David?"

He regarded me for a second longer, and then turned to Dr. Bill. "Well, if you'd like a copy, I'll gladly give you one. That would double my sales for the month." He let out a coarse laugh, and then turned his eyes back to me. I had been watching him from the corner of my eyes, but then stared at the carpet again when he looked back. "How about you, Rachel? Are you writing anything?"

"No, not right now." Oh God, I wanted to tell him more. I wanted to sound bright and engaged! *No, I haven't yet gotten published, though I have a lot of work I've collected through the years. Would you like to take a look?* Instead, I just stared at the carpet.

"Well, nice to meet you," he said to me, and then to Bill, "talk to you guys in a bit." And then he turned and was introduced to someone else. I exhaled the breath I had been holding since he had taken my hand.

I have to admit, I was actually glad when he turned. I had lost the ability to form words, and I was just feeling stupid standing there. When he left, I could breathe freely again. But his forceful presence left a void, a black hole where he had just been. I had never met a man like him. While I met many cultured intellectuals in New York, especially at these parties, I hadn't met someone of his type. I'd met writers, publicists, artists, and even television news anchors. I had met some gorgeous men, whose drive for art and literature inspired me. They were beautiful in a "city" way. Up on politics. Well-spoken. Knew everybody. Connected. Lean in an artistic way. Scruffy beards. Uneven, grown-out hairstyles. Most of the men I found *really* attractive were gay. Like Dr. Frank. I had fallen in love with him during his first lecture on *As You Like It*. His smile was bright, and his eyes were open. He was slim and handsome and nice.

Though I had only shaken hands with him, I knew David was different. I knew he was not going to be a thoughtful, head-in-the-sky intellectual. His leanness was from being outside, from fighting nature. His hand was warm and rough, as if he had just been chopping wood, and his grip was firm but gentle. He leaned forward toward me, displaying none of the subterfuge or affectations of a city man. His skin was burned from the sun and chafed by the elements. There was something primal about his energy—a wolf among golden retrievers, a lion that escaped from its handlers. He had a natural force that only he himself could contain.

But I was just teaching fifth graders. Sweet as they were, I rarely found myself intellectually stimulated. I worked hard, but my job wasn't pushing my mind or my art. I wasn't fully engaged as I had been in college. All around me that night were people who were at least using their full faculties, and I suddenly felt so small in that room. Perhaps I should have circulated…used the mind I knew I had and engaged people with my insights into literature and politics. Baldwin. Chaucer. Faulkner. I was well-read and sharp…I could've held my own with any of these people.

And yet in that small, busy apartment I found my eyes wandering over to David. As I met other people and shook other hands, my eyes searched for him. My gaze found his shoulders over the shoulders of others. I saw his mop of unkempt hair through the other heads. I heard his deep voice above the din of others. And every time I saw him I felt my stomach jump. I felt a tingle down my spine. Oh, I had it bad, I knew. And, worse, my concentration was shot. Instead of meeting professional people and working the room, I was trying to stand where I could see him, or finding myself distracted by his proximity. The cool veneer I had cultivated so well was gone. I was an insecure little girl fumbling every meeting.

Disaster. I gave up.

I poured myself a double screwdriver in the kitchen and walked out to the narrow balcony. It was a cool spring evening in the city. From their balcony I could just see the edge of Central Park. I stood there, cussing at myself, drinking my too-strong drink. Wasted evening. Wasted opportunity. I didn't have fun and I didn't make any connections. Instead, I was a giggly schoolgirl checking out a guy I shook hands with. *It was his fault.*

Maybe I was just going to be a teacher forever.

"Mind if I join you out here?" I knew it was him before I looked over my shoulder. Now my heart was in full flight. I could hear my heartbeat in my ears, and it was galloping!

"Sure, no problem." I tried to play it cool, but was sure he saw that I wasn't.

"Tired of the party?" He had moved next to me, and was looking out over the same cityscape. The balcony was small enough that we were assured nearness. I didn't look at him, and continued to stare out to Central Park.

"Just wanted some fresh air."

"You can just see the park from here." He was looking out.

"Yes, I love their view. Such a great city."

"Yeah." His answer sounded unconvincing.

"You don't like the city?"

"In measured doses. It's great to spend time here…New York has it *all,* and then some. But I'm tired of it after a couple of weeks and need to travel."

"Where are you from, David?" I was trying to fill the quiet with chatter.

"New York." He gave a light chuckle. "The Village, originally. Now just across the park."

"Oh? But you don't like it?"

"It's great to be home. Great to see family. Great to visit with friends. But I want to be back out, exploring. Taking pictures. Writing. I'm already getting the itch."

"Where's your next adventure?"

"Tanzania. Soon."

Damn! He's already leaving. "Tanzania? Wow. What will you be doing there?"

"A piece for *Nat Geo*. Gonna spend a week on safari. Lions. Zebras. That kinda stuff. Also going to see if I can meet with some of the local tribes around Mount Kilimanjaro. Get some campfire dance shots. It's part of a larger piece. A few of us are working on it. We're including maps, herd migrations…gonna be big. I leave in a week."

A week. "That sounds so exciting." It truly did. Mt Kilimanjaro. *The Snows of Kilimanjaro* was one of Hemingway's best. Of course, I thought a walk through Central Park was pretty exotic. It thrilled me to think of him out among the lions…a predator among predators.

"So what about you? Frank mentioned you're not writing much right now."

"I'm teaching. I just graduated a couple of years ago, and I took teaching as something to do while I sort out what I want to write." I knew I was lying, and I hate to admit I was embarrassed about having not written. *Yeah, I'm a failure…all my promise and potential is spent teaching kids to craft a paragraph.*

"Is there a specific genre of writing you're most interested in?"

"Well, I've always enjoyed poetry the most of all, but poets usually starve, especially in this town. I've written lots of short stories as well, but nothing has been published yet." *Do you need to be so honest, Rachel?*

"The most important lesson I've learned over the last couple of years is that money isn't as important as doing what you want. I'd rather be hungry and doing what I love than unhappy and successful."

"Yeah, you're right…I should…I need to get back to writing, that's for sure."

"So why don't you?"

"Write?"

"Yeah."

"Well, I gotta pay the bills. Trying to save for a mortgage. I have written a bit, but just can't devote as much time as I should." It was weird that I was telling a stranger so much. I was not the type of person to open up to people I didn't know.

"Why not?"

"Well…teaching takes more out of me than I thought."

"Energy, you mean?"

"Yeah. Those kids run me ragged sometimes. I think I'll need to find different work if I want to write more, you know?"

"I do. Sometimes you have to take a leap, and just assume you can succeed. There's no shame in trying and failing. You could always go back to teaching later. A blind leap isn't always a bad thing." He smiled…perfect white teeth.

I remember being amazed at this moment. Inside I was trembling…nerve endings on overdrive. Yet his natural calmness and confidence had me talking with him. My heart was moving fast, but I felt a certain stillness at the same time. It's hard to explain, I think, unless you've been there. I was purposely avoiding eye contact, though, and looking out to the city. And sipping my drink. Maybe the drink made the difference.

"What type of poetry do you write?"

"Well, my poems tend to reflect what I see as some of the ills the US is going through. I think our country is in a slump right now, and it seems many of us can't get moving…we're stuck. Maybe we're at a crossroads. Don't know. I also try to focus on eternal themes, like peace and happiness. And justice. I like poems to mean something, and not be just decorations. Poetry should be…dangerous."

"I think it's great that your work stands for something." He had turned his shoulders and was looking at my profile. I couldn't quite turn my head to return his gaze. "Are you from New York?" I was glad he changed the subject.

"Queens. I live with my father." *Crap…why did I mention that?*

"Ah, and do you teach there also?"

"Yeah…it's home. But I love it here in Manhattan. If I can break away from teaching, I'd like to move here."

"So do you mind if I ask? What's your heritage?"

"You mean my race?"

"Yeah, I guess."

I paused and considered the question. If it was somebody else, I might've been offended. "My dad is black…from Atlanta originally… and my mom was British."

"Where in Britain was she from?"

"Birmingham."

"Ah, a Brummie! I've been there. Tough city…hardworking, blue collar. Kinda like the Bronx."

"I've never been there—to Birmingham."

"No?"

"No. My mother was pregnant with me when my parents came back to the States. Dad was in the Army during the war and they stayed there for a while after. But it was hard for them, so in the 50s they moved back so Dad could start his business. And here I am. My mother used to promise to take me England, but she passed a while back."

"I'm sorry…"

"It's okay…I was twelve."

There was a long, uncomfortable silence. I nervously sipped my drink, which was nearly empty. He spoke again.

"You shouldn't worry, you know."

"Worry?" I turned my face to his. His eyes glittered at me.

"Yeah. I see in you the same fear I had just after I graduated. 'What will I do? Where will I go?' I know the fear. You're not doing what you want to do, and you're worried you never will. Things are tough right now with this economy, but it will improve. I think you should take a chance. I was afraid to take the leap myself, but I eventually found my way. You will too."

And the way he said it, I believed him. Instantly, and without reservation, I knew he was telling me the truth. He was so direct and confident, I would never be able to doubt him.

"I know…I need to. I guess I'm afraid of that first step. Or leap…"

"Listen, I gotta go. I'm meeting my sister for brunch tomorrow. I was wondering, though, if you wouldn't mind having dinner with me tomorrow night."

My heart started slamming inside my chest now…I felt a huge rush. I tried so hard to sound confident and calm. "Sure. I'd love to." My voice broke when I said it. I hadn't been on an actual date in a long time. Darnell liked to have me cook for him.

"Great. I'll get your number from Frank and call you. Does seven o'clock sound okay?"

"Sure. Yeah, fine."

"Okay, see you then." I was facing forward, watching the city. Trying to pretend this was no big deal. But it was. He moved past me and then into the apartment. I didn't move. Now that he was gone, I could relish the flush and the tingling feeling all over my body. I could feel my blood coursing through me. A gorgeous man just asked me to dinner. Confident. Handsome. A bit of mystery. Every woman's dream, right? It's safe to say I was crazy for him already. I stood on the balcony and giggled softly to myself...I was giddy with the thrill of it all.

I finished my drink and looked out at the city. I didn't go back in for some time. I was enjoying the little fantasy I was having about David. In my mind, I ran through all the scenarios. Dinner. More dates. Hearing his stories. Taking him to meet my family and friends. Engagement. Marriage. Having his children, all of whom had his dark, hawkish eyes. Growing old together. Yeah, I was in deep already.

I had no idea, though, what was in store for me...for us...

On our date the next evening, David continued to impress. So as to avoid David meeting my father, I was waiting for him out on the street, down half a block. My father had no hang-ups about my dating, but still I was living at home, and I knew there would be questions about any man I was going out with. Plus, he knew Darnell, and I wasn't ready yet to have those worlds collide. So I lied to him and told him I was walking to a friend's house. He was already asleep in his chair when I slipped out the door.

When David pulled up, he got out and moved around the car to open the door for me. I first noticed the car…a blue convertible Corvette. I didn't know cars then (still don't!) but I knew what a Corvette was. I was very impressed, and told him.

"It's my brother's car. He lives in Jersey. He let me borrow it." *So he borrowed his brother's car to impress me?*

As he opened the door and I climbed in, I could see him up close. He had combed his tousled hair, though it was still a little wild. I could smell aftershave, and his face looked smooth. His black sport coat covered a white dress shirt. He then surprised me more.

"You look gorgeous!" he said as I slid into the seat. I was wearing my only good little black dress. I wore the highest heels I had, as he was much taller than me. I hoped I wasn't wearing too much perfume. Or too little. I had spent the time on all the little details a woman does on a first date—hair, nails, makeup, shaving. I wanted everything to be perfect, no matter where the date went.

He made sure I was in before he closed the door. He walked around to the driver's side and slid in himself. The smell of the leather seats and his aftershave made me lightheaded. If he would've slid over and kissed me, I would've let him take me right there, but he didn't. He started up the car, and then looked at me. I saw him stare at my legs, and then work his way up.

"You really do look beautiful tonight, Rachel."

Two comments on my looks! "You look great too, David," I said. *Crap. I was trying to play it cool.*

We moved into traffic. He looked so cool behind the wheel of the Vette. Unfortunately, the wind blew my hair in all directions. I pulled it into a ponytail and held it for the rest of our drive.

"Sorry…should've put the top up," he said, smiling.

I had spent a lot of time on my hair, and would've normally been very upset. To David, though, I said, "It's no problem…don't worry about it." My hair was so wild that it took me a lot of time to make it perfect. Too bad…it was already chaos tonight.

We crossed the Queensboro Bridge, and the water looked so beautiful. Moving through the streets, I took in his movements driving the very powerful car. He had a lean gracefulness in everything he did, even driving. Each movement of his arms. Each gear shift. Checking mirrors. He was graceful and sleek. Everything he did looked so perfect.

When we pulled up to Sparks Steak House on 46th Street, I felt like a movie star. A valet took the car and parked it. He gave me a moment to collect myself and adjust my hair, while he simply looked at me and smiled. That confident smile! I'm sure most women will understand what it's like to be with an extremely handsome man. There's a certain pride a woman feels when she's with a man *that* beautiful. In many ways, it's a validation of us. *This amazingly gorgeous man could choose any woman, and he chose me.* I imagine it's similar for a man with a beautiful woman on his arm. He held the door for me, and we entered the restaurant.

Sparks looks the same now as it did then. A long bar with

hundreds of bottles of all types. Small tables, too close together. We were shown to our table by a middle-aged man with a large belly and leering smile. Though a bit noisy inside, the steaks cooking smelled amazing. David took my wrap, hung it on the rack near the door, held my seat for me, and then seated himself. There was a buzz of conversation and the clink of silverware on dishes.

As we ordered, we kept the conversation light. Family. Life in New York. When our steaks arrived, he surprised me again. He was pulling a small white card from his shirt pocket.

"I hope you don't mind...I have a friend who is a literary agent. I told her I knew someone who was putting together a poetry collection. She said she'd like to talk to you about collecting your work and publishing it. Are you interested?" He handed me a card. *Stella Metz, Senior Partner, Abercrombie Literary Agency*. He talked to them on my behalf?

"David, *Abercrombie* is a top literary agency."

"They're okay. They represented my book last year. It bombed, so maybe Stella owes me one." He chuckled lightly.

"Well, it's a tough market right now." Like I knew anything about it? Meanwhile, my head was reeling. *An agent wants to talk to me?*

"Nah, I think nobody really wanted a picture book of my travels. It was a vanity work. But you know how it is...we feel compelled to create, right? How's your steak?"

"It's delicious...too big, though...I can't possibly finish all this."

"Well, just do your best." He flashed that smile again.

"David, I feel awkward...being referred to Stella Metz like this...I mean..." That was the first truly honest thing I'd said up to that point.

"Why would you feel awkward?"

"Well, I haven't ever collected all my poems, and many aren't good enough, I think."

"Frank told me your work was very insightful...and Stella will help you collect them and focus them. She's good at helping writers refine their work." He spoke as if it was already decided.

"Well, and I like you..." *there, it's out now,* "and I hate to feel like I'm using you."

"Rachel, no matter what happens between us I want to help you. And I hope that maybe there's something more for us. But for now, consider this just a friend helping a friend. *Most people* get jobs and book deals and other career support from friends and connections. So why would you be any different?"

I didn't know how to reply. I had so many thoughts swirling in my mind. "Thank you." It sounded so hollow. Inside, I was a torrent of conflicting feelings. And did he really say, *And I hope that maybe there's something more for us*? That little validation meant a lot.

"There you go! You're welcome. Now, I think we need another bottle of wine."

And why not? He was right…getting published was and is about having connections and knowing people. Why not enjoy this connection? Still, I was so interested in David…falling quickly for him…and I hated to add business to our relationship.

I was too embarrassed to shovel down the entire steak, but the wine was tremendous, and I probably drank a little too much. I found myself giggling awkwardly at everything he said. I knew I was probably a bit too tipsy. I also knew I drank too much because I was losing my nervousness. Still, whenever I looked into those dark eyes, I felt he could see every secret inside me. I found myself too often looking away from his steady gaze.

"Rachel, I know this is probably a bit forward of me, and I want you to know that whatever your answer, I totally understand." *Oh, the vibe got heavy all of a sudden.* "I'd like to take you back to my apartment. I'm very attracted to you."

There was a very awkward silence that seemed to go on forever. Remember, this was 1979. The rules were very different then. "David, we just met. I think it's too soon." My protest was weak…very weak. Had he insisted, I would've said yes. I knew I wanted him, and I knew I would give him anything he wanted. But I was also thinking long term, and I didn't want him to think I was a loose woman. A woman who slept with someone on a first date had a horrible stigma in 1979. I was no virgin, for sure…but the free-love days were gone.

"Sorry, I understand. And I really appreciate your honesty."

"Don't be sorry. When the time is right, it will happen." *Crap again! I gave myself away already.*

He smiled at me. I smiled back. I tried to hold his gaze with my own, but I again looked away. Looking at him directly was like looking at the sun.

We finished our wine, and David paid the check. He put my wrap around me, and we went out to the street. The Corvette pulled around, and we were on the road. This time, the top was up. I was surprised when I found we were on the Brooklyn Bridge.

"Where are we going?"

"I thought we'd go sit at the Bridge Park. Is that okay?"

"Sure, that's fine."

The view from the park was and is amazing. We sat and watched the water and the majestic bridge. The breeze picked up a bit, though, and I found myself shivering. When he felt me trembling, he pulled off his coat and wrapped it around me. Corny, right? Not in the 70s. These little things made a huge difference in those days. No man had ever put his jacket around me like this before, and it felt amazing.

And his coat smelled like him. I wrapped it around me. I smelled him all over me, and it made me incredibly aroused. I felt like his arms were around me, and I wanted that. I wanted to have him wrapped around me so badly it ached. I put my head on his broad shoulder, and he tilted his head on top of mine. Even though he was only in a dress shirt, he felt so warm next to me. I smelled him…I drank in his earthy smell. I felt the world turning all around me. I felt a burning inside me. Deep inside me.

I was consumed by him at this point. I was intoxicated with his scent and his warmth. His voice reverberated through me. His touch lit me on fire. I couldn't fight my feelings a second longer. I turned my head up to him and kissed him. His lips met mine, and I felt myself melting to his kiss. His soft, firm lips sent warm shockwaves through my shivering body. His tongue met mine. I put my arm behind his neck and pulled him to me. He wrapped his strong arms around me, and we were pressed against each other in hot, passionate kissing. His face warmed—he felt like he was on fire. I was melting against his heat; no longer cold, I was warm in all the right places. I felt my now-heated blood coursing through my veins. In one place, I felt hot. My body was awakening. The predator was about to have his prey.

I was no virgin, but I was relatively inexperienced. I had only been with a few men, and none of those was satisfying. I honestly didn't enjoy scx that much, and thought it wasn't something I would ever really enjoy. Sex was overrated, in my mind. All this fuss and bluster about fifteen minutes of sweating and discomfort…instead, I thought it was a duty for a woman, there to please her man. Darnell, my current boyfriend (or "guy I was dating") had never brought me to orgasm, and other men had left me mostly unsatisfied. But I felt like it could be…would be… different with David. His touch moved me in a way I had never experienced. It sent a fire through me. His lips were passion and need… desire and fire.

This was the pivotal moment when everything was about to change. This moment redefined my entire life. Had I rejected him at this moment, I can't imagine how different my life would've been. Had I asked him to take me back to my home, I would be a different person than I am today. You'd have to have lived in this time to truly understand the leap of faith I was taking at this moment. I would take many other leaps very soon.

"David, take me back to your place."

"Let's go."

I was dizzy with thoughts and emotions on the ride. I couldn't believe I was going to sleep with a man I had just met. Good girls *never* put out on the first date. We had to be chased. Courted. Flowers, movies, and chocolates. Good girls didn't go back to a man's apartment. I hardly knew him! Who was this guy? What would my father say? What would Darnell say? Those are such silly societal pressures, but in 1979 they were lodestones.

But I was in heat. I felt my body radiating warmth. I was wet. I was tingling. I was ready. I had been aroused a bit in the past, but had never felt *this way* before. The men I had slept with before were rough and awkward and didn't understand a woman's body or needs. They simply wanted to rip my clothes off, get inside me, and finish. I never enjoyed that, but I honestly thought that's what sex was. My girlfriends would tell me about having orgasms, but I was rarely even close. I often found it painful. As a man forced himself inside me, I would usually wish it were over. It was usually over just as I was starting to feel good. Sex and I hadn't gotten along. I understood myself well enough to know it was arousal that is the key, and I was most certainly aroused now. I *knew* this would be a different encounter than all the others.

I looked over at David. He was driving a bit aggressively, and we were moving through traffic too quickly. I still wore his coat, and could see the toned muscles under his dress shirt moving with each turn of the wheel. His lean, athletic build looked so intriguing. I wanted to touch it. I wanted him to touch me. For the first time, I was craving the touch of a man. He wouldn't have to force his way into me…I was ready.

"We're just a block away." He smiled as if to reassure me.

"Okay." Now I felt awkward. We were close. I was going to give myself to a man I barely knew. I was hoping this would not be another mistake. Even if it was fast and uncomfortable, I felt it would still be worthwhile, because it would be with *him*.

He was, of course, amazingly beautiful.

In the elevator up, he pressed into me, and began kissing me. I was already accepting him. As he pushed against me, I leaned back, and opened my legs to him. *It* pressed against my belly. He kissed my mouth and then my neck. I was warm tingles, head to toe. I drank in the smell of his hair. He pressed his hand on my breast, and I could feel myself getting wetter. I pushed myself against his leg…I *ground* myself against his leg. I wanted him to have me. I wanted to feel him inside me.

He fumbled with the door and I was ablaze…panting. Once inside, our clothes flew off of us. When I saw his chest, I gasped. His body was so smoothly muscular. He was darkly tanned all over. His muscles were lean, but he looked powerful. Muscles moved sinuously under his dark, tight skin, rippling under the light dusting of hair. I fumbled with my nylons, removing them but stayed in my bra and panties…*thank God I wore a nice new set!*

And then he was on me. His hot kisses smashed into my lips as he expertly removed my bra with one hand, and then his hot mouth was on my breasts. His new whiskers chafed my skin in the most pleasant way while the heat of those kisses and nibbles set my body raging… flaming…as if I would immolate…spontaneous combustion. I was dripping at this point. I didn't need foreplay. I wanted him in me… immediately.

I pushed him away and slid backward onto his bed. He was on me like a panther. He again began kissing me roughly, then again down to my breasts. I expected him to enter me, and I felt more ready than I ever had. But he suddenly slowed down. His kisses turned softer. Slower.

Teasing. His hot breath made my soft hairs stand up on end. *No! Don't slow down! I'm ready!*

And then he moved down. He began to kiss below my breasts. Then down to my stomach. As he kissed his way down, he gently tugged at my panties. I lifted my hips, and he slid them down. Self-consciously, I pulled my legs tightly together, even though I was hotter and wetter than I had ever felt before. But his hand slid between my thighs, and he pressed them apart. I couldn't resist his touch. His strength. His heat. I wanted him to do to me whatever he wanted. I wanted to give him all of me.

And then his mouth was on me. I had never experienced a man's mouth on my sex, and I was very nervous—at first. But his hot, rough face pressed into me, and I relaxed and let him. His lips opened me. His whiskers tickled and burned. His tongue pressed into me. He knew exactly where to go and what to do. Immediately wave after wave of warmth moved through my body: my toes were curling, my body was jerking. I felt electric sparks hitting my brain, and I gave in to them. I couldn't fight the feeling. I welcomed the warmth. I welcomed the burning and wetness. He was consuming me, and I wanted him to. Oh God, how I wanted him to! I wanted his mouth to take in my entire sex.

My first real orgasm with a man hit me like a bolt of lightning. It felt like cresting the first big hill on a roller coaster, and then it was that sudden precipitous drop, hurtling down too fast to comprehend. I remember my head slammed back against the bed and my entire body convulsed. I began to shake, and every inch of me was both fire and ice. My mind disappeared. I wasn't Rachel Walker. I was on a cloud. I was underground. I was in Heaven and Hell at the same time. Warm, soft clouds and burning hot fire. Every inch of me was consumed and reborn in that moment. I was twisting violently, unable to control my movements. And I drifted…panting…

"You okay?" I heard him ask. His voice was so distant.

"Yeah….yeah…" and I realized I had been far, far away. How much time had passed? It could've been hours. I drifted back to earth, and he was still passionately kissing me, but avoiding direct pressure on my sex…he knew I was tingling too much. He knew my body so well already.

"David, I want you inside me." Though I was already breathing heavily, I knew I wanted his sex in mine. I wanted him to take me. He had just given me the greatest pleasure I had ever felt, and I wanted to repay him. He looked up at me and smiled. He slid his way up my body, pausing to kiss me coming up, the way he had kissed me going down. But I was too excited…too overwhelmed from my intense orgasm. When he kissed my breasts, I felt hot red pokers through my body. No, I wanted his body. I grabbed his upper arms and pulled him up. I needed it right now!

And then his mouth was on mine. And our tongues returned to their familiar spots, battling each other. I could feel his hardness against my thigh. I opened myself to him, and he was between my legs, without breaking our kiss. *It* was coming soon.

I wanted it. I needed it.

I reached my hand down and grabbed his hardness. It felt so urgent. It felt so thick! I opened my legs as wide as I could and guided him into me. The tip of him found my opening, and began to push…to drive into me…slowly, but relentlessly. Taking my moisture. Pushing gradually. Distending me. As he began to enter me, I gasped. I was so wet he was sliding in easily, but his thickness opened me more than I had ever been opened before. I felt the pressure, pushing me inside out. I felt so stretched. I could feel his hot strength pushing me wider than ever before. He was much larger than anybody I had been with. I felt a moment of fear as he pushed himself into my softness. I was wrapping myself around him, and feeling the joyful tension already building inside me.

But he was so slow, and so careful. And I opened wider to accept him. He moved in, just a bit at a time, and each time my body accepted his inward movement. Each push brought a rasping gasp from me. Electric fire roared through me. Each movement sent a hard shot of flame up my spine and down to my feet. My head was burning. His body felt like hot coals on me. We were already sweating, but we were just getting started.

And then he was all the way in me. He gave me a second to accept this fullness. I felt distended to the limit. Then he began to move. Slowly. Grinding his hips into me. His mouth pressed into mine at the same time, and I felt myself burning inside like I had never before. Every movement in or out sent burning shivers radiating through my body. I felt so warm.

So wanted. So complete. I wanted to be here forever, with this man on top of me. Consuming each other. Is there ever anything as good as that feeling? Warmth through your entire body? A man's strong body moving over the top of you? I felt so feminine yet so powerful. So alive. Every nerve ending was prickling and sparking. My body was stinging and burning. The sensations were almost too much…right to the edge of what my body and mind could handle.

He was moving more rapidly now. I felt his thrusts through me, driving inside me. I grunted with each push in, and gasped with each movement out. He felt so forceful, like he could break me if he pushed just a little harder.

And then he lifted up and pulled my hips onto his thighs, as he knelt upright. His gorgeous, predatory eyes looked into mine, like an eagle about to strike. His lean body was above me. I was throwing my hips up to meet his thrusts, and the urgency was building…that tightening that builds inside, and that you feel could break you into pieces. It felt like he was picking up the tempo, and it felt to me like he would finish soon. I wanted him to. His thrusts were intense and powerful, forcing the wind out of me. Our bodies were slapping together, and we were pouring sweat.

Then he pulled out, and turned my hips with his rough hands. I rolled over. He pulled me up on my knees, and he entered me from behind. I had never done this before. I opened myself as widely as I could. His exigent thrusts felt so deep I had to pull away just a bit. He sensed this, and changed to more shallow, but no less powerful movements. I was more open than I had ever thought possible. Each pounding thrust send his testicles slapping against my clitoris, and I was building to another massive orgasm. He could feel me building, and his thrusts became more grinding, driving more pressure to the right spots. And then it started. From his hot penetrations, the waves of pleasure began to align, and then *Pow!*

Fire shot through me. Hot, furious fire hit my brain like an internal burning sledgehammer. I pushed against him to get every wave of that pleasure. My eyes were slammed shut and I screamed out into the pillow. I was all fire and ferocity and pleasure. This orgasm was different than the last. Instead of letting go to pleasure, I was punching pleasure in the mouth and forcing it to do my bidding. Again, I disappeared…I was in another place. Heaven and Hell…my new vacation spots. Floating on clouds of white, and burning in flames of red. Again, I drifted off, and lost sense of time.

After it was over, I was quivering, crying out to each of his now slowing thrusts. The pillow was wet from my tears.

I was panting loudly. I was exhausted. I was ready for him to finish. I had never experienced anything like this…wanting someone to finish. Sex had always been over too soon for me to enjoy. I didn't know if I was strong enough to have another orgasm from him. I felt like I might not be able to come back.

His hand pressure on my hip caused me to roll over onto my back, though in my exhaustion I moved very slowly. The entire room was spinning. I expected him to enter me and finish quickly, and I was going to be so happy and grateful. Instead, I found him moving his body around, and he was lowering his manhood to my face, while his own face went back to my overwhelmed womanhood. I almost refused him…I knew I didn't do this well…I had been told…but he was already pressing himself to my mouth. I was also burning all over, and thought I would be too sensitive to his lips again. Yet, his hot mouth was again opening me, and warmth was flowing.

He looked so large that I didn't think I could, but I knew I could not refuse David—not anything. I would do anything he wanted, whenever he wanted.

So I took him in my hand, and then guided him into my mouth. I wanted to do well. I wanted to pleasure him. He had given me pleasure like I had never experienced before, so I wanted to give him the same. But he was so large…he was so thick…I could only just work the top of him into my mouth. I tried though. I pushed him into my mouth and tried to emulate my body as closely as I could…open and wet. I bobbed my head up and down. I heard him grunt, then raise his lips off me…the first sounds I had heard him make…" Oh yeah, Rachel…that's so good!"

So I attacked it with more fervor. I moved quickly, and reached my hand up to massage his length and heavy testicles. They were tightening up to his body. I tasted our salty and musky liquids…I drank us. He was drinking from me. It was passion and madness all over my body. I had never experienced anything close to this before.

And then he moved around quickly and was inside me again. He locked his mouth onto mine. We tasted each other once again. His body was pressed on me tightly. My legs wrapped around his hips, as tightly as I could make them, twisted around him. And now his thrusts were urgent. Powerful. Deep. He was burning hot, and he was dripping his sweat all over me. His sweat was sweet to me, and my body drank it in. My arms slipped over his wet back and shoulders. He drove himself into me. I pulled him deeper with my legs. I could feel the heat of his kisses building more intensely. At first our mouths fought each other. Then, his kisses became a bit distant…less controlled. I could sense he was stiffening and nearing his own climax. He swelled even larger inside me, and as he did I felt my own hot burning waves beginning to build yet again. Not as forcefully as before, but still warm and tingly and flowing. I embraced those waves. I rode those waves. I now knew how to ride them, thanks to David.

As he began to grunt his pleasure, I did the same with mine. We were both grunting and slamming our hips against each other. My nails dug into his slick, muscular shoulders. He lifted his head and his eyes rolled back. We were both together and miles apart. His body began to jerk uncontrollably. I felt the burning hotness entering me…warm and wet and slippery…and I rode my waves to smooth, rolling pleasure. My final orgasm went between my toes and my brain in an even, flowing river, and I felt him thrusting his final pushes into me. Instead of the searing rage of my previous orgasms, this one felt like lying on a beach and letting the warm water lap over me. It seemed to go on forever.

He collapsed onto me.

I lay there, my vision finally clearing. Smelling his hair and tangy sweat. Feeling his panting breaths on my shoulder. Our sweat melted together. His hardness began to soften just a bit, and I was finally able to breathe. I was feeling the muscles on his back. His sweat rolling off of him in rivers. Sweat from his shoulder ran into my face. I put my chin above his shoulder to take in deep, warm breaths. The throbbing in my body softened…softened…became more distant.

He lifted his head up, and smiled down at me. His hair was damp. His hawkish eyes were now soft and glassy. Our sex was all over each other. He said, "Hi. You okay?"

"Yeah, I'm good." And I was. Better than good. I had never felt so pleasantly warm. So whole. So complete. Not the shy, shaky, nerdy girl.

Not the weak little thing who cried too easily and didn't believe in herself. I felt like a woman. Confident. Relaxed. Vulnerable and strong at the same time. It was a wonderful feeling, and I wanted to feel this way forever. He had given me more than incredible sex…he had made me a whole and complete female. Sexy. Sensual. Warm. Loved.

Yes, I wanted to feel this way forever. Never let it end. I was already in love with him. Sure, part of it was the postcoital buzz. But it was more. Much more.

He kissed me, this time softly. Lightly. His lips took the last of my strength. Then he rolled off of me, and pulled me onto his shoulder. I felt the coolness of his orgasm dripping out of me. I pulled the blanket over me, but he kept the blanket off, letting his sweat cool on him. I looked down, and saw his lean, smooth body. Darkly tanned, and just a bit of black hair spread around. A body of motion. A body of doing. His large penis, now softening, glistened in the bedroom light. I took in his smell, now musty and sweaty, full and manly. My head rose and fell with his now slowing breath.

And then I drifted off to sleep, fully satisfied. It was a deep sleep. A marvelous sleep. A complete sleep. All my fears, all my insecurities, all my doubt…all gone.

For now, at least.

"Rachel, what the fuck are you talking about?" Darnell's brown eyes always narrowed when he got angry, and they were slits now. I could see his jaw muscles flexing. Though light-skinned for a black man, his face darkened with rage.

"I said I don't want to see you anymore. We've been growing apart for a while, and I want to just end it so we can each find someone else." I was trying my best to avoid responding to his anger and aggression with the same.

"Who's the brother?" he said, a bit too loudly. We were in the teacher's lounge. Though alone, people were walking by outside. The last thing I wanted was for others to hear our discussion.

"Keep your voice down, Darnell."

"Don't tell me what to do, Rachel. *Who's the brother you're fucking?*" His voice was harsh and accusatory. I didn't need this at my job.

"I'm not going to do this here, Darnell. I'm not going to fight here at work."

"I'm just asking you to tell me the truth." His shoulders and neck were flexed. His voice rasped like metal scraping concrete.

"Truth? I caught you kissing Melanie last year...how about that truth?" Honestly, I didn't care about that any longer, but I was trying to put him on the defensive. He was unapologetic.

"For fuck's sake, Rachel...I told you that was an accident...we were drunk...you and I got through that last year..." He looked exasperated, first throwing up his hands and then placing them hard on his hips, looking away as if a small child had said something embarrassing.

"*You* got through it...*I* never did. But it's not about that, Darnell. I'm just ready to move on." I made eye contact with our science teacher, Misty, as she walked by. Her face told me she understood what we were talking about and she sympathized with my plight.

"And you're not going to tell me who the brother you've been fucking is?" Again, voice too loud.

I'd had enough. "Goodbye, Darnell." I stormed out of the lounge. As I left the room, I noticed a few teachers standing just outside the door. They tried to pretend that they hadn't been listening. I felt my eyes roll in disgust, though I wasn't sure if it was about Darnell or my eavesdropping peers.

Later, Tiffany came by with a cup of coffee. She taught across the hall from me. Tiffany had been a college basketball player at Georgia Tech, so she towered over me. I was sitting with my head in my hands at my desk, pretending to grade homework.

"You okay, Rachel?" She handed me the coffee. "I heard about what happened."

"Yeah, I'm fine." I took a drink. "Darnell is such a prick sometimes."

"You've known that for a while."

"Yeah." I smiled at her. I felt better having her there to talk to. She knew Darnell better than most, and knew his reaction wasn't uncommon.

"So?" she asked.

"So what?" I looked at her innocently.

"Is there another brother? Are you seeing someone else?"

"Wow!" I laughed a bit. "You're going to believe everything you hear?"

"Well, there must be someone. You kept dating Darnell even though you knew he was cheating on you. Then you suddenly break up with him today? I'm no fool..."

"Well, you know I was never crazy about him anyway. He was just someone to go out with."

"Sure, but plenty of marriages have started that way."

"Yeah."

"Well, c'mon then…you have class in fifteen minutes."

"What do you want me to tell you?"

"Are you seeing someone else?" Her eyes bore down on me, and she wasn't going to let me off the hook. She could be very demanding when she wanted to be. She must've been fearsome at GT!

"Not sure…maybe…I have a potential I'm working on, and I just wanted to make sure I'm one hundred percent available, in case it develops." Obfuscating, I know.

"Oh my God! That's great, Rachel!" She was as loud as Darnell all of a sudden.

"Shh! I don't want this going around."

She looked around, and whispered, "Sorry!" Then, she added, "I'm just happy for you."

"Thanks, honey, I know. I really appreciate it. I don't know if this one is going to be what I've been looking for, but he's very intriguing."

"You *must* give me a few details…I just *have* to know!" She sat on the edge of my desk, waiting to get my gossip.

"His name is David, and he's a photographer and adventure writer. And that's *all* I'm going to say about it. Now leave…I have to prep for class."

"Okay, but if this develops, I have to meet this David!" She slid off my desk, and started to the door.

"It's a deal…now go!"

Tiffany had left me with a smile. I had stopped thinking of Darnell, and was now thinking about David. My life was indeed looking up. I was anticipating his call, and looking forward to our next date. I was still a bit sore from the night before, but it was a sore I was enjoying. Every time I moved in my chair, I could feel that wonderful ache, and I thought of him.

I looked out the window. My life was different now. I saw a happy, more satisfied life ahead of me. And in my purse I had the card of one of the most respected literary agents in New York. I couldn't wait for David's next call. He was all I could think of.

Three days later, I had not heard from him. And I was furious. When he had dropped me off the morning after our night together, his last words had been, "I'll call you tonight."

But he hadn't. I had stayed in that night and watched the phone. Waiting for it to ring. After the harsh words from Darnell, I really wanted to hear his voice. I knew he had my number, and if he'd lost it, all he had to do was call Dr. Frank. Why wasn't he calling?

But by the next night the absence of his call was something I couldn't ignore. He hadn't called for the second night in a row. Was I the only one who felt something? Was it just me who felt something amazing between us? Was this just a one-night-stand for him? Was I just another notch on his bedpost? Did he get everything he wanted and now wanted nothing more? Did I disappoint him sexually?

By the third night, I felt very used. Like a piece of meat. And I was angry. And hurt. So many emotions hit me all at once. Looking back, it seems silly, doesn't it? This was a gorgeous man with an amazingly interesting career. He was a hot commodity. What woman wouldn't want him? I had given it away on our first date, before we had a chance to develop love. What did I expect?

But I wanted him. Badly. And I wasn't going to let myself turn into someone's "piece." He was going to hear about it, at the very least.

I did something I could have never imagined before. This just wasn't done in my day.

I took a taxi to his Upper East Side apartment. I took the elevator up. I saw the corner where we had kissed passionately. I went to his door. *What if he's in there with somebody else?* Well, if he was, then I was going to at least know. That's the worst part of being in a situation like that...not knowing. If he had called me and told me he was married, at least I would have known. If he had opened the door that night and had a girl with him, at least I would have known. I'd have probably egged his apartment, and then been done with it.

But not knowing? That was the worst. It was maddening.

I knocked. Movement inside. I could feel him move to the door, and I knew he was peering through the peephole. Then the door opened.

As soon as I saw his face, I was ready to forgive him. There he stood. Dark t-shirt, pajama pants, gorgeous black eyes, beautiful smile. I hate to admit it, but I was so smitten with him...face, body, soul...that even if he had been in there with somebody, I would've forgiven him had he asked. His face, though, showed surprise and a hint of sadness.

"Hi, Rachel. You didn't call...you okay?"

"Hi, David. *You* didn't call. You said you'd call me three nights ago."

"Come in, come in..." he said nervously. I entered with my body tense, trying to put on a tough veneer...but probably failing miserably. I have to admit I had barely looked at his apartment the last time I was there. We had gone straight to the bedroom, and then rushed out the next morning. This time, I looked around. On his wall were some of the most amazing photos. My eyes were drawn to them. Instead of sitting, I walked to the wall near his sofa and looked at the pictures that were there. I remember clearly the black-and-white photo of a dark, old-world church with the sun setting behind it.

"Do you like that picture?"

"Yes, where is it?"

"That's Saint Vitus Cathedral in Prague. I was writing an article on the Astronomical Clock in the city square, but felt so drawn to this old church. It...spoke to me, I guess."

He had walked up behind me. I turned and faced him. He smiled, but when he saw the look on my face, the smile faded.

"What's wrong, Rachel?"

"You know what's wrong."

"Because I didn't call you?"

"Well...yeah...of course. I'm not a one-night-stand. I trusted you, David." My voice was harsh...scolding. I was channeling Darnell.

"I didn't say you were..."

"Then why didn't you call me? You said you would."

"It's...hard to explain...sit down."

I didn't though. I stood there with my arms folded and glared at him. My mother had a hot temper, and I felt the way she must've felt when she scolded me.

"Please...Rachel...sit down. I'll explain."

I glared for a second more, and then sat down on his overstuffed sofa. I noted that his apartment was fastidiously clean. Maybe there *was* someone else.

"There is something I have to tell you."

Oh no, here it comes. Wife. Fiancée. Gay.

"It's not easy to talk about. I wanted to talk to you, but I lost my nerve."

"Are you okay?" How quickly I switched from anger to concern. That was the power David had over me.

"No, this is very hard."

"Are you married? Fiancée?"

"No, nothing like that."

Oh, thank God! "Then what?" He was standing in front of me. I could see his face twisting. He was wrestling with something. "It's okay, David. I'm a big girl. I can take it." That was probably a lie. Definitely a lie.

"It's a bit embarrassing...hard to talk about it."

"David, I've heard a lot," I lied again. "Just tell me."

"There's something in me that's hard to talk about. I want to tell you, but it's hard to discuss...you need to prepare yourself."

"David, come on...just tell me." I was impatient now. I was mostly worried he was married, and since it wasn't that, I figured I was ready for whatever he could tell me.

I wasn't, though.

"I feel such a strong connection to you already, Rachel. You're beautiful, smart, and interesting. I felt our lovemaking was so incredible."

Oh thank goodness...so he felt it too! "Then what? What can't you tell me?"

"Oh, this is tough..."

"Just tell me, David, Jesus Christ."

"I have..."

The Clap? Syphilis? "What?"

"I have...exotic tastes." He was looking away. "Exotic."

"Exotic tastes. Food?"

"No, no...exotic...*sexual* tastes."

I sat there for a second, looking at him blankly. *Exotic sexual tastes? What the hell could he possibly mean?*

"David, I don't understand. What do you mean?"

"Sexually. I enjoyed our lovemaking so much. You were incredible. You felt so right to me, Rachel, but regular sex isn't enough for me."

"Regular sex is not enough? David, what on earth do you mean?" *Was I not enough for him? What does that mean? Why won't he just come out with it?*

"Regular sex...I need *more* than regular sex...I like sex in different ways."

"Well, I'm willing to try things. We did a few positions last time...we can try anything you like. Why didn't you just ask me?" *This seemed like an immensely stupid conversation at this point. I had no idea what he was referring to. I was so young and naïve.*

"No, Rachel...you don't understand. This is so hard..."

"Then just say it, David! Fuck! C'mon!" I rarely swore in those days but I was really frustrated at this point.

"I like what people consider 'kinky.' I like things most consider weird. I like things most people don't like. I want to do things sexually a good girl like you would never do. I didn't tell you because I didn't want to scare you away. I didn't tell you because I fell for you already."

He fell for me?

"But regular sex gets boring to me, and I have to do other things.

I'm sorry, but I've tried…these desires don't go away…" He was looking away, avoiding eye contact. He looked like one of my students who was caught cheating.

"Like what? What things sexually do you do that someone like me wouldn't do?" I was not prepared for what he was about to tell me. At this point in my life, I hardly even knew about regular sex. I was about to receive the shock of my life.

"Are you sure you want to know?"

"Yes…of course!"

"Okay, don't get mad. I warned you. I enjoy things most people consider perverted. Some things are still illegal in some states. *For example*, I like sex with multiple people. I like sex in groups and in public places. Exhibitionism. Threesomes. Swapping. I like *all* things sexual. Anything between consenting adults excites me. And I feel compelled to do them."

"What do you mean? You want to have sex with other people?" Tears were already falling out of my eyes. Hot ones.

"I want *us* to have sex with other people. Together. But I know you wouldn't do things like that…you're a good girl. This is why I avoided talking to you. It's hard to explain. This conversation usually ends my relationships." He handed me a box of tissues, and then sat next to me on the couch.

I was wiping burning tears out of my eyes. *Why can't I just have a man? I finally meet someone beautiful…inside and outside…and he's a pervert? A lecher?* I honestly felt like I was losing the love of my life in this very moment. We only knew each other a couple of days, but I felt like no man would ever replace this one. He was too gorgeous. Too intelligent. Too sensual. Too talented.

"David, I don't understand what you're telling me. How can you have a relationship and have sex with other people?"

"To me, sex needs to be…adventurous. I want a normal relationship with a woman…with you. But sexually, I need to have exotic sex. Try new things all the time. Wild, sexy, sexual things. That wouldn't always involve other people, but that would be part of it. Do you know what swinging is?"

"No." Swinging was not something people talked about in the 1970s.

"Swinging is when people exchange sexual partners with other couples."

"So you would want to have sex with another woman?"

"Yes…" more hot tears shot out of my eyes, "while you would have sex with other men."

"But…I don't want sex with other men. I want sex with you."

"I understand, Rachel…I understand. You're a good girl. The *best*. I totally don't blame you. Believe me, I usually get this response."

"Usually?"

"Yeah, I've had to have this conversation before. It's not easy. I didn't want to have this one with you though…"

"Why not?"

"I felt like you were maybe 'the one.' You are special to me. But I have tried to lead a normal sexual life and simply can't. Eventually, I find myself needing it. Like I'm a drug addict or an alcoholic or something. At some point I seek it out. I figure it's better to tell you now and save us from a much more painful conversation later. I had to tell you now so I wouldn't fall more madly for you, and then lose you when I couldn't be without you."

Fall madly for me? "But why can't you just focus on me?"

"You see, here's what happens to me. I meet someone, and we enjoy healthy sex and fall in love. Then I find myself feeling these desires…desires for adventurous sex. Sometimes, I have only shared a little bit of what I'm interested in, and the girl might try to satisfy that. But it's never enough, you see? I need to keep pushing the boundaries of sex. Sex with you was amazing…the best…but I know that in a couple of weeks I'll find myself wanting to try new things with you, and I'll keep pushing until you hate me."

"You can't stop? You can't get help?"

"I don't want help. I desire these things. Why shouldn't I have them? It's part of me…part of who I am." He was looking down at his hands.

"What types of things have you done?"

"Oh, you don't want to know. Many things. With many people." I didn't want to know, but I was so immensely curious…I had to push a little.

"Just name me one thing you've done."

"Just one?" He paused, and thought for a second. "One thing I like is to attend orgies. Do you know what an orgy is?"

"Like the Romans?"

"Yeah...many people, all having sex with each other."

"Men and women?"

"Yes, men and women have sex together in orgies."

"I mean, do *you* have sex with men and women?" I had wanted to know but now I really didn't want to know.

He paused, looked down again, and then looked me in the eyes. "Yes, I have and I do, though I prefer sex with women."

"So if we had sex with another couple, you might have sex with both of them?"

"I have before, yes."

There aren't words to describe how I felt in that moment. I had never heard of bisexuality...I had barely even heard of homosexuality. All of this was very sudden. I was shell-shocked, I think.

"This is all very hard for me to understand."

"I know...you see now why I was so hesitant to talk with you about this. This isn't easy. Do you understand?"

"That I understand."

And I did. This was a long time ago, after all. People didn't talk about sex like this...especially when they were young and had only gone on one date. While it was destroying me that a man I had already fallen for was telling me he wanted sex with other people, I totally appreciated that he was being honest with me. He could've lied and then dumped me when he got bored.

"Rachel, you are so special to me. I meant it when I said I've fallen for you already. I hope you know that you'll always be someone I care so much about. I hope we can always be friends."

"David, wait. Before you write this off, I want to think about it, okay?" My words formed reflexively. I didn't know what I was saying but I knew I had to consider ways to preserve my relationship with David.

"Think about what?"

"I want to think about what you told me...think about it some."

"What's there to think about? I can't change, Rachel. I'm who I am."

"That's not what I mean."

"What then?"

"I might be willing to do some of those things with you, David. I might be willing to try some of those."

"Might?"

"Well, I'm not sure…I have to think about it. This is all so new to me. I've never thought about swinging or anything like that."

"You would have to understand…it's not just one or two things. It's *everything*."

"Everything?"

"I want to do everything…nothing off limits…nothing out of bounds…"

"Nothing?"

"Nothing between consenting adults. I want to try it all…all…"

"That's a lot to get my head around. But I will think about it, David. I will."

"I don't want you to do anything you aren't comfortable with, Rachel. I'd rather us part as friends than find you hate me later."

"Let me think about it. I'll call you." I said that on purpose.

I felt betrayed…and in some ways I wished he hadn't taken me out. This was a lot for a young woman in those days. I didn't even want to think about many of these things. Sex was stigmatized back then. Even still, I guess.

But I did think about it. David called me a cab, and I went to my room that night with my head faltering…swimming in thoughts. I was shocked by what I had heard. But, perhaps, just a little intrigued. It's hard to imagine that I was a woman who had only experienced her first sexual orgasm a few nights before, and yet was thinking about joining a man on a sexual exploration that violated almost every principle I was raised with. What would my father think? I was raised in a Christian household. We attended church every Sunday, and were good Protestants. How could I even consider what I was considering?

But David was breathtaking. Beautiful. Unique. Confident. A man I wanted to be with.

On cue, my father knocked on my bedroom door.

"Hi, baby girl. Are you okay?" He was standing nervously at my door.

"Hi, Daddy." I didn't answer his question.

He moved into the room, and sat on the edge of my bed.

"Why are you crying? Did somebody hurt you?"

"I can't really talk about it."

"You know you can tell me everything."

"No, I can't really talk about it, Daddy." And I couldn't. How would I talk about something like this to my father? *Well, Daddy, my new boyfriend likes to have sex with men and women and attend orgies and threesomes. What do you think I should do?*

He sat there for a bit, and then walked to the door. "Don't forget that I love you, and will always be here for you."

I didn't reply. I wish I would have.

I felt like I was standing on the edge of a high bridge, looking down into yawning blackness. All I could see down there was darkness and uncertainty. On the bridge was my same old boring life. My same old loneliness. If I jumped into the blackness, would I die? Part of me said yes. That darkness below was fear. But part of me felt that I hadn't yet really lived. If I jumped, I could hurt myself—I probably would. But if I stayed on this lonely bridge and went down the lonely highway in front of me, I might never experience life fully.

And isn't that at least part of a suicide? Jumping off a bridge? Isn't part of it that you desire to see what's waiting? Experience newness... different-ness. You hope that what's waiting for you will be a better life. I don't think anybody who commits suicide thinks the afterlife will be misery and suffering...or they wouldn't do it. They're hoping for a *release* from their current suffering, and maybe just assuming that whatever waits for them is better. Or couldn't be worse, anyway.

So is what I did a type of suicide? Or, instead, like alcohol and drugs, a *slow suicide?* Self-destruction? Destroying the old me? Tossing myself off a bridge and looking for an afterlife of love and acceptance?

I don't look at it that way. Instead, I look at it as someone finding someone she loves, or at least could love...and then being prepared to do anything to keep that person. Today, people would call that co-dependent, I guess—facilitating someone's behavior or addictions or whatever. Maybe it was. I'm no doctor. But I'd also be lying if I didn't admit that I was a little bit sexually excited. While I was worried David would lead me to things I couldn't do, I was also excited about some possibilities. The 60s had awakened our country to the idea that anything could be. The 50s were black and white, but the 60s were sparkling Technicolor. We were almost now to the 80s, but my life was still dull and gray. I was leading a sheltered life…a sparse life. Was I missing out? How would I know if I didn't try?

While I was very sexually inexperienced, I was no prude. My thoughts revolved around meeting a great guy and being with him exclusively. Still, that doesn't mean I hadn't had the occasional fantasy of multiple partners. I had heard whispers of sexual oddities and wondered, if only a little, what it was like. While I never imagined doing these things, it didn't mean I was disgusted by them. Well, some of them, perhaps, but not all.

Control. That was what I really needed. If I wanted to keep who I was, I needed to keep myself from being coerced or forced into something I wouldn't want to do. That, I thought, was how it should go down. I had to exert control from the outset.

I called David very late…or very early. After a few rings, I heard the line click, and heard his breath. "Yeah? Who is it?" His voice was dry and foggy.

"Hi, David. It's Rachel."

"Oh, hi, Rachel. It's two o'clock…you okay?"

"Yeah. I just wanted you to know I thought about what we talked about."

"Yeah?"

"Yeah."

"Whatever you decide is okay with—"

I cut him off. "I decided I want to try those things with you, David. I want to follow you down the path you're going."

Silence, except for shallow breaths.

"David?"

"Yeah, I'm here. You sure?"

"Pretty sure. I'll give it a try, anyway. But…I have one condition."

"Okay…let's hear it."

"We take it slowly. One thing at a time. Don't rush me. Don't push me. Don't coerce me. If we reach a point where I can't go any farther, then I will just stop, okay?"

"Yeah, of course…sure."

"I mean that, David...this is non-negotiable...don't put pressure on me and don't put me in situations I'm not ready for."

"Got it...yeah."

"Okay. When are you leaving for Tanzania?"

"Day after tomorrow. Can I see you tomorrow?"

"I probably won't have the strength. I'm meeting Stella tomorrow in the afternoon. I'm taking her all my poems. And I have homework to grade. Let's just get together when you get back, okay?"

"Yeah, okay."

"Goodnight, David."

"Goodnight, baby."

I didn't know what was ahead of me, but I had just jumped off my nice, safe, lonely bridge. The air was already rushing around me. I was falling, plunging into the unknown depths...the cavernous darkness below me. I was curious to see where I would land. Fearful? Absolutely. I was petrified...yet excited at the same time.

Part II : Lepidoptera

$(\mathcal{W})$e were walking in Central Park, holding hands. The sun had just gone down, and it was getting a bit cool. A soft breeze blew on my legs, and up my peasant skirt. I felt warm tonight though. David had just returned from Tanzania. He was burned brown, and was tired from the long flight. But he had called me as soon as he had arrived, and said he couldn't wait to see me. I liked being his first thought.

He was telling me stories of his adventures over the last three weeks. He had seen lions eat wildebeest. He had baked in the hot sun of the grasslands. Been soaked by tropical rainstorms. Climbed up Mt. Kilimanjaro, high enough to touch the snow. He had watched native dances and eaten Tanzanian food, even though he didn't like it much. Everything he did seemed so romantic...exotic, to use his word. I listened breathlessly to everything he said.

As we walked and he talked, I imagined him in these places. Camera around his neck, notepad in hand. Taking down the sights and smells and tastes of East Africa. A modern-day Ernest Hemingway, tasting foreign lands to inspire his art. Being a mix of African and English, I hadn't yet been to either ancestral continent. I knew I must travel to the landmarks of my heritage, or at least what I knew. David, though, had been everywhere.

"What really gets you in the Serengeti is the dust. In the dry season, it's enough to choke you. It's in your eyes, your ears, your nose. All you want to do is take a long shower and change your clothes. Then it rains and you're slopping through mud."

"How did you stay clean out there?"

"Well, you can't. We'd wash in our tents, using a bowl and sponge. I changed clothes a few times, but never enough. Felt like the dirt and dust and mud were everywhere."

We walked along and saw the darkness enclosing us. We sat on a bench, near the Dakota and the 72nd Street subway. That towering Gothic building sat like a gargoyle over us, watching us. Its dark mystery made me think of European cathedrals, or vampiric castles.

It was a quiet night, and few people were around. I took his arm and leaned on his shoulder. I knew he was tired from his long and numerous flights, and I didn't quite know what he was expecting upon his return.

"So, Rachel, how do you feel about everything we were talking about before I left?"

"What do you mean, David?" I asked. I knew, but wanted him to say it.

"You know...the talk we had...are you still okay with it? Have you changed your mind?"

"No, I haven't changed my mind. I guess I just don't know how it'll start."

"Start?"

"Yeah, I mean, are you gonna just walk up to random people and ask to have sex? Do you have people you already do these things with?"

"Random people? Ha ha!" His laugh surprised me. I felt he should've been a bit more concerned about my feelings, and I probably scowled at him.

"Well, I'm just not sure how all of it will work, if you know what I mean." I wanted him to help and support me, I guess. I was waiting for him to guide me.

"There's nothing that has to work so much as we just need to figure out what you're willing to try and get started. For me, there's nothing I don't want, so let me know how you want to start and we can.

We don't have to start immediately, but at some point we'll need to kick things off."

"I'm pretty nervous…I'm afraid I won't be able to keep up, or that you'll want something that I can't do. I have lines I can't cross, I think…"

"Well, we'll have to see how that goes, I guess. I want to be sure to honor your boundaries." He was looking out to the street. We were at the edge of the park and the Upper West Side. A soft breeze was blowing, and it felt so luxurious. I loved the nature to the one side of me, and the Gothic stone-and-iron to the other…like I was balanced on a knife blade, between two worlds. I guess I was, really. I *was* sitting on the boundary between two worlds—my old, simple, plain, uncomplicated life and a brave, fascinating, scary, dark world I knew nothing of.

And there I sat.

During the last few weeks, I had spent much of my time trying to think about all the possible scenarios, and what I would and would not be able to do. There wasn't anybody I could speak with…how do you ask a friend about something like this? Yet, I knew I needed more information. I went to the public library and found a few books on fetishes, but nothing was helpful. I considered myself completely heterosexual, so I thought I would draw the line at lesbianism. It seemed so foreign to my life that I felt that was a line I would never cross. I had no idea…

Other than that, much of the work seemed to be on David's side. Swinging? Orgies? Those were things he would have to set up and execute, and I could opt out of anything I didn't like. I didn't know what to expect, and I didn't know how to take the first steps myself.

I was not horrified, though, as many people might have been. I didn't consider anything so horrific that I would lose my mind (or perspective) if the subject were proposed. Certain fetishes didn't excite me in any way, but at the same time I didn't consider anything I read about to be gross or evil. Those judgments didn't exist within me.

"So how about you, Rachel? How did it go with Stella?"

"It went well…"

"Yeah?"

"Yeah…I brought in all my poems and a few short pieces. She read through many of them with me. She showed me what would be marketable and what would not. I signed a development contract, and have been working on more poems."

"Yeah? That's great! Did you get a check when you signed?"

"A small one. A thousand dollars. Poetry doesn't sell that much, after all. But I've written several more poems while you were gone. I sent the latest to her yesterday. Hoping to hear back in a few days."

"You should've delivered them in person!"

"Oh, I hate to be pushy. She can read them at her leisure. That'll also give me some time to write a few more. I think I'll need eight to ten more poems to finish a good collection, at least as she viewed it."

"Well, I think it's fantastic, Rachel. I'm so proud of you."

"I would've never even started if it wasn't for you, David. Thank you."

"No, don't thank me."

"But I must…"

"No, it's nothing really…you wrote those poems."

"Without your push and introduction to Stella, I would still only be dreaming about writing. Now, I'm putting together something that *could* get published."

"Well, you're more than welcome." His smile was bright and warm.

"Well, I really want to thank you in a special way." As I said this, I reached over and put my hand on his crotch and began to massage him. Immediately he stiffened. He looked me in the eyes, then leaned his head back and began to breathe steadily. I continued to stroke him, and he became even harder.

Breathily, he said, "I think we'd better go back to my place…"

"No," I said, "not yet." I unzipped his pants, and found his hard manhood. I began to stroke him faster and squeeze between strokes. He looked at me knowingly, and then closed his eyes. I could see him flushing.

I scanned the area. There were a few people in the general area, but nobody was watching us. Central Park West was a little busy, but our bench was below street level, and there were some trees between the road and us. I felt my courage rising.

Could I go further? Could I do this? He looked so handsome with his head back. His jagged face and lithe body were so perfect. I was so excited that I was giving him pleasure. I wanted to do more. I wanted him to have what he wanted. My bit of reading on fetishes taught me just a couple of things, and I was going to use those. I was going to get things started tonight. I was going to go places I never thought I could. I decided in that very moment.

Was this for him or for me? If you had asked me then, I would have told you it was entirely for him. If you ask me today, I will share ownership. Maybe I wanted this as much as he did. Maybe more.

David looked at me with surprise when I pulled him out. His head swiveled around, and he had a slightly panicked look on his face. *Good!* Maybe he wasn't as adventurous as he thought he was. Maybe I could surprise him!

And he was so big and thick! It took some maneuvering to get him out of his pants. But when it was free, I wanted it. I wanted to pleasure him. I wanted him to have a taste of the immense pleasure he had given me. I wanted him to see I could be bold and adventurous. I wanted to show him that I wasn't afraid. I, too, could be out on the knife's edge; I too had courage.

I could have wings and fly.

I lowered my head down, and took him into my mouth.

I felt so excited! The danger! The fear of being caught! What would everybody say? In my head, I was expecting a police car to screech up or whistles to blow. But I wasn't going to stop. And I began to take him in earnest. I took him as deeply into my mouth as I could. He put his hand on the back of my head, and applied just a bit of pressure. I was taking all I could, and letting him hit the back of my throat. It felt so nasty and dirty and exciting and sexy. I wanted him to come in my mouth at that very moment.

David was moaning now. I could feel him getting thicker the more I took him in, and it became harder to perform on him. His head was back, and his lidded eyes looked to the stars. When I could, I scanned around, and nobody was looking at us. We were out in public and yet in our own world. People were busy going to dinner or taking a walk or on their way to visit friends. They didn't know a man and woman were sinfully at work on this quiet bench.

By now, I was much more excited myself. While I thought this moment was going to be for David, I was incredibly turned on. The more I thought about someone catching us or even someone watching us, the hotter and wetter I became. The risk and anticipation of it were very erotic.

Danger. Fear. If you haven't tried them, you're missing some incredible sensory sensations. Natural aphrodisiacs were pumping through my veins.

I had wanted David to finish in my mouth, but I became so aroused I couldn't control myself. I slid my right hand down, and then up my long skirt. I was already very wet. When I touched myself, I knew I was already close. I was smoldering with pent-up pressure and excitement. It had been weeks, after all, but it was more than that—I was taking control. I was leading us into danger. And I liked that feeling.

I had to have him in me.

David looked up when I released him from my mouth. I quickly jerked my panties down and then off. I moved my long peasant skirt as I climbed on top of him. He didn't look shocked at all. Instead, he held me off just a second while he slid his pants down a bit. I positioned myself over him, and then I took him inside me.

I was instantly near a thunderous orgasm. I was already shaking from the intensity. My knees were on either side of him, and I grabbed onto his shoulders. I began to rock and squeeze him. He felt so large in me again, but I was so ready for him I knew I was soaking his crotch. I was so close I began to ride with speed, and I was quickly grabbing the undulations of fire that ran through me. I looked down, and David's eyes were staring at me like he would devour me right there. He began talking to me through gritted teeth.

"That's it, baby…fuck my cock…fuck me with that hot, wet pussy…"

I was so intensely energized that his words put me over the edge. I leaned my head back and gasped my intense, burning orgasm. My brain and body were on fire, no matter the cool breeze blowing on me. I wanted to shriek, but held that back. I knew my gasps weren't much quieter though. I bit my lip hard, and grunted and panted like I was sprinting.

And a funny thing happened. I began to secretly *hope* that someone would catch us. That's right! I *wanted* someone to walk up and shout at us. I wanted the police to be called. I wanted to be vilified and ridiculed. I wanted to be humiliated. I wanted the world to know I was a whore…a slut…the type of girl who would have sex in Central Park with a man she hardly knew. I wanted that ridicule. I wanted to be *that girl.* I grabbed on to the dark side, and rode it.

While still burning in my climax, I yanked open the top buttons of my blouse in a fit of passion. I was lost…I was not there. Someone else was doing this. I lifted up my bra and stuffed my breasts into his mouth. The cool night air hit my nipples and kept my orgasm burning. It would not stop! David chewed on my hard nipples fiercely, and I let out a shriek of pleasure and pain. I was riding so hard now I was afraid I would hurt him or me.

And I wanted it all. I smashed his face against my breasts. I was grinding my body onto his. And still he talked to me…still he growled at me.

"Fuck that cock, Rachel! Fuck that cock hard! Everybody can see you! Everybody knows what you're doing!" His voice was too loud but I didn't care.

I slowly came down from my fierce, massive climax…and I was trembling…weak…but the intensity was still there, and I knew I could get another one. I was lost in dark passion. I had *surrendered* to the darkness…and I had liked it.

And then his head pulled away…his eyes rolled back, and I knew he was close. The sight of his beautiful face flushing with pleasure put me over the edge again, and I immediately began another…just seconds after my last one. I was riding and sweating and grunting and trembling, and then the fire began. As the hot pulses of pleasure rolled through me, I threw back my head and let out an uncontrolled shriek. Full volume. I didn't care…I was in this moment and there were no others. I heard David grunting hard and his burning wetness filled me. I wanted all of it, and rode him with all I had. I was only tingling and burning and shrieking. I lost all control…I was only my climax.

And then I heard voices. My vision was blurred with tears, but I looked around and saw people looking and pointing at us. I could see people moving.

"C'mon, Rachel, let's go…"

I climbed off onto wobbly legs, and felt his issue running down my thighs. He pulled up his pants and put his slick penis away, while I hastily buttoned my blouse. And then he grabbed my hand and we took off running. I was dizzy and could barely control my legs; they moved without my volition. His hard grip pulled me forward. Despite this mad moment, I started laughing. I was trying to button my blouse, but with my breasts bouncing and swaying I was having little luck. Yet I found it immensely humorous…running through beautiful, tree-lined paths, with David's semen running down my thighs. Breasts swinging, blouse open. Who was doing this? Me? It was some insane burlesque, not *my* life. Nobody who knew me would have believed that I was in this situation in this moment.

And *I* couldn't believe it! I had just had sex in public. I had just exposed myself to the whole world. I had lost myself in passion in Central Park, of all places. Anybody who looked would've seen my breasts and David's penis. And yet I had orgasmed immensely…more powerfully than I had ever imagined. I had experienced a type of pleasure I hadn't felt before, partly because it was coupled with that sense of danger. That sweet sense of fear.

We ran, laughing and panting…my sandals were terrible for running, so I took them off and ran barefoot. We eventually reached a line of trees that led to the Lake. We followed them, and then tried to act nonchalantly. As we did so, we heard people running nearby, but they went away from us.

I realized too late that I had left my panties on the bench, and I again began to laugh loudly. David looked at me, and laughed along with me. We were panting and tittering like little children.

He put his arms around me and said, "I love you, Rachel."

I leaned into his arms, still lost in laughter.

*W*e grabbed a taxi a few blocks down, hoping nobody would recognize us. We giggled the entire ride. We went back to David's apartment and cleaned up. I felt so deliciously dirty, wiping his semen from my thighs. I was giggling in the bathroom. I ended up taking a quick shower.

And then we were back out into the city. It was a beautiful night, and I wanted to be free and out and living in this amazing concrete jungle. I was feeling alive and in love with life.

I needed new panties, though, so we took a taxi to Fifth Avenue. Once inside the taxi, David leaned over and planted a warm kiss on my lips. I was so energized! I felt like the moment in the park had transformed me. I grabbed him and pulled him to me, pulled him hard against me. He began to kiss me strongly, and I kissed back. We lost ourselves in our kissing. His whiskers scratched my face, and I drank in his deep smell and expensive cologne. I loved his rough, strong body against me.

I sneaked a peek and saw that the driver was watching us in his rearview mirror. I smiled leeringly at him, and then returned to kissing David again. I began to lose myself in his kisses. I began to lose myself in the moment. More to the point, I *let* myself be lost in those kisses. I was soaring…I was a sparrow flying fast over a mountain, feeling the updrafts hit the underside of my wings. I wanted to go higher.

And I felt like a new me. I know that sounds a bit silly…corny even…one wild moment didn't make me a different person. Yet, in many ways, I was new. Reborn. Energized. Free. Freed from a prison, perhaps of my own making. I guess part of it was throwing off the societal pressures that were heavy on women in those days. Women had to sit with backs erect, smile at men's humor, be pretty and sweet. Clean and restrained. Thoughtless. Pure. Never too happy, never too sad. Always keeping our thoughts and ideas to whispers among friends.

Yet now I was venturing into a new realm, a new reality. I was going where women didn't go in my day. I was taking a course most would never dare sail, out into the dark ocean to find new lands. I loved the trepidation. Breaking through barriers is never easy.

So as I was kissing David, I took his hand, his warm, strong hand, and placed it on my breast…the one closest to the taxi driver. I felt him squeeze so gently at first, and then more strongly. I began to get hot. Another quick peek and I saw the driver was watching us still. His eyes flashed between the road and the mirror. Those darting, sinful eyes! I decided to give him a show. I would fill his mirror with something he had never seen in it before.

I pulled back, and began to unbutton my blouse, my eyes burning into David's. Just a few buttons, but enough to provide access. David slipped his hand in, bypassed my bra, and squeezed my bare breast. His rough hand made my nipple hard. I tilted my head back, and he began to kiss my neck with passion. His kisses woke my skin, and I tingled all over.

I pushed him back, and looked again into his deep, black eyes. I leaned back against the door, opening the remaining buttons on my blouse. I then inched my skirt up, showing my smooth thighs. David fixed his gaze on me…his eyes were flaming, as if he meant to incinerate me with the heat of his ebony stare. And then he was on me. His hot mouth smashed against mine. His strong hands were grabbing my breasts, which were now throbbing. And then I felt his hand slide down. I wanted his rough hands all over me. I wanted every inch of my body to be scraped with his hot, callused hands.

I noticed that the taxi was not moving. I thought we might be at a light, but I was enjoying his ministrations too much, losing myself to his touch. My body was prickling all over, and I was so excited to know the driver was probably watching us.

David slipped two fingers inside me, and we could both feel how soaked I was. His fingers were so insistent…strong and rough. I pushed back against them. I began to burn all over my body. Hot, deep ripples were spreading through me and over me. Through our hot panting, I heard another mouth panting. I felt motion, not with David and me, but near. I was so caught up in our passion that I didn't want to even consider what this other motion could be. I pushed myself over and over against David's rough hand. I pushed my breasts against him. I ground my mouth on his, and fought for his tongue. Oh God! I was on fire. I could smell my sex. The windows were fogging from our breath. And still that extra motion was nearby, near us.

Though I was immolating in my furious passion, I guess curiosity eventually got the best of me, and I had to find out what was causing this other movement. My eyes were slammed shut, but I forced them open just enough to peek through the bottom of my lids. The driver had pulled to the side of the road. His head was turned, and he was watching us directly. He was masturbating, though I could only see the motion of his shoulders and not his erection. I could now hear, though, a moist, slapping sound that matched the rhythm of his movements.

Though he was a balding, paunchy man in his forties, it made me so hot that he was watching us and pleasuring himself. I decided to give him something to enjoy. There was no more pretense—we all knew the score.

I began to moan with my passion now. I continued to push my wetness against David's hand. The added thrill of being watched enhanced the tingling sensations flittering through my body. I could feel the beginnings of a climax, though it was off in the distance. I let it stay there…I wanted to build this one slowly…it was there when I needed it.

I then found my hand on David's crotch. I pulled at his zipper, but couldn't get an angle on it. He kept his hand inside me, but pulled the other off my breast. He unzipped himself, and opened his belt buckle. I dug into his crotch and pulled at his thick penis. It was already so hard, and dripping with excitement. I pulled it up and stroked it hard, yanking on it…pulling it toward me. I used his moisture to wet the tip. I heard the subtlest moan from our driver.

I wanted David inside me again. I wanted to feel his large manhood pressing into my body. The angle, though, just wasn't right. I pushed against his chest, forcing him to slide back. He understood, and moved back against the door, still facing me. I then lowered my head to his crotch, and took him into my mouth.

Though we had just made love a short while before, he was absolutely rigid…maybe even stiffer than he had been earlier. I moved up and down on him, and could feel him growing even larger, and throbbing in my mouth. I couldn't see it, but I know David made eye contact with the driver. I know this because the driver said, "You're a lucky sonofabitch, man!" in a heavy Brooklyn accent.

He was enjoying the show! Good! I pulled my hair and threw it to the other side of my head. This gave the driver the full view of my efforts to pleasure David. My saliva ran down his length, and I purposely slurped to make more of a production.

And I went at it with gusto. I bobbed my head up and down, over and over. I used my hand to pump his shaft, and drive him as deeply into my mouth as I could take him. David leaned his head back. To give the driver a better show, I used my left hand to fully expose my breasts. I then slipped that hand down to my crotch, pulling up my skirt. I began to rub my aching clitoris, first with one and then two fingers. I was sucking David with all I had, but it did feel good to have pressure. My orgasm wasn't nearly as far away now. It was becoming more imminent now. I knew it would overwhelm me soon.

To help it, I inserted two fingers. I was so open and wet that I could hear the damp sounds. And it felt so good! I was burning from my own heat. My face was on fire now. I knew the driver was enjoying it too, because I could feel the car moving even more with his vigorous pumping. His breath was quicker than David's. I could hear his moisture…I could hear that he was close to an orgasm. I decided to help him get there.

I pulled the two fingers out of me. I looked into David's eyes, and slowly, languidly, put those two fingers into my mouth, tasting myself. I let out a long "Mmmmm" as I did so. My tangy juices still had a hint of David's musky flavor.

"Oh shit, man!" I heard the driver shout, and then, "Un un un un un." I could hear his squirting strokes. I could hear his climax, and it set me off on my own. I pushed my fingers back into me and came... violently. I lifted my head up and shouted, "Oh fuck!" and twisted under the massive, extreme peak. It was shorter than the one earlier, but just as intense...maybe more. The taxi was spinning in my brain, and I was riding the pleasure as it raced through me. My head swam, and thoughts whooshed through my brain.

When I had finished, I looked up, panting heavily. David was looking down at me with a smile on his face. I could smell the driver's semen. I suddenly felt a bit self-conscious, and immediately sat up and began to button my blouse. David, too, began to put himself together, though he was still engorged. He hadn't finished, so it took some doing.

The driver had a hand-towel and was cleaning up his dashboard and steering wheel.

"Uh, I hope you don't mind...I'm gonna drop you off here. Fifth Avenue is one block up. I gotta get home. Fare's on me." His face was slack, and he looked exhausted.

We got out, and walked into the night air. David put his arm around me.

We found a shop called Mandy's just a few blocks down Fifth Avenue. David was feeling very sexually agitated, as he hadn't been able to climax in the taxi. I liked him on this edge, this agitated state of interrupted orgasm, but I could see he clearly wasn't feeling very comfortable. His pants were just too tight. I saw a hungry look in his dark eyes, and I knew he wanted to take me home and ravish me. I was enjoying the tease, and wanted to torture him just a bit more.

When we entered Mandy's, I saw they had quite a variety of panties and other under-garments. However, now that I was there I wasn't ready to lose the nakedness under my peasant skirt. It was such a free feeling...such a dangerous feeling. This was a new experience, and I was enjoying it. The cool evening air moving up my naked thighs had felt so erotic. I was in no hurry to lose this feeling. Instead, I went to the shoes. David grumpily followed me. I guess he assumed I was just going to shop and ignore his ache.

As it was late at night, the store was empty, except for a very young salesman. He came over and asked if I needed any help. "We close in about twenty minutes" he warned us. I looked at some heels. Though I normally don't like very high ones, I suddenly felt the urge to try some on. After all, I was breaking lots of my own rules tonight. Why not push other boundaries?

I asked him to show me a pair of black stilettos in a size seven. I sat down while he came back with them. David was drifting around the store a little. He was probably wondering why I was trying on shoes when we came here for panties. Maybe he was walking off his erection.

The young man knelt in front of me to help me try them on. I caught David's eye and gave him a devilish wink. As I did so, I began to shift in my seat and let my skirt ride up. The salesman must have been around twenty...probably a college student. He did his best to stay focused on my shoes, but it wasn't long before I caught him sneaking a peek up my skirt. I pretended to be interested in these shoes, looking at them from different angles. My movements opened my legs to him. I knew he could see all the way up my skirt and straight into my womanhood.

He blushed. Hard. His face was sanguine and his eyes were large; he was sweating instantly. I looked at David, and he also flushed. He was watching us without breathing.

"What do you think, David, do these shoes look good on me?"

"What?"

"These shoes? What do you think?" I stood up suddenly, and the spell was broken for both of them. David looked into my eyes and then down at my shoes.

"Uh, yeah...they look good."

"Hmmm...I don't like them." I saw another pair...they were ugly, but it wasn't the shoes I was interested in. "Do you have those in a seven?"

"Ummm...let me check..." the young boy hurried to the backroom.

I smiled at David, and he leered back at me, lust pouring through his veins.

"Did you like that?"

"Yeah...I did..."

"You did?"

"Yeah...I like everything."

The salesman was back in a minute. I noticed that he was actually just about to be good looking. His face was shiny and pimply...youth, after all. But when his face cleared up and he lost his nervous twitchiness, he would be a handsome young man.

He knelt down in front of me again. Before I sat down, I ensured my skirt was up my thighs already, so that when I sat he could see clearly. I pulled it around the back a bit, which elevated it in the front.

He made no pretense about focusing on my shoes. His eyes flitted back and forth between my feet and my sex. I kept my legs wide for him. His hands were shaking as he slid these shoes on. They were horrible brown things, but I pretended to be ambivalent about them.

"Oh, I don't know...what do you think, David?" I stood up and modeled them. I walked to a mirror and looked at myself wearing them. I was careful to toss my skirt around a little, to show some thigh.

"Um, I don't know. Maybe you should try another pair." David was in on the game now.

"Yeah. How about these wedges? Do you have those in seven?"

The boy was in the backroom again. I could see David's crotch bulging. His face was dark now. I knew he was aroused. I was enjoying this little game, and I could feel the excited shivering in my belly, the goose bumps on my arms and back. I heard a few boxes fall in the back, and I smiled to myself.

The young man was back. I again sat with my skirt up, this time bunched halfway up my thighs. As he knelt down, I gave him what he wanted. This time, he never took his eyes off my crotch. He moved ever so slowly, putting the shoes on my feet. They were wedges, and could slip on quickly, but he made it a very slow process. His hands were very hot and wet, and trembling visibly. I looked at his crotch, and could clearly see his erection was straining to be free. In those days, men wore very tight pants, and it seemed as if he was about to rip out of his khakis.

I was never a popular girl. I was never the sexy girl. I wasn't the blonde cheerleader who dated the quarterback. Never the homecoming queen. I was the nerd who outworked everybody. I was a teacher, for God's sake! I had never unleashed my feminine power before. Yet here I was with a young, soon-to-be-handsome salesman kneeling in front of me, and a stunning boyfriend, and both were watching me with lust and desire. This was entirely new for me, and, I'm afraid to say, I reveled in it. The tease. The heat. The desire. I was making them want me. I had the power. I had the control. I could stop it and start it at any time. I guess it was immature of me, but this was something I had missed growing up. I had never been a girl who could tease a man until he begged for her. Most girls work that out in high school, but this was totally new to me. So if I seem to have been acting badly, I can only say that I was blooming late in my sexuality. I make no apologies.

And I was feeling very sexy, and that's never wrong. So sexy, in fact, that I was immensely wet with anticipation. I didn't know how far I would go, and already I had crossed a hundred boundaries I never thought I could. Yet I also knew I wasn't about to generate an orgy in a shoe store.

"Gee, I don't know. None of these are doing it for me. Do you have anything else…something you think would look good on me?" I asked with innocence in my eyes. I shouldn't have bothered, as the young man's eyes were focused elsewhere.

"Um, yeah…" He stood up, slowly tearing his eyes away from my swollen sex. He was in the backroom again. As he did, I pulled up my skirt even higher. There was no more pretense. I was fully exposing my wet sex to a young man. When he came back, he immediately focused on my crotch when kneeling before me. I might as well have been naked, as my skirt was bunched up around my waist.

"What shoes did you bring me?" I asked with feigned interest.

"Um, yeah…." He pretended to be reaching for a box of shoes.

"Or would you rather look at my pussy?" I asked.

He looked up at me for the first time in a while, enlarged eyes like a child with his hand in the cookie jar.

"Oh, sorry…it's just…"

"It's okay…I know you were looking at her. Do you like her?" I cooed my words.

"Yeah!" He sounded too overexcited. A quick glance at David showed me he was curious about where this was going also. His bulge looked absolutely massive in his pants. His arms were at his side, and he was leaning forward. Had the young salesman looked at him, he probably would have felt intimidated by his presence…but he avoided David's stare completely.

I slid my hand sensuously down my stomach, and then began to tease my first two fingers around my now badly swollen opening. I was absolutely dripping. As I moved my fingers over it, they became slick with my wetness. I began to play, slowly at first. The young man looked like he was seeing God for the first time. I wondered for a moment if he was a virgin.

Then when I knew I had his full attention, I slipped first one, then two fingers inside me. His mouth dropped open. His eyes glazed over. His face drew closer to me. I began to move my fingers in and out, spreading my moisture, which was practically gushing out of me. He put his hand on my thigh, which surprised me at first. His hand was clammy. I didn't push him away.

I looked over at David, and he was rubbing himself through his pants. His eyes were focused on my fingers inside me, and the boy watching me. His eyes darted between us. The smell of my sex was in the air, and there was thick tension in the room. All I could hear was panting. The salesman was now pushing against his own crotch with the heel of his hand. His pants were straining under the pressure. He had a large wet spot.

I'm not sure what the salesman expected, but I wasn't about to do anything with him. Instead, I wanted to see if he would respond the way the taxi driver had. I pulled my two sopping fingers out. His eyes followed them. I then placed the two fingers in my mouth and tasted myself. Immediately, I saw his eyes roll back. His face flushed even more, his head tilted back, and he grunted his orgasm loudly. I could see the wetness growing on his crotch.

This might sound very odd, but his orgasm excited me incredibly. Why? I had brought a young man to climax without touching him in any way…simply by showing him my body and providing some teasing play. For a woman who felt out of place, I felt immensely empowered. I was a sexual tigress, and I wanted to let out all that I held inside me.

However, it was time to go. I looked up to David, who was still touching himself through his pants.

"Let's go," I said, and we walked to the door.

I looked back at my young friend, and he was still on his knees where I had left him. His face was red, and his chin was down to his chest.

*W*hen we got back to his apartment, David nearly dragged me upstairs. I wouldn't have it, though. It's hard to describe, but I was so on edge... so worked up...I wanted this night to go on forever. It took some doing, but I talked him into getting the Corvette. His brother was still out of town, and David had been keeping it at his place, as his building had a secure car park. When we walked to the garage, David was clearly agitated, but I wasn't giving up the control I had just gained. I felt like we had switched roles, if only for tonight...I was the one making the decisions, and I liked it.

Out on the road, I saw his frustration through his clenched jaw. "Where do you want to go?" He looked like a small boy who didn't get his toy.

"Take the tunnel...let's drive into Jersey," I directed.

"Jersey?"

"Believe me, I'm going to make it worth your while." Moving through Midtown, I noticed it was nearly one o'clock in the morning. My energy was high, and I felt I could be out all night.

As we entered the tunnel, I reached behind my back and unfastened my bra. In a flash, I pulled my top off and exposed my bare breasts. The cool evening air produced rigid goose bumps all over my body. The wind blowing over my naked torso was so exhilarating! I was young and new and fresh. I was alive. I was primal. I was a woman who was waking up—mind, body, and spirit. I wasn't about to slow down. I wanted to go faster and faster. My naked breasts drank in the night air.

And David immediately perked up. As we moved through the tunnel, I was studying the faces of the drivers coming the other way. I saw eyes grow large. One man honked his horn. Once out of the tunnel, he opened it up and we were racing down the highway. I sat up high in the seat and held my arms over my head. My body was on display for the whole world to see, but I was not embarrassed at all. My skin was crackling with electricity. I shrieked out…baying to the night air. Never, ever could I have imagined I would feel so alive and sexual and raw, racing down the road in a shiny, fast car, a beautiful man behind the wheel, and my nakedness catching the wind of the night air. My hair flew out behind me. I was Lady Godiva…unashamed for the first time. I was the goddess of the night, and the wind worshipped my body as it whipped around me.

We took an exit outside Newark, and we slowed. I sunk back into my seat. David drove until we found a row of trees away from any buildings. I asked him to park and turn off the car.

And then I was on him. My mouth smashed into his. I shoved my breasts hard against him. I put my arms around his neck and pulled him hard to me. Our tongues fought each other. I took his between my lips and sucked on it hard. Then I pulled his face down to my naked breasts, and pressed my nipples into his hungry mouth. I was attacking him…I was taking sex from him. I was a hungry lioness taking her prey.

I was so immensely keyed up. I remember never wanting sex more than I wanted it at that moment. The park. The taxi. The shoe salesman. The naked ride. My whole body was intense sensation, and I was ready to explode with the merest touch. Every nerve ending of my skin was alive…they burned so much it felt like I was being stung by a thousand bees.

I pulled back from him and began to rip at his pants. He helped me get his buckle undone, and then I had him out. His large cock looked angry, and he was already dripping. I wanted that in me so badly. I straddled him, and forced him into me hard. I was so excited he slid in easily, and I had a shuddering orgasm almost immediately. As I climaxed, he bit down hard on my nipple, and my mind flew thirty thousand feet in the air. I was in the clouds over the Andes. I was rain on the high desert. I was snow in the Himalayas. My body and mind floated above the world and saw every flower, every tree, every blade of grass.

And then I became fury.

I began to grind myself on him with all that I had. I was slamming myself down with acrimony. David was already growling at me. He was talking, though at first I couldn't make out what he was saying. Then I realized he was critiquing the show I gave him.

"You loved it when that boy came, didn't you?" I knew his mind was feeling nasty, and he wanted me to feed his fire. I was ready to pleasure his body and his mind. I was ready to take him down any road he wanted to go but not by following him—I wanted to lead the way.

"You liked that, baby? You liked me being a dirty girl? You like me being a tease?" I hummed softly into his ear.

"Oh fuck, yeah…you made me so hot." His voice was so deep and primal…he was a bear…all instincts and anger and aggression.

"Oh yeah, I can feel it. You're so hard inside me. Give me that hot prick. Fuck me with it, David. I want your hot come inside me."

"Yeah, you made that boy come too, didn't you, you bad girl!" I could feel him expanding inside me, and I knew he was close. I could feel him about to burst inside me. *Oh, that made him hot, did it?*

"Oh yeah, that boy touched my legs and wanted to lick my pussy…you know he did…maybe I should have let him…"

That was all it took. David threw his head back and began a deep, groaning orgasm. I felt it burning inside of me, like his seed was gasoline. It burned and ached inside me. His orgasm set off another, shorter one in me. We were groaning and burning and panting, our heads turned up to the night sky. We were coyotes in the desert night. My hair thrashed his face. I squeezed my arms around his neck and panted up to the moon.

And then a sharp light was in my eyes. "What are you two doing here? *Jesus H. Christ!*"

We were so lost in ourselves we hadn't noticed a police car pull up next to us. The officer had turned the squad car's side spotlight on us. It was blindingly bright. I immediately scrambled for my clothes. I heard both officers get out and slam their doors. David began to swear under his breath.

"I'm going to need to see some ID," the first officer said. His partner stood a bit off, resting his elbow on his gun belt. We obliged … though I threw on my blouse before I dug into my purse. The same officer read our information over the radio. I noticed the second cop had a nasty leering smile on his face. I suddenly felt incredibly dirty. His sickening expression judged me…and I hated judgment.

"Looks like we ruined your fun," said the leering cop. We didn't answer, and kept dressing.

After a bit the first officer returned. He handed back our IDs. "They got no priors," he said to his partner.

"You're not gonna let 'em go, are you, Sarge?"

He didn't answer his partner. "Look, what you guys did may seem harmless, but this is a residential area. Just up the street are some good families. If one of their kids came down this street and saw what you were up to, that wouldn't be good. I'm letting you go with a warning this time. Don't come back here with none of that shit, okay?"

David was quick to reply, "You got it, sir."

"Drive safely, folks."

We backed out, still hearing his partner protesting. He apparently felt we deserved a harsher punishment. Or did his lascivious smile suggest something else? I'm glad I never found out.

We drove home in silence. David drove the speed limit the entire way back. I don't think he exhaled until we were in Manhattan.

When we were in the elevator, I looked over at David. He looked back at me. When his eyes met mine, I broke out into the silliest laughter I had experienced since I was a little girl. I laughed and laughed until we reached the door of his apartment. He didn't so much as smile, and instead looked like the boy who got caught cheating on a test.

I called in sick the next day, and we spent a long morning lounging in bed. We held each other and talked softly. Outside, I could just hear the traffic of the big city below us. We drank orange juice and listened to the morning news on the clock radio.

I finally broke the ice. "How did you feel about last night, David?" I asked, studying his face. I wondered if his view of me changed. Did the sobering morning bring a new perspective on us? Did I lose the veneer of "the good girl" and become a raving skank worthy of derision?

"You mean the cops?"

"No, I mean everything we did…Central Park, the drive, the shoe salesman…"

"It was incredible…you surprised me…you were more than I had hoped for."

"Really?"

"Well, yeah…those are the type of experiences I yearn for. Surprise…liberation…uninhibited actions…doing whatever crazy thing we can think of. But avoiding the cops would be wise in the future." He smiled. "Neither of us need that in our lives."

"So when the salesman touched my thigh you weren't angry?" I was studying him carefully, looking for signs of judgment.

"I was hoping you'd go further…"

"Seriously?"

"Yeah."

"Like how much further?"

"I was hoping you'd let him go down on you or something like that."

"You wouldn't have been jealous that a stranger was doing that to me?"

"Jealous? Well, I think that is part of it…it's one of the many emotions I go through. Jealousy, hurt, anger, attraction, excitement…it's a jumble of many emotions…all at incredible speed."

So far, his face and movements betrayed nothing surreptitious.

"But don't you later feel that jealousy stinging you?"

"Well, here and there…but I also feel intense excitement at the same time."

"That's hard for me to understand, David. The thought of you with another woman makes me feel very jealous and angry, and I don't know if I'd get over it." I had to let him know my feelings, and we had to talk this out. "I've tried to picture us swapping and doing other things, and I only feel like I would be angry and vengeful." His face darkened a bit.

"Well, I understand. Last night, though, you were pretty wild. You don't think you can let that spirit out in different situations?"

"I'm not sure…I try to imagine it, and it's cloudy…"

"I get that…we call this 'the life' and it's not for everybody. If you can't do some things I will definitely understand, like we spoke about before I left. But…you have to admit last night we were having a blast, yeah?"

"At least until the cops showed up…then I felt humiliated." He rolled over and looked me in the eyes.

"Well, that was a first for me also…but last night was one of the best nights of my life. I felt so free and alive…" He looked a bit wistful.

"Me, too, but I don't ever want to experience the humiliation of the police again, okay?"

"Yeah, let's avoid sex outdoors…for a while anyway." He laughed softly to himself.

"So are there places where we can do these things safely? Is the life safe from arrest?"

"Oh, of course…especially here in New York. Plus, I know some great places overseas. Europe is much freer with sex than the US."

I have to admit I was intrigued, but I was also jealous thinking of David flying around the world, having sex in random places with random people.

"In Tanzania also?"

David let out a big laugh, eyes up to the ceiling. "No, not in Tanzania, silly Rachel. In Tanzania I was fighting bugs and disease and lions."

Okay, I felt better. "But how do you learn about places where these things happen? How do you learn about all of this? Most people, I think, never know such places exist." I really was curious.

"Well, it's like a network of people. We share information with people we trust. In the US, you have to be careful because in some states this life is illegal. Not in New York though…here you'd be amazed at who you see in these types of gatherings."

"Like whom?"

"Politicians. Celebrities. I've seen many."

I was intrigued.

"Studio 54 used to be the place, and you'd see rock stars and celebrities all over. Cher. Bowie. The upstairs at that place was basically a giant orgy. But it has become quite a drag recently, and you have to watch out for people taking pictures. I avoid it now. Plus, I'm not into drugs, and there's a lot of that there…too much…"

"Have you ever been with any celebrities?"

"A couple, but I'd rather not talk about it. Maybe another time."

"Okay. But can I ask you some other questions?"

"Shoot."

"How did you find yourself in the life? What got you started? Nobody just starts out this way, I'm sure." I know now that I sounded awfully judgmental but I was young.

"Well, I think I probably always had a very strong sex drive, and was naturally curious about everything. That's how I started with writing and traveling."

"Okay, but how did you start sexually? Did you just one day find an orgy and jump in?"

"No, nothing like that," he said, chuckling lightly.

"Well, c'mon then, tell me about your sexual experiences. I'm curious."

"Are you going to try to psychoanalyze me? 'David, you're a pervert because…'"

"No, nothing like that."

"Believe me, it happens a lot. Every woman I'm with thinks she can cure me of 'this disease that's inside.'" His fingers were pumping the quotations. "I can't and don't want to be cured. I like the life. It makes me happy. I'd be bored to tears living any other way."

"What were your first sexual experiences like?" I was sure there would be something in there that I could pick up on. I guess I was already guilty of what others had tried in his past. Would knowing make anything different?

"Well, I started early. I was always intrigued by sex and the human body. When I was ten I was already masturbating. I remember being at a pool on hot summer days and seeing girls with only a swimsuit on used to give me the most painful erections!"

"Who took your virginity?"

"Well, I lost it very early…I was fourteen. We had a neighbor on our floor. Mrs. Crinshaw. Her husband was a bus driver. He worked long hours, putting in overtime to make a few extra bucks. Mrs. Crinshaw told my mother that she needed a hand with a few chores, and asked if I wanted to make some extra money."

"Chores?"

"Well, she told my mother I could change some light bulbs, or load boxes in closets…stuff like that. I did one day, and she paid me five dollars. That was easy money. So I would always ask her if she needed any chores done, and she would have something for me to do. One day, she asked me to stay after and talk."

"Talk?"

"That's what she said." Wry smile. "She went into her bedroom and came out in a nightie. She was an older woman…probably forty-five or so…but she wasn't unattractive. She was slender. She had a beautiful face, though it was lined with the years. Still, she was thirty years older than I was."

"What did you think when you saw her in the nightie?"

"I was a bit surprised, as you can imagine. I was only fourteen, after all. She asked me to sit down next to her on the couch. I did. She began to tell me she was lonely because her husband worked so many hours. She told me she just liked to hold a man from time to time. I didn't know what she meant, but I had never sat that close to a woman before...except my mother."

"Then what happened?"

"Well, she asked if I would hug her. I did. She then kissed me on the mouth. It surprised me, but I was excited as well."

"You were only fourteen...I can't believe a woman would take advantage of you like that. It's perverted, don't you think?"

"Well, believe me when I say I am conflicted about that whole period. If that were my son, I would be furious. But...I was a horny teenager, willing to do anything. Still, she was not the type of female I had envisioned losing my virginity to."

"Then what happened?"

"When she kissed me, she put my hand on her breast. It was the first time I'd touched a breast, and I became very excited. She let me squeeze her breasts for a while. Then she took me into the bedroom, stripped me, and we had sex."

"Regular sex?" I guess I wanted to know all the details.

"She pulled me on top of her and put me inside. I didn't last very long. I don't think she really enjoyed it. I think she was just so horny she had to have something."

"So that was it? You came? Then what?"

"Well, she cleaned me up and sent me back home. I came back the next day after school and then the next day...and every day for a while."

"You let her take advantage of you?"

"She wasn't taking advantage of me, really. I guess in the legal sense she was. But I was happy for it. I was so glad to have someone to have sex with that I would've been there every day, if I could've. But her husband was home on the weekends."

"Did he ever find out?"

"I don't know. At first, she made it sound like they never had sex anymore. Later she admitted that they did have sex. I even heard them once in a while."

"How did you feel about that...them having sex?"

"It was a lot of conflicting feelings, of course…I was so young. None of my classmates could get so much as a kiss from a girl, and I was having sex five days a week…sometimes two to three times a day. She was also teaching me. She taught me positions and techniques…how to hold myself back…Ruby was a good teacher."

"How long did you and her have sex?"

"It was for over a year."

"Really? A year?"

"Yeah. We did it all the time too. I was so horny then. We must've done it nearly a thousand times."

"You never got bored of it with her?"

"No…I was fourteen years old having sex regularly. Plus, she was great at getting me turned on. She and her husband had a large collection of magazines and books. They even had a few early porno movies and a projector. That was really rare. So we talked a lot and had a lot of sex. She was the first person to tell me about the life and all that."

"Were she and her husband swingers?"

"She never told me so, but I have my suspicions. She would always couch it as, 'some people like to do this…' so I never knew for sure. She knew a lot about everything so I imagine they did some things in their day. Maybe he even knew about his wife and I. I'll never know."

"Why did you stop?"

"I started seeing a girl at school, and Mrs. Crinshaw found another play-toy in the neighborhood. He was older than me, so perhaps she wanted a man instead of a boy."

"Were you hurt?"

"Nah…I had really enjoyed the sex and what she taught me, but I had done everything I could with her…there was no place left to go. She was married, after all. I *definitely* missed the regular sex. It was hard just to get a handjob from a high school girl. But yeah, it's not your usual deflowering story."

"No, it's not…"

"So here's the part where you say, 'Ah-ha…now I know why you're a pervert, David.'"

"No, I wasn't going to say that," though there was a part of me that registered it that way, I guess.

"So what about you, Rachel? How did you lose your virginity?"

"A woman never tells." I looked away.

"No way are you getting away with that!"

"David, I don't have much to tell you. It's more embarrassing than anything."

"Back seat of a car? Janitor's closet in high school?"

"Under the bleachers."

"Yeah? Details?"

"Oh, next to your story it's so bland."

"Well, I told you, so you need to share yours, don't you think?"

"Well, only because you insist."

"I do, I do…"

"Remember, I warned you. My first was Elroy Johnson. I told you I was the nerdy girl. Elroy was the class clown. He was the skinniest guy you've ever seen, and had the biggest Afro in the school. People used to call him 'Black Q-Tip.' One day we were studying by the football field…we went there to get away from the others who would tease both of us non-stop. Football practice wasn't until the afternoon." David's eyes were riveted on me. "So we were studying and I guess Elroy started flirting with me. He told me he had never kissed a girl, so I let him kiss me."

"How old were you?"

"Sixteen."

"Was this your first kiss also?" He seemed like he wanted to know every single detail.

"No, but I hadn't kissed anybody for a long time."

"Okay, go on…"

"So as we kissed, he began to touch me all over. I was shy, but I let him. It felt good to have somebody touch me, and he was such a nice guy…shy like me. And he had a nice smile. We both felt so awkward and out of touch with our classmates…so unwanted. He touched me and then started pulling on my clothes."

"Right there on the football field?"

"Well, next to it, but yeah. I kept pushing his hands away, telling him we'd be spotted. He convinced me to go under the bleachers, as nobody would see us there."

"Nobody was nearby?"

"No, we didn't see anybody. We went under the bleachers and

kissed more, and he began to touch me all over. I got very excited, so I lay down and let him play with me more." I could see David's erection growing. He was enjoying this! That seemed very strange to me, but I loved his largeness. I smiled as I continued, and I wanted to excite him more. "When I lay down, I pulled off my panties so he could see my pussy. I pulled up my blouse so he could suck on my nipples."

"Did you like it?"

"Oh yeah, of course I did. I was getting wet." Actually, I had been too nervous to get excited, but I wanted David to enjoy the story.

"Then what happened?" He was touching himself now, slowly moving his hand up and down his length.

"He pulled his penis out, and I touched it. It was the first time I had touched one. I didn't know what to do, but Elroy pulled my hand up and down it, showing me."

"Was he big?"

"He was long, but not very thick, I guess." I could see he was imagining what we were doing, so I was dragging out what was a very short story. "I stroked my hand up and down his shaft, and I could feel him getting harder in my hand. I was enjoying how stiff it was."

"Then what? Did you suck him?"

"No, I was too shy. I lay there stroking him. I didn't know penises dripped when they got excited, so I thought he had already climaxed. I was so naïve!"

He was stroking himself faster now. His eyes were focused a thousand miles away. "Then what?"

"He said he wanted to put it in me. He asked if it was okay. I thought he was finished, so I didn't understand. I said okay, but didn't think he could. I was so wet, but I was very nervous also. He put himself in me."

"How did it feel?"

"It hurt so badly. I was clenched so tight, and part of my hymen was still intact. It felt like a knife inside me. He was so excited, though, that he came almost instantly."

"He came inside you?"

"Yes. I had never felt that before, so I thought he had peed in me. When he pulled out there was all this white stuff all over."

"A lot?"

"It seemed like gallons, but it wasn't, of course. I suddenly remembered that I could get pregnant and got very scared."

"How did he react?"

"He pulled his pants back up, ran over to his books, and then ran back to school."

"He left you there?"

"Yeah...left me with his come and my blood and all the responsibility."

"Did you guys ever do it again?"

"No...after that, Elroy never talked to me again. He had been my only guy friend, and he would turn and walk away whenever I was near. We didn't speak again until after we graduated."

"Did he ever tell you why he wouldn't talk to you?"

"No, but I know he was just abashed by his quick performance. It was just a couple seconds. He must've felt as embarrassed as I did by the whole thing."

David moved on top of my body and entered me.

David rode with me in the taxi the next morning. I would've normally taken the subway, but he was going to stop by a friend's place on Long Island. It was an act of providence.

The taxi ride was long, and there was some unexpected traffic. Still we were soon pulling up to my house. I thought it might be a good time to introduce David to my father, but was afraid to ask him. I was hoping he would volunteer to come inside when we arrived.

As we pulled up, I looked at David for a second, waiting for him to kiss me goodbye. Instead, he said, "Let me walk you up." I didn't protest. He asked the driver to stay, and then we slid out of the car.

I hadn't seen Darnell at all. I just heard his voice as we started up the walkway to my home.

"So...this is the dude you're fucking. I didn't know you liked white boys, Rachel." I knew the voice without turning, but I did anyway.

I saw him standing there, chest bowed, fists balled. He was here to fight. Even at a distance I could smell the alcohol on his breath.

"Darnell, what are you doing here?" I shouted. David stood next to me. He exuded confidence, and I knew he would be there to defend me without question.

"I've been waiting for you. All night. You didn't come home last night." He took an unsteady step forward. His clothes were ragged, and his hair was a mess. Darnell was normally fastidious, so I knew he had to be very drunk. Darnell was more careful about his appearance than I was about my own. "Now you come waltzing home like a whore after her trick."

"Hey man, watch your mouth," David commanded. I could feel his body go rigid.

I grabbed his hand. "Don't, David," I warned. I knew Darnell was here for trouble, and I didn't want David to be hurt by my stupid ex-boyfriend.

"You talking to me, white boy?" Darnell shouted. "Who the fuck do you think you are?" He slurred heavily, and his words were mistimed. Sloppy drunk.

"I'm her boyfriend, in case you couldn't tell."

Darnell took another step forward. "No, I'm her boyfriend, asshole." He jerked his thumb at himself.

"You're my ex, Darnell...we broke up." Oh, I was so worried about what David would think about all this.

"Bullshit, Rachel. You know better than that." He took another unsteady step. I could tell he was up to no good. His slow steps were to put him in a position to strike David. Or me. Or both of us. Darnell wasn't subtle. He had never hit me before, but I had never seen him this drunk either.

"Darnell, you'd better leave." I turned to David. He was locked on Darnell: two men, both showing their status and position. Both coiled like snakes for a strike. I tried to step in the middle, but David's forearm blocked me.

"Step back, Rachel. If he wants a fight, I'm ready." He was very self-assured, and I loved that about him. I felt so safe. I did not, though, want it to come to blows.

"Listen, motherfucker," Darnell commanded, "You don't know what Rachel and I have. It's something special. You need to take your cracker ass off this lawn, get in your taxi, and drive the fuck away."

"I'm not leaving, Darnell. I'm here because she wants me here."

"Suit yourself," he said, and then his fist was flying toward David.

David, though, had seen it coming. He stepped back deftly, then threw his own punch over the top, hitting Darnell flush in the mouth. Darnell landed backward on the ground with a thud, and I saw his upper lip was split. He spit blood onto the cement, and then stood up, stepping back from David. David stood coiled, ready for another attack.

Darnell stepped farther back, and again spit blood onto the cement.

"Okay man, okay…you asked for it." Darnell reached into his back pocket, and produced a small pistol. "Now you die, motherfucker!" He stepped forward now, and pointed the pistol at David's face. I shrieked in horror and stepped backward. The taxi peeled out and raced down the street.

David, though, didn't budge. "Go ahead, Darnell. Shoot me."

"I'm gonna shoot you in that big mouth, motherfucker!" Darnell shouted. I could see his hand shaking, but he was just feet away and probably couldn't miss at this distance.

"What are you waiting for then? Shoot!" David stood perfectly still, with complete confidence. He showed not an ounce of fear. His gaze was steady, while the pistol wavered.

"You die today!" Darnell shouted. Now it seemed as if his courage had flagged, and he was using his words to bolster his courage. David saw it too.

"So what are you waiting for, Darnell?" David shouted. "Shoot me, asshole! Pull the fucking trigger!"

Darnell stepped forward again, and the gun was nearly touching David.

And then David struck. With catlike speed, his right hand punched Darnell's wrist, while the other hand flicked the gun from his hand. The gun skittered across the cement to the street's asphalt. David threw another punch, and this time hit Darnell on his right eye. He fell again to the ground, this time flat on his back.

"Darnell, what in God's name are you doing?" This time it was my father. His deep, gravelly voice was followed by the *clack* of his pump-action shotgun.

Darnell, now bleeding from his eyebrow, turned to look at him, shamefaced.

My father stepped down the curb, neither raising nor lowering his gun.

"Darnell, look at you. What have you done to yourself?" He

seemed to pity him, but I could see his hands squeezing the shotgun. I worried he might shoot Darnell where he sat.

"You don't know how I feel about her, Mr. Walker."

My father stepped up to us, and we all stood above Darnell, regarding him. Darnell suddenly seemed very small. Insignificant.

"Daddy, this is David."

They shook hands. We heard the distant siren of a police car. Darnell spit blood one more time.

The cloak-and-dagger aspect of New York swing society at this time reminded me of old, cheap war movies. Coded messages. Smoky meeting rooms. Foreign accents. All it needed was black-and-white film and Humphrey Bogart.

The first swing club David took me to was in Midtown. Downstairs, we met the doorman. David said, "I'm here to collect rainwater for Madrid."

The doorman looked at him, then me, and said, "Twenty-fifth floor," as he pulled open the door for us. In the elevator, we had to use a special key. David inserted it, pushed the "25" button, and then put the key in his wallet.

The Trojan was a rather ironic name for a swing club because, in those days, nobody used condoms. However, many people did dress up, some as ancient soldiers of Troy. Others dressed as witches or priests. Most though, like us, didn't wear costumes, and instead just wore dark clothes and hoped nobody would recognize us as we entered. The Trojan was an entire floor of the building, which normally held five large apartments with views. The rooms radiated out from the elevator landing. From the elevator, they just appeared like regular apartment doors.

Inside, they were all interconnected, and adorned in over-the-top toga-party chic. The music was loud and the marijuana smoke was heavy.

I was shivering, but I wasn't cold. I didn't know what to expect. I think I assumed that I would walk off the elevator and somebody would drag me into the bowels of Hell. Instead, I saw two nicely dressed men holding drinks and talking. David and I shook hands with both of them. The first man was introduced to me as Miguel, and I was told he was the "overseer of events." He made sure rules were enforced and nobody acted belligerently. The second man was very slender with long hair. He said, "Billy," as I took his hand. His handshake was very effeminate. When we entered the door closest to us, David said, "Did you recognize the long-haired guy?"

"No."

"That's Billy Allison. He's the singer for Blue Monday."

"He looks so different in person."

"Yeah…he usually wears makeup for his shows."

"Do you know him?"

"Not really, but he gave me tickets to their Radio City Music Hall show last summer. Nice guy."

As we moved into the first room, I saw a long bar and a collection of different styles of chairs. Bean-bag chairs, swivel chairs, white and metallic chairs, red plush chairs. One chair looked like a Louis XVI, and another looked like something Andy Warhol would perch himself on. We took a seat at the bar, and I ordered a wet martini. David ordered a Manhattan.

"This isn't what I expected," I confessed to him. I had to raise my voice over the music.

"How so?"

"All these people are talking to each other."

"Yeah. What's wrong with that?"

"Nothing…I just thought everybody would be fucking."

He let out a huge laugh. "Many will, but some just come for the vibe…the openness…"

I still felt a little prickly about being here, so I probably asked the next question with a touch of anger in my heart. "Have you slept with anybody here?"

"In this room?"

"The people who are all sitting here."

He looked around the room. "No, I don't recognize anybody. Doesn't mean we didn't, but I don't recognize them." For some reason that made me feel good. I started to turn to take a sip of my drink. Then he shocked me again. "But I had a threesome with Billy and another girl once."

"With Billy? You had sex with Billy?"

"Well, I think we were more focused on the girl, but we all had sex together, so yeah, we did."

"Is Billy gay?" I still was grappling with sexuality. Sad that I was letting silly things like that define me…and us…and others…

"No, he was giving her the business pretty well, so I guess he's bisexual."

I knew in my mind that this also made David bisexual, which at this time carried a huge stigma. I had enjoyed our romp in the park and our outdoor adventure, but this seemed like a whole new world to me. In my heart, I was still a good Christian girl. Never in a million years would I have imagined I would be in a Manhattan swinger's club, figuring out my boyfriend swung both ways, if only sometimes. I thought people went to Hell for these types of things. Yet, here I was. I told myself it was for David, but was it? I was good at transference, so I stuck with it.

Still, I was changing very quickly. I was here after all, wasn't I? I guess I was quickly losing my prudish feelings, but I probably wasn't ready to move as quickly as we were moving. Nor was I ready to throw off the shackles of my religious and cultural mores. When he talked to me about coming here, I resisted at first. I told him I wasn't sure I was ready, and it was only the disappointment in his eyes that made me acquiesce. The control I had enjoyed so much the week before was gone, and I felt awkward and slightly hurt. David had assured me, though, that we would only do things at my speed. If we didn't do anything on this trip, that would be fine. We could simply watch and have a few drinks. He said, "You call the shots, Rachel. If you want nothing to happen, nothing will happen. When you say go, we will." Still, I felt like I would've rather been finding a way to flash my tits to unsuspecting strangers.

"So what do you think so far?" David asked me.

"Well, I'm still trying to understand why they call it the Trojan."

"When they first built this place, it had an ancient-Troy feel to it. Columns. Shields. Swords. Stuff hanging everywhere. Some people complained that all the decoration was too much, so Miguel had them taken down. Still some people like to play dress-up, and historical names help that. A few people like to wear sheets and coronets. When this gets closed down they'll rename it something else, and everybody will have to find another way to dress up."

"Closed down?"

"Sex clubs are still technically against the law. Ultimately, somebody tells the police and an investigation is launched. Rather than face lawsuits and possible arrests, they'll simply close this down, find a new fake ownership group, call it something else, and reopen it somewhere else."

"So who *does* own it? Not Miguel?"

"No, not Miguel. I heard it was owned by one of the Saudi royal family…somebody told me once that there's a prince who frequents here, and that he was bragging that he was the true owner. Dunno. Could've just been a drunk Iranian for all anybody knew."

We finished our drinks and then ordered fresh ones. We took these new drinks and moved out of this room. The bar area was surrounded by a stone-finished wall, with hanging beads showing the entryway to another area. Very 70s.

The light behind the hanging beads was dark red.

Hell was waiting for me after all.

We passed through the beads. On the other side there was a large area with pillows and silk throws. It almost seemed Moroccan. On these pillows were couples and more. People in various phases of nudity. Some were smiling and laughing. Some were kissing. Nobody, though, was having sex. David and I pulled up on pillows, in a corner away from others.

"David, I thought people would be having sex here." I counted, and there were thirteen people in this room. The room was large enough that we couldn't hear what anybody was saying. The music was not blaring but still muffled the distinct sound of a person's voice.

"Well, this is where people get to know each other a little better. If they want to have sex they're asked to go to the private rooms. These pillows wouldn't last long if they were covered in come." He said that a bit too nonchalantly.

Near us, there was a very slender, dark-skinned black man, an Asian woman, and a red-haired white man. The red-haired man was very large—tall and muscular...not like a bodybuilder, but in a lean, athletic way. He was absolutely huge compared to the other men in the room. He had a beautiful smile. David saw me looking at him.

"Do you recognize him?"

"No, should I?"

"That's Mark Freeman, the wide receiver for the New York Giants."

"I don't follow football." This man was intensely physically attractive. Beyond just his size, he had a confidence and grace about him. His shirt was open, and I could see his large chest muscles moving.

"He's a great guy...do you want to meet him?"

"Maybe later."

I watched the three of them talking. They seemed so comfortable here. They were sipping drinks, smiling...completely at ease, as if they were at a family barbeque. But they were all flirting. The woman, a very delicate, fair-skinned woman, was smiling through her narrow eyes. Her gaze flitted back and forth between the two men. The black man was quick to laugh, and he was sitting very close to her. As I watched, he leaned over and kissed the woman. She returned the kiss passionately. Mark put his very large hands on her breasts and began to massage them. The woman then turned to him and kissed him, pulling his face to hers.

"Aren't they a beautiful threesome?" David asked me. My eyes were riveted on them.

"Doesn't Mark have a wife? He's so handsome...surely..."

"That's his wife he's kissing." I looked again, and the woman turned her head back to the black man. She pulled on his lips, sucking each one into her mouth. Her hand drifted down to his crotch.

"He's sharing his wife with another man?" I asked, stunned.

"Yeah...they're in the life."

After kissing for a bit, they got up and began to move to the next room on the other side of the beads. They spotted David and me.

"Hi, David," the Asian woman said. Mark smiled at us.

"Hi, Keiko...hi, Mark...how are you guys tonight?"

"We're good," she replied with a wry smile on her lips. "This is

Abeeku...he's new to the Trojan." Abeeku smiled at us.

"This is Rachel, my girlfriend." It felt good when he said that. "This is her first time here also."

Keiko smiled at me, but she obviously had other things on her mind. Without another word, they moved through the beads and into the next room. The light glowed blood red as they moved through the beaded curtain.

"What's on the other side?" I asked.

"They're moving to the private rooms."

"To have sex with each other?" I guess I shouldn't have been shocked, as we were in a swing club...but still...it just seemed so far from what I knew of life and relationships.

He looked at me, no doubt incredulously. "Well of course, Rachel."

"I mean, I know that's why people are here. I just can't imagine the man sharing his wife with another man."

"That's the life, Rachel. That's how it works."

"How do people have sex in threes, though? I guess I never stopped to think of the mechanics of it."

"Mechanics?"

"Yeah, I mean...she only has one vagina...do they take turns?"

"Do you want to watch?"

"Oh God, no...that wouldn't be right."

"Well, if they want privacy, they'll close the door. Most people don't, though. That's part of the thrill. Didn't you enjoy eyes moving on us in Central Park?"

"Yes."

"Well, they likely do too. If they wanted privacy, they'd go to their own homes. Instead, they're here."

"I don't know..."

"Well, c'mon...let's go take a look. We can leave if you want."

We got up and moved through the beaded curtain to the next room, which was really a collection of smaller rooms in a broad semi-circle. Each had a door, but only one door was closed. We walked by one room after another until we found them. The room had a king-sized bed. They had put down sheets and bedding. We stood by the door. I felt so dirty looking in, but my eyes were drawn by their moving bodies...by

Mark's masculine body. I couldn't have looked away even if I had wanted to.

On the bed, I saw Keiko lying open. Her husband was between her legs, and obviously doing a good job of it, based on her moans. She was busy, though, as she had Abeeku's manhood in her hand. He was standing next to the bed, and between moans she was taking him into her mouth. He was pushing his hips to her, trying to get her to give him undivided attention. He had the longest penis I had ever seen, and she was doing her best to give it the attention it deserved. Her breath rasped, and I think she was near orgasm. Her husband was pushing his tongue deep inside her. Still, she pumped the large dark shaft, and sucked on it when her ragged breathing allowed. I could hear her husband talking to her, but with his mouth in her nether regions I couldn't understand what he was saying. He then slid two fingers inside her.

I saw David shifting from foot to foot. He was worked up already. His hand was on his crotch and his eyes were taking in everything that was happening. We could both smell the heavy scent of sex in the room.

And then I heard her orgasm. She began to grunt deeply, and then a low mewling cry. She let go of the long shaft in her hand, and put both hands in her husband's hair. She thrust her hips against his face. I saw her eyes roll back, and I knew exactly where she was. She was lost in the ecstasy…lost in the passion and pleasure…lost in the waves rolling through her body and mind.

And then they changed positions. Her husband moved to her side and began to kiss her, while massaging her breasts. Abeeku mounted her. She obviously had a bit of difficulty with his size. She had to move her hips around to work him in. I could see her sex as he moved into her… she was open and spread as wide as she could be. He patiently worked himself in, and her eyes reacted to the pressure inside her. Once in, he began to move slowly. Her husband ministered to her breasts, but had his gaze was locked on the man between his wife's legs. His eyes focused on their union. He was taking it in. I wondered what he was thinking. I wondered how he could watch someone pleasure himself inside his wife. I had so much to experience yet. I was immensely excited though, and I felt myself becoming sexually energized.

And then he began to move more aggressively. His long, slow thrusts gained strength. His butt muscles clenched and relaxed. Though slender, he too was muscular, and his dark skin shone with sweat. The muscles of his arms and back rose, like a cat stretching. Because of his length, his thrusts required a lot of hip movement. Keiko was panting and sweating. Her hands grabbed the muscular arms of her lover, and her heels hooked his thighs. Her husband leaned back as his wife pulled her lover down onto her. He slipped a hand on her breast, but he was outside their sex. He didn't seem to mind, and was still focused on their union.

I was even more excited now. I had never watched other people have sex like this. Though I know David had, he was now grinding his crotch with the palm of his hand. I could feel my dampness increasing, and I know I was sweating sheets...not sexy, but I couldn't stop. I almost felt like I was having sex with them. We were so close we could hear every damp, slapping sound. We could hear the fast breathing and smell the musky aroma of sex.

They changed positions again. As they changed, Keiko made eye contact with me...just for a second. Her eyes had the lost look of someone in the throes of sex, but I sensed her sparkling at me. Maybe I read too much into it, but I got the sense that she enjoyed the fact that we were looking at her. She enjoyed performing for us.

Mark lay down on his back. His wife took a sixty-nine position over him. His head and her crotch were pointed to the door, and I could see how distended she was. She looked so swollen and open. The other man entered her from behind. This position surprised me, as it put his large testicles into her husband's face. Again, neither seemed to mind. As he began to move in her again, the red-haired man was licking at her crotch fervently. I later noticed that he would occasionally let his tongue glide over the shaft of the man inside his wife. This caused a fevered pitch in their lovemaking. Both she and her lover neared orgasm quickly. Though I had never seen a man pleasure another man before, I found this position very exciting, if strikingly odd to my very traditional eyes. I immediately looked to David, and wondered if he had done something similar to this. Based on his burning focus on them, I assumed he had. His palm was pressing hard against his crotch now.

Soon they were moving very quickly. The strokes came quicker. The woman could no longer focus on her husband's manhood, and instead tilted her head back and stared into infinite space. She began to grunt again, and then there was the whining cry. Her lover held her hips roughly and was slamming himself into her.

Abeeku growled loudly, and then he threw his head back and shouted; large droplets of sweat flew out of his curly hair. Mark continued to lick feverishly, first on her clitoris and then on her lover's dusky testicles. This seemed to prolong their orgasms. Her cries and his grunts filled the room. Hot sweat dripped everywhere.

I had never seen anything like this, but I was immensely hot. I could feel my moisture soaking my thighs. I grabbed David's hand and said, "Let's find a room." He nodded and pulled me along the semi-circle until we found a vacant room. There were folded sheets inside. We hastily threw them on the bed while ripping off our clothes.

David slid onto the bed, and I was on him instantly. I took him into my mouth and attacked his body savagely. I was burning! I was forcing him very quickly into my mouth while using my other hand to squeeze his testicles. His erection was furious, and he was dripping a large amount of fluid. He rolled me over and made to move down on me, but I was too worked up.

"I want you in me *now,* David" I commanded. He obliged. I was so wet that he slid right into me, despite his girth. As soon as he was in me, I was already near orgasm. I wanted it hard and fast and immediate. "Fuck me, David…fuck me hard," I demanded. I twisted my legs around him and bucked and pulled him against me. He began to slam himself inside me with passion and anger. I pulled his mouth down onto mine. As our tongues battled, I felt my orgasm building like a hurricane. I wanted that orgasm so badly. I rode the hot swells inside me, and I felt an explosion that wracked my body intensely. I could feel the undulations slam into my brain with each thrust of David's hips. My nails dug into his back. I cried out into his mouth. I shouted out my passion and my fury and my desire. I let it all out. Every stroke was fire. Every stroke was pleasure. It felt like this orgasm went on forever. I was floating on the waves of the universe. A solar storm. I felt hot tears pouring down the side of my face and into my hair. This was the most intense orgasm I had ever felt, and it didn't want to end…it felt like it would go on forever. I let it last…I rode it as long as it wanted to go. It felt like hours.

As I came down from the stars, I felt David again. He had been maintaining his strokes to maximize my pleasure. I opened my eyes, and he was smiling down at me. "You okay?" he asked.

"Yeah," I replied. I was more than okay.

But now I wanted to pleasure him. I had never finished a man orally before, but I knew I wanted to do that with David. I pushed his shoulders off me, and pinned him down on the bed. I slid myself down his body. I took his heft into my hand, and grabbed his swollen testicles with the other. I then slammed my mouth down onto him. I took what I could of him, and moved as rapidly as possible. I squeezed with both hands. I wanted to taste him. I wanted to give him the pleasure he had always given me. I could taste both of us on him, and it was a musky, sharp flavor. I looked up at him, and his eyes looked into mine. His hands were in my curly hair. His muscled stomach and chest looked so amazing to me...so manly. I could see him twitching and jerking with my aggression. He was enjoying it as much as I enjoyed giving it.

Perhaps it was his already excited state, but I felt him swell just a bit more, and I saw his eyes lose focus. He began to groan...a deep, hollow groan. Then his hips began to jerk, driving himself into my mouth even more. His explosion of semen surprised me with its force, but I wasn't about to stop my pace. I squeezed even harder and forced my mouth down on him with all I had. Hot, sticky saltiness poured into my mouth, and still I continued to take him in. Each thrust of his hips was a new hot ejaculate. He grunted with each thrust. I pulled and squeezed and swallowed with all I had. I wanted this to be the best orgasm of his life. I continued to squeeze and pump even as he began to relax. His eyes were slammed shut and his grunts were soft now, but still I never stopped. I squeezed ever drop out of him I could.

He softened a little, so my motions became a bit softer as well. I didn't stop though...I continued to move my mouth and tongue over him, and could still feel him twitching between my lips. I looked up and saw him looking at me and smiling.

"Thank you, Rachel...that was amazing."

I took him out of my mouth and asked, "You liked it?" It was, after all, the first time I had ever done that.

"It was perfect."

I grabbed a small towel that was in the room. I wiped my mouth, and then I lay down, with my head on his shoulder. We both drifted off to sleep.

Just imagine! I watched a multiracial three-way in a Manhattan swing club, had swallowed my lover's seed, and now I was falling asleep in this den of iniquity. My life was in a place I had not anticipated. While it wasn't what I had expected, I didn't hate it like I thought I would. I was living on a sexual edge I didn't know existed just a few weeks before. The sharpest edge, balanced so delicately. Desperately.

*W*hen we awoke, I thought we would head home. Instead, David wanted to stay and have a few more drinks. I reluctantly agreed. I was very tired, and had a lot of thoughts swirling in my head. I couldn't lie to myself and pretend I didn't find what I had seen intriguing. Still, for a young woman with little sexual experience it had been a lot to take in. What would my friends and family think if they saw me here? I was in a confused state of mind. Overwhelmed, perhaps, at my own actions...at my willingness to participate in things I would've considered abhorrent just weeks ago. And guilt? Yeah. Guilt that I had become excited by what should have repulsed me.

We dressed, and took the sheets and towels to a large, drop-in hamper. I wondered who had the unfortunate task of cleaning up all these sex-covered sheets, and was glad it wasn't me. I guess the monthly dues made sense after all.

We grabbed another drink and then began to walk around the club. As we passed the semi-circular room into the next room, I was in for another surprise. This room was filled with sex toys of all types. Vibrators. Dildos. Creams. Oils. As with the other room, smaller rooms moved out in a semi-circle from a larger center room with pillows. This room was colored red and gold, and everything here, except the toys, was in some shade of those two colors. With the light dimmed, much of the gold seemed to glimmer.

I asked David, "Are all of these clean?" indicating the sex toys.

"Yeah. We're required to clean them after use. Club rules. There're cleaning supplies in each room. Just to be sure, I'd clean them again before use." He winked at me.

As we began to move into the last area, I happened to peek into the room nearest the beads. I saw a heavyset man on his hands and knees. A woman had a dildo strapped onto her, and she was entering him from behind. The man was letting out soft cries. She was saying humiliating things to him. "You love being fucked in the ass, don't you, little bitch? You love being my little whore, don't you?" I realized there was still so much I didn't know and hadn't seen. It was a big world I had just entered.

The last large room, also arranged in a semi-circle, was for bondage and sadism. There was a collection of handcuffs, whips, gags, blindfolds, and shackles. In one room, I could hear a whip being snapped and a woman crying out. This room made me nervous, and I asked David if we could leave it. He saw the worry in my eyes, so he took my hand and we worked our way back to the bar in the entry room. We ordered another drink.

"Why did you panic in the Bondage Room, Rachel?" David asked me at the bar.

"I don't know. I don't like the idea of pain in sex."

"Well, the whips and things are usually used lightly…"

"I don't know…seemed so scary…like a medieval torture room… like the Tower of London or something."

Another laugh. "Okay, I hear you. Don't worry…I'm not really into that, as I've said before. I've done it once or twice and it's not really my bag."

"So there is something you don't do?" It was my turn to laugh.

"Well, let's just say it's not my favorite. There isn't anything I *won't* do."

I wasn't surprised he said this, but these words slowly sunk into my mind. *There isn't anything he won't do? What has he done in his lifetime?* I shuddered at the idea of all the things he must have done (with so many people) through the years. We were in the days before we knew about AIDS. Still, nobody wants to think of their lover having lots of sex with lots of partners.

As we sipped our drinks, we watched some of the other people who were in this area. Near us sat an older, paunchy, middle-aged man with two women. The first woman seemed to be his own age, and, though well-kept, had the lines of many years on her face, matching the streaks of gray in her hair. The other woman was much younger, probably my age, and her long, straight blonde hair shimmered even in the dim lighting. They were sipping their drinks together, and chatting casually. The younger woman was young enough to be their daughter, though they looked nothing alike.

After a while, they all got up together and moved through the beads into the next room.

I turned to look at David. He was already looking at me.

"You don't think…" I began then thought better of it. He looked at me for a bit, then replied.

"What? That they're going to go have sex?"

"Yeah."

"Sure they are."

"But they're old enough to be her parents."

"And?"

"Well, it just seems kinda, you know…"

"Well, first you have to know that the younger lady is a pro. She works here many nights. Second, you can't blame them for wanting a younger partner, can you?"

"She's a pro? Pro swinger?"

"No, a prostitute…professional gal."

"They have prostitutes here?" I scanned the room over his shoulder. "How do you know if they're prostitutes?" I probably said that too loudly.

"Well, I know that girl because I've seen her here often. Sandy is her name. She's a top-flight girl…expensive call girl…she charges three hundred for a session."

"Three hundred dollars?" In 1979, that was a *lot* of money.

"Yeah. I've heard she's worth it, though I've never seen her in action. Do you want to go watch?"

"No, no…I just didn't realize."

"Well, most people here are not. A few professionals, though, work this as it's a great way to generate business. Their customers here can translate into business outside, if you know what I mean."

"How many pros do you think there are?"

"I've only seen a few. Sandy is the only one I recognize tonight. So far, anyway…the night is still young. And yes, there are a couple of gigolos who work here also."

"Really?"

"Yeah. I don't see any right now, but if I see one I'll point him out to you." He gave me a snarky smile, as if that was what I was looking for.

I sipped on my drink a bit. Prostitution had such a horrible stigma in those days. Prostitutes were the lowest of the low…selling their bodies for money. Whores. Streetwalkers. It all seemed so dirty and seedy. Yet, the young woman I had just seen was beautiful and seemed clean…not a girl perched on stiletto heels in a mini-skirt working a street corner, which is how I envisioned prostitution.

As we sat there sipping our drinks and watching people, I felt a man move into the seat next to me. He ordered a drink, and then turned to me. "Hi, pretty lady. Name's Buzz." I turned and looked at him. He was in his thirties, and was a bit heavyset. He had on a sport coat and open-collared white dress shirt. His hand was extended to me.

"Hi." I shook his hand.

"Now, you're not going to tell me your name, pretty lady?" I couldn't recognize his accent, but it seemed a bit South.

"Sorry. It's Rachel."

"Nice to meet you, Rachel. Is this your first time here? I don't recognize your face."

"Yeah, first time. My boyfriend brought me here." I turned to introduce him, but David had turned and was talking to a man on the other side of him. They seemed to know each other.

"Ah, David brought you here? How long have you known him?"

"A month or so." *Minus the time he was in Tanzania.*

"Okay." I knew he was doing the mental math and judging our relationship. "So do you like what you see?"

"What do you mean?"

"The club? The life. Do you like it?" He was leaning toward me now, and his hot alcohol-breath was in my face.

I decided I didn't like him judging me. "I was in the life before I met David."

"Really? I've never seen you around."

"Yeah, I just moved to this part of the world." I felt David get up. When I looked, he had walked to the side of the bar and was talking to a few people.

"Oh, where were you before?"

I thought of the US map. "Arkansas."

"Arkansas? Really? You don't strike me as a girl from Arkansas."

"Why? Because I'm black?"

"No, that's not it at all. You just seem like a city girl."

"We have cities in Arkansas too." I could only name Little Rock, and I was prepared to answer that if he asked. He didn't.

"Now, don't go taking offense, pretty lady." Now I heard a bit of a twang in his accent. "I'm just asking. Trying to get to know you is all."

"No offense taken." I lied again. This banter thing wasn't my game. *Why isn't David here?*

"So do they have anything like this in Arkansas? I know they don't in North Texas."

"No, nothing like this."

"I know the guy who owned this apartment before he sold it to the prince…this used to be five different apartments, but they knocked out the walls and made them all one."

"That must've been expensive work."

"Well, money wasn't an issue for him."

I looked around again, and David was talking with two men and an athletic-looking brunette girl who looked younger than me. They were laughing and sipping their drinks. David was standing next to her, and I immediately felt the burn of jealousy.

"So what are you looking for tonight?"

"Me?"

"Yeah…what are you and David doing? Are you looking to swap or swing or pick up an extra?"

He said it so quickly I wasn't sure what he was asking me at first. "I don't know what you mean?"

"Well, pretty lady…I was hoping to get a chance to have some fun with you. Would love to bed you. I'll bet you're a vixen in the sack."

I knew I was in a swing club. I knew that's what people were here for. Yet never in my life had a man propositioned me for sex like this. Before I realized what I had done, I had slapped this big Texan across his mouth. I stood up and stomped over to David, who was staring at me incredulously. I grabbed his arm and pulled him to the door. "We're leaving."

I didn't say a word on the ride home. I was fuming inside. In my mind, I blamed David for putting me in a situation where a man could proposition me like that. I know, I know…we were in a swing club, a club wholly devoted to people meeting and having sex. All I had to tell that man was that I wasn't interested and that I wanted him to leave me alone.

Yet that moment made me feel cheap. Made me feel like a piece of meat. I was hurt and angry and sad. No woman can be happy if she feels cheap.

And I was going to be heard.

Back in David's apartment, I was flushed. David saw my eyes and didn't ask me any questions. I got ready for bed, still not talking. I was overly fussing every detail. I was cursing under my breath. David kept his distance.

As I folded down the bedding and slid under the covers, David finally spoke to me, though from the doorway to the bedroom. Perhaps he was preparing himself in case I threw something at him. That probably was a good idea.

"You do know that the Trojan is a swing club, right Rachel?"

"It's not that." I had so many things I wanted to say. That was all that came out.

"Did Buzz say something uncalled for?"

"What?"

"Did he call you a slut or something?"

"No."

"You made us leave so suddenly I didn't have a chance to find out what he had said."

"He told me he wanted to sleep with me."

"Yeah?"

"Yes."

"What else?"

"What?"

"What else did he say?"

"He asked me where I was from and all that."

"I mean, what did he say that made you so upset?"

"He asked to sleep with me. I told you already."

"That's it?"

"Yes...but that's not it."

"What was it then?"

"You should've been by my side. You should have been fending him off. Instead you were trying to connect with that pretty brunette."

He let out a huge laugh, which made my face burn hotter. "The brunette?" He laughed again.

"You know who I'm talking about."

"Yes, I do. I wasn't trying to do anything with her."

"Like you said, you were in a swing club." I folded my arms and looked away.

"Okay, Rachel. First, the brunette is a photographer for Life magazine. Denny Harrison. One of the best. I was talking with her about work things, and was going to bring you over to introduce you to her. Second, she's a lesbian. She comes by the club for the relaxed atmosphere, but she never has sex with men. Her lover is going to meet her there later tonight."

"How do you know she's a lesbian?"

"I work with her lover. She went with us to Tanzania. She's a film engineer. Michelle is an old friend of mine and a great person to work with."

"I didn't know you traveled with women on those photo shoots." I probably meant that vindictively, trying to regain control of my anger.

"Of course…women work in this industry also. But I would never sleep with someone I work with…it would create too much tension." He sat down on the bed. I faced away from him, with my arms still crossed. "Now, as for this guy who propositioned you…it's a swinger's club… people proposition each other. You can simply say no thanks and that's it. If he continues beyond that, you tell me or tell someone else…we don't stand for behavior like that. It's a private club. We pay a membership fee. If people misbehave they are out without question."

I was still feeling angry. He spoke again, and I felt him moving closer to me. He was right behind me now. "Look, Rachel…we don't have to go to that club again. I don't care. But you also know where I'm coming from. You can choose however you want to do things, but you know that I *need* those activities because that's who I am. I can't change. But that club is just a location. We can be wherever you want."

"Will I be in trouble for slapping that man?"

"Well, they'll probably give us a warning…if he complained. If not, then no problem."

"I'm sorry I reacted that way." I was cooling down now and starting to think logically. "I felt so alone and vulnerable, and jealous of you and that girl."

"Why were you jealous?"

"Because I love you, you asshole!"

"Then trust me not to proposition a woman without your permission. Did you notice that throughout the night I never once moved on anybody? We watched a lot of hot action, but I was only with you. I would never pick up someone unless you were on board." And then his arms were around me, and he kissed the back of my neck. I turned to him. I kissed him back.

"This is all so weird still, I guess," I said.

"I understand. Believe me, I do."

"Do you?"

"Sure. It's just who I am…but I know how it looks. I get that most people don't get it."

I fell asleep in his arms that night, but it took a while. I had so many thoughts running through my mind. I felt so confused, yet excited at the same time. Excited? Yes, most definitely. I had seen some incredibly sensual and sexual possibilities in a private club in New York. I had seen beautiful bodies and incredible sex. I found myself turned on more than I thought I would be. Yet I felt dirty…whorish even…and wondered if I was losing my identity. Who would I be if I spent time in places like that?

But it was me who jumped off the bridge, wasn't it? I was falling into the darkness, and it wasn't always bad. Or was it? Was I falling or flying? Doesn't falling feel like flying, at least at first? Was I bound to be crushed on the rocks below, or would I sail on the updrafts? Was I becoming someone I never wanted to be? Did that even matter?

Part III : Transfiguration

few days later, David and I were having coffee. I had come directly to his place after work, and we were listening to music. I could hear the phonograph scratching through the vinyl grooves. I think it was Bowie. We sat quietly for a while, when David spoke.

"Rachel, I've been waiting to hear what your father thinks of me. I only met him that day with Darnell. He isn't mad at me or anything, is he?"

I was surprised by the question. "No, of course not. He told me he was glad you were there to protect me. Darnell was armed and dangerous."

"Okay, glad to hear it."

"You have to understand my father, David. He is very quiet. When I'm home with him he hardly ever says a word. He works very hard running his business, and when he comes home he's tired and doesn't have much to say. He has always been the strong, silent type."

"What was your mother like?"

I wondered if he had a reason for asking these questions. "Well, she died a long time ago. I was twelve. My memories are fading some. She was always very busy. She cooked and cleaned and did everything, plus she would manage Daddy's books. I always remember her doing something."

"That's my brother, Jake—the one in Jersey who lent me the Vette. He's a workaholic. He is always doing something, and I think he's working himself to death."

"Well, I guess my mother did just that. One day she just collapsed. Stroke. She was cooking my father dinner when I was at a friend's house studying. He smelled the food burning. She fell by the stove and was already gone when he found her."

"I'm sorry, Rachel. That must have been tough."

"Thanks. Well, I was lucky. I had my father, still. But…losing my female role model just before my teen years was a challenge. I had to learn about things like bras and periods on my own. Wasn't easy."

"No aunts to help you out?"

"No. Daddy's family's in Atlanta. And you know my mom was from England, and I never really spoke with that side. Guess I should look them up some day."

"You really should."

"I keep telling myself I will. I'd love to see the place my British family hails from. I have my mother's address book with all the family information. But you know how it is…so much to do all the time. And I don't know anything about Birmingham."

"I know, but you really should visit. I'm sure they'd get a kick out of your mom's American daughter."

"Well, not sure if they know I'm alive. Mom never talked about them."

"There's a reason I'm asking you about this, Rachel."

So there it was. "What is it, David?"

"I actually need to fly to London to take a few photos…some freelance work."

"When are you leaving?"

"Well, it's no hurry. But I was thinking that you might like to go with me, and then we could take the train to Birmingham and meet your mother's family. What do you think?"

Of course I was surprised. "David, I can't afford that." It was a weak protest, I guess.

"It's okay. My treat. I can probably get the magazine to reimburse me for your seat if I claim you're my assistant. They're good about that."

"David, I would love to go, but are you sure?" My heart was beating fast now, thinking that it might really happen.

"I'm sure, and it's decided. Work out your schedule, tell me when you're able, and then I'll talk to the magazine's travel agent and get our tickets."

"If you insist," I smiled.

"I do…I do!"

My father helped me pack, and he made sure I took sweaters. "It's always cold in that damned country," he said. "Felt like winter every day." I felt him hovering as I packed. I knew he had things he wanted to tell me, but couldn't just say it. He was like a teenager at his first dance, standing there awkwardly, trying to find the words.

When I finished packing, he carried my bags down the stairs.

I stood near the door waiting for David to pull up.

"What's wrong, Daddy?" I asked.

"Honey, don't take anything they say personally, okay?" He was looking away from me.

"What do you mean?"

"Well, they don't know you…don't be surprised if they don't take a shine to you right away. They're nice people; it's just that they view the world differently than us."

"How so?"

"Well, it's just different is all." I heard his Georgia twang. "They never thought much of me, but I couldn't hold it against them. Those were different days, you know."

I heard David pull up. "Okay, Daddy, I gotta go."

"I'll carry your bags out."

The flight over seemed unbelievably long. I tried to sleep, but just couldn't get more than a few minutes of shut-eye. David slept comfortably most of the trip, while I was alone with my thoughts. His snores aggravated me, and reminded me that I was still awake. I tried to read, but couldn't concentrate.

I had always wanted to see the old country with my mother. See where she was born. Have her show me the landmarks of her youth. Where she had played. Where she had first kissed a boy. I wanted to experience her life with her. Instead, I was disconnected from her youth almost completely, and my memories of her were already a bit distant. I would never hear her tell me, "This was my church growing up," or "I was born at this hospital." It was a void in my life I knew I would never fill. Yet here I was on a plane, flying to the land of her birth. My mind was a maelstrom.

As I considered images of her, and the life I would never know, I began to cry. I cried softly so as not to wake David. But the tears were deep ones. I cried for the loss of my mother. I cried for the loss of our time together. I cried for the absence in my life, and the emptiness in my future. She would never cry at my wedding. She would never kiss her grandchildren, or read them a bedtime story. I felt the hole in my life as a deep wound that would never heal.

So on this never-ending flight, I poured my heart out on paper. I wrote the poem that was to earn me the most recognition out of my collected works. It began:

A mother's tears fall to parched, barren land
A man can never hope to understand
What in the depths of her heart she sees and knows
Summer sunshine, winter snows

When we arrived, I was spent. I had written the first drafts of two poems, but hadn't slept and was physically sore from sitting. When we entered the room of our hotel, I lay down for what I thought would be a short nap, but instead I slept through the whole night. While I slept, David sneaked out quietly and took the train to St. Paul's and took some lovely images. We would add those images to his apartment walls, and several were published in multiple magazines. He was truly an artist, and I still regret not being present when he took those pictures.

We hopped the morning train to Birmingham. I had the address of relatives I wanted to meet, starting with her sister Emily. But what I really wanted was to feel my mother and her life when she met my father. I hoped I would find a piece of her there, I guess. I had dreamed of cheery British cottage homes and loving hugs from cousins and aunties. I thought we'd sip tea while I regaled them with stories of America.

I wasn't prepared for the gloom of Birmingham. It was a factory town at this time, and smokestacks sent black clouds billowing skyward. The town consisted of brick factories and small, lower-middle class row homes surrounding them. Unkempt children roamed the streets. It was miserably windy and cold, even in summer.

David and I stayed at a rundown hotel near the center of town. After seeing the city on our first day, we drove to my mother's oldest sister's house the next morning. It was hard to find...one row house in a forest of row homes.

Aunt Emily was a dowager, living alone after the death of her husband a decade before. She was several years older than my mother. Her little home smelled of mothballs and ammonia. She was squat and a bit humped, but her face and eyes were definitely my mother's. When she met us at the door, I explained to her who I was.

"You're Veronica's daughter then?" Her accent was very thick. Her eyes flicked up to mine, over me, and then to David behind me.

"Yes, Aunt Emily. I flew all the way here to meet you. I had always wanted to come back to meet Mom's family. Sorry I didn't call first...it's just..."

"She died some time ago...why are you visiting now? I wish you would've called, you see..."

"I wanted to, but I thought it would be better to meet in person." I flushed.

"You know, it's not that I'm not happy to meet you; it's just that Veronica and I weren't very close."

"Oh, she never mentioned that."

"She wouldn't have, I'm sure. I never approved of yer father. I didn't approve of English ladies marrying the darkie Yanks that were running around here...mixing our blood like that...making little half-darkies..." and her pale eyes shot up at me.

"Oh…" I was slapped by her words, and couldn't think of anything to say.

"You're a pretty gal and all, but us Whartons are pure Anglo-Saxon, goin' back a thousand years or more. I never understood why she'd want to bed that beastly father of yours."

David began to tug on my arm, but I was rigid now. "My father isn't beastly, Aunt Emily. He's a very nice man. He took very good care of her…"

"During the war, there was lots of them blackies running about. Many local girls had a fling with them…you know, because of their size and they had money from Roosevelt. But they were always careful not to get pregnant…no good girl could raise a darkie child like that…"

David interjected, "Rachel, we need to go…"

"Aunt Emily, I can't believe you're not happy to see me…"

"Don't take it personal, love…I just hadn't heard from yer mother in twenty years and then her half-breed daughter shows up on me doorstep…"

The tears were burning out of my eyes. I couldn't register these words from my own flesh and blood. I had flown all this way for this?

"Aunt Emily, it was nice to meet you," David said, loudly, this time insistently pulling my arm. "Rachel, we gotta go right now."

With one final look at my mother's sister, I turned and walked back to the car. The door shut behind me. I never saw my mother's family again.

In the car, I started sobbing openly. David drove with one hand on my shoulder. He offered comforting words, but to little effect.

"Don't you dare let them judge you, Rachel. You see now why your mother left and never came back. Don't let ignorance define you."

But I just sobbed. I had always dreamed of meeting my British family. I had grown up without them. Now I did indeed know why she had left. I now knew why she didn't speak of them. They had left because of the ignorance and hatred of a small community in a poor neighborhood in a factory town. I was glad to be rid of it…but the sting was deep. I was a mess even as we checked out of the hotel, turned in our car, and took the train back to London.

To cheer me up, David booked flights to Paris. Instead of spending a few days feeling sad and dejected over my mother's ignorant family, we flew to the City of Light and spent three nights just off the Champs-Élysées. We shopped, brunched, and strolled the beautiful streets of Paris. The pain of Birmingham and the beauty of Paris put more words in my mind, and poetry flowed from my soul. Darkness. Light. Contrasts and colors, shade and morning sun. Out of my heart poured words I didn't know I could write. Pain is definitely the best teacher, I suppose. I was producing some of my best work. David knew when I was "in the zone" and would leave me to my words and verses. I felt so fortunate to have someone who understood my need to create and my need for solitude when I worked.

What most impressed me during our time in Paris was that David never once talked about or even mentioned the life. He was attentive, and treated me beautifully. We slept in, ate amazing food, drank too much wine, shopped, and strolled through this beautiful city. We saw every detail. The Louvre took my breath away; I wanted to create art like the masters whose work adorned those walls and halls. Paris was and is an inspiring city, and several of my best poems through the years owe themselves to her. The seeds that city planted in my heart still produce flowers to this day.

I fell in love with David over and over again on this trip, and I felt I wanted to give him more of myself, and more of what he wanted. I wanted to give him the joy he gave to me. He was such a noble person: he stood by me; he protected me—physically, mentally, and emotionally. His strength made me stronger. He was a great stone foundation, and I wanted to build upon it: a life with him, a future with him. His foundation would hold up much, I knew.

On the flight home, I told David, "I'm ready to take the next step with you, David."

"Next step?"

"You know...*the things you need.*" I used code, as I didn't want anybody nearby to hear.

"Oh, okay then. Great! So what do you think you're ready for?" His dark eyes looked into mine as I considered.

"Well, I wouldn't mind something with that football player we saw at the club..." I spoke in a low voice.

"Mark?"

"Yeah. Him and his lovely wife. Do you think you'd be able to set something up with them? Or should we just try our luck at the club?"

"Well, I can call them when we get back."

"You have their number?"

"Yeah."

I wasn't really surprised. "Okay, that would be great."

He was still looking at me, and his dark eyes regarded me. "You sure you're okay with moving forward?"

"I am; are you?"

"I am always ready."

"Okay. I can't make too many promises…this is all still so new to me…but I promise you I'll try."

"That's all I can ask."

"I love you, David," I said and we kissed.

Later, he fell asleep again, leaving me to my thoughts. No poetry came out of me this time. I looked out at the white clouds and blue water.

I have to admit my heart was racing, and when the doorbell rang, it fluttered. My hands were visibly shaking, palms clammy. David answered the door, and in walked Keiko, followed by Mark. David wasn't a small man, standing around six feet tall. But Mark towered over him, and was immensely broad in the shoulders. He was physically intimidating. Keiko was dressed in a black miniskirt and beautiful silver top. She wore a demure smile and her eyes sparkled. Mark wore jeans and a dress shirt with the sleeves partly rolled up. Summer was here, and the humidity was making everybody dress lightly.

"Mark and Keiko, you remember Rachel, right?" David asked as he introduced us. Keiko gave me the "girl hug" and kiss on the cheek. Mark took my hand and also kissed me on the cheek. He was strong and manly, and as a woman I had to say I was again struck by his physical presence. His light copper hair and light eyes were in stark contrast to David's dark jagged features. They were a study in contrasts, those two. "Please, everybody, sit down…I'll bring the wine," David said, as he led us into the living room.

We sat, and David began working on the cork. I was dumbly smiling at this beautiful couple. She sat close to her husband, and his

large arm was around her shoulders. Keiko had very majestic features…
long, straight hair, slender in the waist, and very feminine curves. To me
she looked like a princess. I initially tried not to consider that David was
probably going to have sex with her tonight, yet I couldn't help but think
about it. I was already feeling the sting of jealousy. Next to her petite
body and features, I felt giant and gangly. Yet when I looked at Mark, he
was looking at me and smiling. His look made me blush. His size and
physical power were intriguing to me. While David was a hawk, Mark
was a lion.

David returned with the wine. "Well, you're all so quiet," he said.

"We were waiting for the wine," Mark responded. His voice was
very deep and resonated through the small apartment.

"Well, here we are then." David poured out four tall glasses,
which nearly finished this first bottle. He had a nervous excitement, and
his smile was broad. He held up his glass, "To old and new friends." We
clinked glasses and drank. I was so keyed up I nearly finished my glass
in the first swallow. I put the glass on the coffee table, as I was afraid
everybody would see my hands shaking.

"David, I absolutely love your photos on your walls. Rachel, have
you seen the pictures from Buenos Aires?" Keiko's voice was very soft,
and she was smiling with her eyes.

"Which ones are from Buenos Aires?" I had spent the night
several times, but I hadn't really devoted a lot of time to admiring his
photos. I was surprised that Keiko would know them better than I did.

"Over here, let me show you." We stood up. She took my hand,
and led me over to the far wall, which was on the opposite side of the
room. Her hand was soft and cool. When we reached the wall, she turned
and regarded me. "Are you okay, honey?" She was looking up at me
with caring in her eyes.

"Yeah, sorry…I'm so nervous."

"You've never done this before, have you?" She turned and
pretended to be pointing out a picture to me. She kept a hushed tone. I
appreciated her candor and her quiet voice.

"No, nothing like this."

"Oh dear. You're not being forced to do this, are you? Sometimes
people feel trapped into it…"

"No, I want to…it's just that I've never done it before." She was pointing to another picture.

"Well, if you don't want to do anything, just give me the word. We girls have to stick together. If you feel awkward or want to stop, tell me and I'll put the brakes on, okay?"

"Thanks, Keiko. That does make me feel better."

"We could always start with watching or a 'soft swap' if that would make it easier for you."

"What's a soft swap?"

"David hasn't told you much, has he? Well, a soft swap is when you play with the other person but don't have sex. Some kissing, stroking...whatever people feel comfortable with. If this is your first time, you could set the parameters. Or we can just not do anything. It's hard the first time...we've all been there. Nobody is born doing this. It takes some practice to work through it."

"Maybe if we started really slowly that would help me. I think just thinking so much about it is making me more nervous."

"Yeah, I know what you mean....but that's also part of the fun... the anticipation..."

"How long have you and Mark done this?"

"We met at a swinger's party. We've always done it. For me, I have about seven years in the life..."

"You don't get jealous?"

"Sometimes. It's important to discuss boundaries and address jealousy in an honest way."

"What are you girls doing over there?" David shouted from across the room.

"Oh David, girls need to talk! That's what we do! Leave us alone!" Keiko playfully scolded. I looked back and saw David and Mark talking softly and regarding us. "Okay, let's go back, Rachel. I'll make sure we take it slow, okay? Remember: tell me if you feel uncomfortable about *anything*, okay? I don't have a problem shutting these boys down at any time."

"Okay. Thank you." She took my hand and led me back to the boys. "Okay, boys, Rachel and I have talked and we're going to take things *very* slowly tonight."

"Yeah, we've already talked about that a bit, Keiko," David began to protest.

"David, no offense, but men don't understand a woman's needs. I'm going to make sure we think about Rachel and make sure nothing goes where she's not ready to go, okay?"

David flushed a little, but for me, Keiko's interest in my feelings was immensely strengthening. I felt more empowered, and I instantly felt a bond with her. How sweet of her, after all, to put my feelings first. I began to relax a bit. The control I was feeling slip away suddenly returned, and I felt more confident right away. I mean, I was still *very* nervous, but I did feel my heart rate slow some.

And I relaxed even more when David opened another bottle of wine. Soon we were talking and laughing. David loved Rod Stewart, and put on his latest album. The music loosened us up more, and we found ourselves talking.

We talked about art, movies, music. Keiko was very well educated in the arts, and she knew about aspects of culture I never knew existed. We shared our backgrounds, if superficially. Keiko shared her upbringing, being born in northern Japan and emigrating to the US as a small girl. She understood, as did I, that being in two societies was difficult. Mark discussed his Midwest upbringing, and then being drafted by the Giants and moving to the Big Apple. David told a few stories from his trip to Tanzania.

As the wine flowed, our mood lightened, and we began to giggle. Mark told some humorous stories from his college days, and the pranks athletes played on each other. I couldn't stop tittering. His deep, resonating voice was immensely attractive, and his dry sense of humor turned me on. I still love a man who can make me laugh.

David put on some Earth, Wind, and Fire, and soon we were moving around the room. Laughing. Eating snacks. Talking about silly things. Laughing at nothing. Admiring David's photos and library.

I noticed Keiko and David were looking at pictures on the wall. I assumed Keiko was talking to him about something as well. I hadn't yet spoken directly to Mark, though we had talked together as part of group conversation. Without thinking about it, I found him standing next to me. His deep voice startled me.

"So this is really your first time, Rachel?" he asked. When I looked at him, his light blue eyes were looking directly into mine. His red hair had fallen down over his forehead. He needed a haircut, I thought, as he looked like his hair had been short before and grew out unevenly. He towered over me.

"Yeah. I'm sorry…I might be a bit of a bore…"

"No, not at all. In fact, someone's first time is a big deal in the swinging world."

"Really?"

"It's kinda like taking someone's virginity. We've all had our first time, and we try to make it a pleasant experience, if possible."

"Ah, I didn't know that." Why hadn't David told me that?

"So you just relax. We don't have to do anything if you don't want. I mean, I'd like to…you're a very beautiful woman. But if you just say the word, we stop immediately and this just turns into drinks with friends." His manly voice and smile made me feel warm. He was so handsome that I couldn't help but feel excited by his presence.

"Thanks, Mark. That helps." And it did, coming from the person I guess I was supposed to have sex with that night. That was part of the drama for me, I think, the expectations. Knowing they weren't there made it easier on me.

"Sometimes it helps if we just play with the person who brought us."

"I don't know what you mean."

"Well, sometimes swinging starts with just being with your regular partner…you and David, and me and Keiko. Then if you feel comfortable we can do a soft swap and work from there."

"That might make it easier. I have to say this is not the way I've ever had sex with another person."

"Yeah! I know what you mean. It's all a bit awkward, especially at first. Normal relationships start with the mutual attraction and work from there. These swings are a bit different, as they start with sex in mind."

"Yes, I guess that's why it feels so weird. I would usually expect a man to take me to dinner a few times before we ended up having sex."

Mark laughed, a deep roar of a laugh. "Yeah! Well, if it helps we can order some takeout to get you started."

I laughed back, and it felt good to laugh with a strong, handsome man. And he really was handsome, in a square-jawed, broad-shouldered, deep-voiced way. What woman wouldn't be attracted to a man like that? His confidence was incredibly sexy, and his physical power was a bit intimidating. Aren't all women both appreciative and yet intimidated by a man's physical power? Mark was bigger and stronger than any man I had met up to that point in my life. He was a force, that one.

David and Keiko returned. They stood there regarding us.

Mark spoke again. "So here's what I'm thinking. When Rachel's ready, why don't we start with our regular partners, and then see what happens from there?"

Now the tension was building again. We were actually planning our sexual congress. My heart started to beat quickly. David nodded agreement. Keiko's eyes questioned mine, and I smiled and nodded in reply.

"Okay, I'm ready," I said. Keiko and I exchanged a nonverbal conversation, and I reassured her with my look that I was ready.

That was a leap of faith. Another jump. Another plunge into darkness. What would I find tonight? I had the sense that my life would never be the same. Would I sprout wings and fly? Or would I dash myself on the jagged rocks below?

19

We took our wineglasses into the bedroom. I nervously stood by David, almost hiding behind him. Mark and Keiko stood on the other side of the bed from us, like we were choosing sides in a battle. We put our glasses down on the nightstand. David looked at me and smiled, and then lowered his head down and kissed me. His kisses were always so warm. I relaxed, if just a bit. We sat on the bed and continued to kiss. Another couple was kissing just a couple feet from me, but my eyes stayed closed, as if I were pretending they weren't there. I could hear them kissing, and then a soft giggle from Keiko. I felt the bed move as they moved.

David's warm hands began to explore my body. I could feel my heart pounding in my throat, and when he touched me my pulse accelerated. My heart beat so loudly that I wondered if everybody could hear it. Yet, his hands were so warm and strong, and I began to surrender to him. His touch made me feel at one with him. I put my hands behind his neck and pulled him against me. Our tongues intertwined, and our bodies began to merge.

I could feel him begin to tug at my blouse. He started with the buttons, and had a bit of difficulty. I moved away just a bit and helped him. As my blouse opened, his hands moved to my breasts. I reached behind my back and unfastened my bra. My cool skin was warmed by his touch, which was now burning hot. That warmth emanated through my body. He tugged at my nipples, gently at first, then harder. I felt my breasts swelling, and I was getting moist. I don't know if it was the sexuality of what was happening, but I was feeling hot and getting hotter.

David lowered his mouth down to my breasts, and took my nipple in his mouth. My breathing came faster now. I couldn't help but peek over at the couple just a few feet away from us. Keiko was already topless, and she was standing in front of Mark who was helping her step out of her black skirt and panties. She was now completely naked. I had seen her naked before, but this time I wasn't a passive observer.

Her body was so slender, and her skin so white. Her breasts were small, but upturned. Her nipples were hard, and Mark now took them in his mouth. Her soft mound of dark black hair contrasted with her very light skin. Though I couldn't see all of her past the massive shoulders of her husband, I could easily see she was beautiful. She seemed even more beautiful than she had in the Trojan. I had never considered myself to have any attraction to women in any way, but I couldn't ignore that she was beautiful. I guess I was staring, because she looked over at me, caught my eyes, and smiled at me. Her eyes then questioned mine, as if to ask, "Are you okay?" I smiled back at her and nodded. I turned my attention back to David, as I felt self-conscious about looking at her.

Seeing Keiko's naked, lovely body had fired me up a bit, though. I pushed David back and began to unbutton his shirt. I tore at the buttons, and kissed the skin I exposed. His dark skin and manly odor made my hormones rage. I wanted him…now. The contrast of his dark, lean, manly frame to Keiko's soft, white, delicate body was entrancing. As I kissed my way down David, I peeked over at her, and again saw her beautiful, slender body, so small and delicate next to the giant who was her husband. He was pulling off his own shirt, and his wide, muscular back dwarfed his tiny wife. Mark's skin was as pale as hers, but he was freckled, whereas she was as smooth and clear as carved alabaster.

I unbuckled David's pants, and fought them down his legs. I wanted him naked and on me. I know now that I had found Keiko attractive and sexy, and to prove myself still a "woman" (whatever that meant) I wanted to have a man's body. Once his pants were off, I yanked down his boxers. He was already nearly fully hard, but I knelt in front of him and took him in my mouth. I did so heatedly, and I heard David hiss his pleasure and surprise at me. His hardness made me feel aggressive. Angry. I took him in with all I had and grabbed his hips to guide him. I wanted him to make me into a woman with his rough body. I wanted to be lost in his strong arms. I wanted to feel his hotness inside me. I wanted him to break me over and over.

But then my eyes drifted over to Keiko. Mark had laid her down on the bed, and his mouth was between her legs. The top of her head was toward me. As he pleasured her, her body arched and squirmed. Her shoulders and upturned breasts twisted under Mark's efforts. Her head tilted back, and I could see her eyes rolling in pleasure. He already had her near the brink.

I pushed David back on the bed. He and Keiko were parallel, with his head near her opened left leg. I climbed on top of him, and pushed myself down on his hard manhood. My knee was right next to Keiko's head. I couldn't help but look down and see her gorgeous body. She had her hands in her husband's hair, and she was pushing herself against his face. Mark was licking voraciously, and his slurping sounds only increased my now maddening desire.

I looked back to David, and his eyes were already on mine. He gave me a large smile. He knew what I had been doing. He knew that I had been admiring a beautiful woman's body. I have to admit that made me feel guilt and shame a bit. I was a straight woman. I was a good Christian girl. I was raised in a loving home. Yet here I was admiring her slender curves, her delicate breasts, her beautiful, smooth thighs. I now had something to prove.

I began to throw myself down on David. I ground my hips onto him, and took all of him I could. My clitoris rubbing on his crotch produced so much pleasure I felt the tingling, burning sensation of an orgasm building quickly. I put my hands on his belly. I lifted my head up. I started riding those boiling hot waves churning inside me. I ground down with all I had. I was completely full of his hardness. The orgasm burned to be let free. Just before I let it go, I turned to look at Keiko again.

Her eyes were smiling up at me. As I started to let my orgasm go, I felt her cool, soft hand touch my right breast. No woman had ever touched me that way, but I wasn't shocked or angry. Instead, my orgasm took control of me, and it crashed through my body like breaking waves in front of a hurricane. Those burning hot and cold waves of pleasure raced through me and set my body twitching, and my hair whipped around me. I didn't yelp, but shrieked with pleasure. I roared like a tigress. The soft hand pulled on my nipple, and then squeezed my breast. And the orgasm continued...I let it wash over me. I let myself disappear within it. The waves hit me so hard I eventually collapsed down on David. Keiko's hand now smoothed the sweat on my back. Her soft, gentle hand moved across my skin, cooling me and relaxing me.

And then Mark was on top of her, and her hand left my body and grabbed his big shoulders. He was such a large man that he seemed to be a giant on that bed. His shoulders bumped my hips. Keiko had to spread her legs wide to accept him. His large, athletic muscles rippled under his tight skin. With my face near David's I could see Mark penetrating Keiko's small opening. Our bodies all rubbed together. Mark's penetrations shook the bed violently, like a ship tossed by a storm at sea.

Mark and Keiko were also a study in contrasts. His massive, muscular, freckled body seemed to consume her tiny, white, porcelain frame. If he was a tiger, she was a little white rabbit. His powerful movements rocked us so hard that I almost feared for little Keiko. He was too big to be doing that to her, but her grunts and groans proved she didn't mind.

I smelled their sex. I heard the wet slapping of their joining. Mark's muscular body ground against David and I, and his sex was just inches from my face, as was Keiko's soft, white thigh. I felt like moving. I wanted to move. But I couldn't. I just lay there on top of David, staring at Mark and Keiko's bodies together. Feeling their joining. Seeing his manhood appear and then disappear inside of her. I could smell her tangy scent. I could smell his musky genitals. His large balls slapped against her butt. I was frozen. It was like I couldn't take my eyes off of them.

David nudged me to move. He then turned me around, and laid me next to Keiko. My head was now next to hers. I opened myself to him, and this caused my legs to intertwine with Keiko's. She hooked her calf over mine. Our thighs and hips rubbed against each other. I didn't look at her...I was afraid what that might mean. David lowered himself onto me. He and Mark were bumping shoulders. He pushed himself into me, and I felt the stretching fullness I loved so much. I felt the electricity of touch. My thighs against hers added to the tension and increased my excitement. My mind wanted to revolt. *This was a woman's thigh I was rubbing against!* I'm a straight woman. Yet the softness of her skin felt so good. Her cool body contrasted strongly with the heat of David's. And Mark's.

I tried to lock eyes on David and his body above me, but found my gaze drifting to the broad shoulders next to us. He was so large. So strong. So powerful. His large muscles rippled as he pushed himself into his wife. His chest was massive and broad, almost unreally so. His stomach muscles stood out like those of a statue. He was a copper-haired Adonis. The woman in me was so attracted to his hard, muscular, powerful body. I found myself looking at him longer than I was looking at David. Both men were so beautiful in their own way.

I had a marvelous study in contrasts in that moment. Mark was white-skinned and copper haired. He was as bright as the morning sun. He consumed space. His gravity was powerful, just like a giant star. David, though, was lean and dark and angular. He was the moon. He was shadow. David and Mark were polar twins, from opposite worlds. And just like the sun and moon, their forces pulled on me. Threw the ocean to my shores. Made seasons within me. It was an immense moment in my life, there in bed with these men. I was never the same. How could you go back to dating some regular guy after having been in bed with these two beautiful men? How would Harold the baker or Bill the plumber ever do anything for me? How would I go back to a guy with a nine-to-five job driving a truck or hanging sheetrock?

And, I wonder now, did Mark and David view Keiko and I the same? Were we polar twins? I was tall, lanky, dark skinned and wild-haired. Keiko was small, delicate, white skinned and straight-haired. We too might have presented those contrasts for those men…there in that bed, so many years ago. Perhaps they enjoyed our contrasts as much as I enjoyed theirs.

"How do you…feel…Rachel?" I heard Keiko say next to me. She was panting her words between Mark's driving thrusts.

I turned my head and our faces were inches apart. Our gasps mixed together. "Good. It's so good." I was feeling the buildup to another orgasm.

"It's great, isn't it?"

"Yeah…great…"

And then she kissed me.

It happened so quickly. Her soft, wet lips met mine. I should have immediately shrieked. I should have immediately demanded a stop to this. Straight women don't do this! But I didn't. Instead, I kissed her back. Her lips felt so sweet and wet. Our lips met and pulled on each other. Then her small, wet tongue entered my mouth. All around me was quiet. I could no longer hear the slapping and grunting of the men between our legs. I could no longer smell the heat and tangy sex smells. I could only feel her mouth on mine. Her softness. Her femininity. Delicate wet lips on mine.

And we kissed. She put her small hand on my cheek, and pulled my mouth onto hers. Reflexively, I put my hand on her, and my hand landed on her soft breast. I didn't recoil, as I would have thought I would. Instead, I squeezed her soft, pert breast. I pulled gently on her nipple. I moved my hand over her lovely, soft breast. And I *loved* the new feeling. It was different than I had felt with a man…with David. It was a whole new set of sensations. And it wasn't bad at all.

Then my orgasm started, and I could not hold it back. Keiko felt me groaning in her mouth, and she reached over to my breasts. She inched herself over, pushing her husband off of her. She turned over, and her mouth was on my right breast; her soft hand was on my left. Her soft tongue hit my nipple and I exploded.

I felt meteor showers inside me, and they ripped through my body and mind. I looked down and saw this beautiful woman on my nipple, but her smiling eyes upturned to mine. It felt so dirty yet so natural at the same time. And my orgasm was like I had never felt before: the heat and hardness between my legs, the softness and coolness on my breasts. It was like two different orgasms blending into one. I arched and twisted my body. I cried. I screamed and bucked. I pushed against David, but it was my mind that was experiencing the most pleasure. David was an afterthought…penetration where I needed it, but my mind was on…her. The roaring flames in my mind and body bore her image. The sparks and torrents tearing through me knew about the soft touch on my body.

As I came down, I saw Keiko's eyes again. She was riding me down those last few waves, and helping me feel the last of them. She knew how I felt. She knew how my orgasm had burned within me. She and I experienced that one together.

"Good one, Rachel?" she asked.

"Yeah…intense," I panted.

"Good, honey." And then she kissed me on the lips again. I kissed back, and I loved it. Then she was on her back again, focusing on her husband. I looked back to David, and his eyes were burning into mine. I could see the same expression I had seen when we had sex in Central Park. He was on fire. His face was dripping sweat.

But now my thoughts were back to Keiko. She was enjoying her husband's penetrations, but she seemed like she was far away from an orgasm. I wanted to help her achieve what I had just experienced. I wanted to give back what was given to me. I had never done anything like this, but I knew I wanted to. Wanted her. Wanted.

"Keiko, I want you to come too," I whispered to her. David was now a thousand miles away to me.

"I'm getting there…"

"I want you to come now," I demanded, as if that would work.

"Then kiss me, Rachel."

And I did. I pushed David out of me. He fell out with a wet sound. I moved over to Keiko, and she was waiting for me with open arms. Mark lifted up as much as he could, but his wet chest slapped against my shoulder. My mouth met hers again. I was kissing her…hard. My tongue pushed into her mouth. It felt so good to kiss her soft lips with passion. My hand was on her soft breast. I squeezed her hard nipple and worked her breast in my hand.

I was in a fever. There was only her and me. I was kissing and squeezing. I felt her beginning to build her own orgasm.

I felt David try to move behind me, but I closed myself to him. This was about Keiko and me. She began to pant regularly. I wanted her to have what I had. I put my mouth down to her small breast, and took the nipple into my mouth. Then I was on the other breast.

"Oh yeah, Rachel…suck my nipples!" she groaned loudly. And I did. I sucked on those hard little nipples like that was all I had in the world. I could feel her moving under Mark, but I wanted to bring her to that orgasm. I wanted it to be *me* that she experienced pleasure from.

My left hand moved down between her legs, forcing my way

between Mark's thrusts. I found her clitoris, though my hand was pinched with each of his thrusts. I began to press on it. Gently at first. Then with more aggression. I was sucking her nipples harder now, and sliding my finger across her with passion.

And then I felt her body jerk. Her head slammed against the bed, and she was twisting and writhing and grinding and mewling. So I pushed harder on her, and faster. Her orgasm exploded more. She squeezed my head to her breasts, and I sucked on them with all that I had. She cooed and cried and twisted under me. She and I rode her orgasm until it finished…until she was twitching so softly, and breathing in short gasps. She was completely relaxed, and her eyes were lidded. I knew where she was. She was floating through the universe, lost in the cosmos. I knew that feeling so well these days. I was proud I helped her get there.

When her dreamy eyes opened, she said, "That was wonderful, Rachel. Thank you."

"You're welcome," was all I could muster. I kissed her again, and then lay back down, next to her. She moved her hand over mine, and we squeezed hands. David was staring at me, and his hand was wrapped around his swollen manhood.

"What do you think, honey?" Keiko asked me.

"About what?"

"Are you ready for a swap, or do you want to stay the way we are."

So there it was. *The* question. I hadn't even thought about having sex with Mark, but now I was faced with it. All three sets of eyes were on me. That felt a bit intimidating, but I felt like I had already crossed a boundary I had never thought I would, so why not go all the way? I was now relaxed and enjoying the sexual energy of the moment. I decided I was ready.

"Okay, yeah…" I said.

"I love you," David said, looking deeply into my eyes. He and Mark changed places, and then Mark was over the top of me. He had a nice, sweet smile on his face.

"Don't worry, Rachel," Keiko said next to me. "You can stop it at any moment."

I expected Mark to replace David inside me, but instead he

lowered himself down between my legs. I squirmed a bit as he put his lips to me, because I was very sensitive. But soon the heat of his mouth warmed me up. I looked down to see his red hair above my crotch, and his beautiful light eyes were looking into mine. David slid in between Keiko's legs, and he immediately penetrated her. He lowered himself down, and three of our faces were close together. David kissed Keiko, and then he moved over and kissed me.

I have to admit this was the strangest moment of the entire night. It was unreal. The man I loved was between the legs of another woman. Yet he also kissed me, just after kissing her. And I had kissed her. The only person I hadn't kissed that night was Mark, but he was between my legs kissing me. I had a moment of surreality. It just wasn't normal for a young, Christian girl to be involved in situations like this. I was in a bed with three other people, and I was having sex with all of them.

But then Mark's tongue began to pleasure me, and instead of thinking about how weird everything was, I focused on his warm, wet mouth. That, I think, got me over the oddity…over the guilt. And Mark was good. His tongue was better than David's, I had to admit. He knew exactly where to touch me, and I was melting on his lips and tongue.

I leaned back and felt the heat of his mouth, and let the warm tingling go through my body. I felt the bed moving as David repeatedly penetrated Keiko. I could hear her soft moans, and I knew the pleasure she was having. I knew the man I loved was having sex with another woman right next to me, and I couldn't yet bring my eyes to look at them…beyond, perhaps a quick peek now and then. Sure, it was hypocritical of me, but that's what was in my mind. This conflict burned in me. Jealousy, green-eyed and ugly, boiled in my heart. It nagged at me. Whispered in my mind. And it built inside me, getting louder and more demanding. I decided to take action and work through the inner turmoil.

I lifted myself up and dove to Mark's crotch. He was still erect. He wasn't as big as David, but he was still a good size and long. I took his very pink penis in my mouth. I realized I could taste Keiko on him, and that made me feel hotter. I took him repeatedly into my mouth, and I received his approving grunts and thrusts in return. I felt his very coarse hands on my back and in my hair. His hands were like sandpaper. No doubt his football career made him immensely strong and required a lot of physical work. He felt like a giant oak tree…rough and solid and towering over me.

I felt his tension building, but I kept up my aggressive tempo. I was bringing him to the brink, so he pushed me down and entered me with force. I put my hands on his hugely muscled arms. They felt so good…so manly. His body felt like iron. He smelled of sweat and expensive cologne. He had so much power that I saw stars with each thrust of his hips. His body was like a battering ram. His mouth came down hard on mine, and I kissed back with passion. His hips pounded against mine, and I felt surging passion in both of us. I looked over at David and Keiko, and saw that her eyes were on her husband. I saw no jealousy…she seemed to enjoy watching what he was doing. David's face was buried in Keiko's hair.

This will sound strange, but I felt more jealousy at this moment. When I looked at David, I felt a sense of shame and anger. Here was the man I loved pushing himself into another woman. Yet a strange thing happened. That jealousy turned to excitement. It's hard to explain, but the "burn" I felt watching him also burned inside me sexually. The more I grew angry with him for having sex with Keiko, the more excited I became, the more I wanted gratification.

I pulled Mark down again and kissed him furiously. I sucked the tongue out of his mouth, and let them both see that I had his tongue between my lips. I moved my hips under him, and pulled on him with my heels. I wanted the dirtiness of it all. I wanted the jealousy-burn. I wanted to have the seed of another man inside me. I wanted his wife to watch me pleasure him. I wanted her to hear my orgasm. I wanted my love to see a stronger man take me.

So I let them hear it. All of them. My own words shocked and excited me.

"Yeah, Mark, fuck me with that big cock of yours. Oh God, you're so strong. Fuck me, baby. Put your come inside me. I want it." The dirtiness of it all fired me up immensely. I was going to be a whore. A slut. I was a dirty girl doing things I could never tell anybody about. I let it all out of me in a barrage of whorish comments. Mark responded.

"You like that, Rachel? Yeah, I'll fuck you hard, baby." I only realized his full strength when he began to hammer me. He was so strong he nearly knocked the wind out of me with each stroke. All of his muscles were moving under his tight skin. I could feel his sweat dripping down on me. My God, he was so powerful. Sex with him felt like wrestling a tiger, which was both scary and exciting at once.

And I wanted more. I pushed him off of me, and turned over. I got up on all fours. I wanted to look into the eyes of his beautiful wife, while her husband entered me from behind. As he pushed against me, I opened up. My thighs pushed against David's. I wanted my boyfriend to feel every thrust. He put me here, after all. Right? He wanted sex with other people, so why shouldn't I give him all of it? Let him feel the pleasure and pain.

Mark again began to pound me. My face was just inches from Keiko. Her eyes switched between Mark's and mine. She didn't even look at David, who was now lifted up…she only had eyes for us. I realized in that moment that she loved it too. I could see her dark eyes sparkling…she had fire and fury in her gaze. She got swept up in the moment along with us, and she told us about it.

"Yeah, Mark, fuck her hard, honey. Fuck her hot pussy, baby!" And then to me, "Take my husband's cock, Rachel. I want to see his come inside you."

I was panting hard now. I was taking his iron-hard thrusts, and I could feel my climax building inside me again. I moved just a bit forward, and found my face brushing Keiko's. She pulled my lips down hard against hers. She sucked on my tongue for all she was worth. I was exhaling each thrust into her mouth. The pounding I was taking was intense. Keiko slid her hand under me, reaching for my clitoris. I slid forward to help her, never breaking contact with her mouth. Only the three of us existed. I didn't even consider David part of this exchange.

When she reached me with her soft fingers, she put me over the edge. Instantly the intensity moved through every nerve in my body. My eyes rolled back. I buried my face in her neck and began shrieking the loudest, longest orgasm I had ever experienced. Her pressure on my clitoris was almost too much, and I felt myself racing across the sky. The combined pressure and the hard thrusts from behind gave me a sensation I never knew possible. Instead of rolling hot waves, it felt like a jackhammer of pleasure, hitting first my skull, then my crotch, and then back to my skull. This intensity threw me into another world.

During sex with David, I had twice experienced a "loss of self"—a sense that I disappeared for a bit and lost consciousness. This time, I completely lost consciousness. I was awakened by Keiko stroking my face.

"You okay, Rachel? Rachel?"

Her voice sounded distant. Like a memory. It took me a bit to find myself.

"Yeah, I'm okay…I just…"

"I know the feeling…amazing, isn't it?"

"Yeah…"

I lifted up, and turned myself over, lying down next to Keiko again. Mark smiled at me and again moved between my legs. I was spent physically and mentally. I was as weak as a child, and physically trembling. I told him so.

"Mark, I don't think I can have another one. That last one was so amazing. I want you to come in me, okay?" I looked at David when I said it. He looked back at me without expression.

"Okay…I'm pretty close right now."

"Good." I was already feeling beat up down there, and didn't know how much more of him I could take. His body was so strong it felt like he could split me in half.

Mark was quickening his motions. I didn't even notice David or Keiko now. My full concentration was on Mark and helping him finish. I wanted him to have a strong orgasm, so I spoke to him. As I thrust my hips against him, I egged him on.

"Did you like me kissing your pretty wife? Did that turn you on, Mark? I loved sucking her titties. She made me come so good when she stroked my hard clit. Did you like that?"

His pace grew faster and faster. His light eyes were glistening. He was pushing into me hard. I knew I would be terribly sore tomorrow, but for tonight I wanted him to have it any way he wanted it.

And then he surprised me. He pulled his heels up under his butt, grabbed my hips, and rolled back onto his heels. He was so strong I felt like I was hanging in the air. With his powerful arms, he slammed me onto his crotch. I was sliding across his thighs like I weighed nothing at all. His granite penis slammed into me with ferocity. We were both sweating freely. His strength excited me…I was in absolute awe of his power.

I saw his mouth begin to hang open, and his face flushed. I knew he was about to ejaculate inside me. I turned and looked at Keiko…her eyes were smoldering, and locked on her husband.

And then he let out a loud, booming cry, and I felt the burning wetness inside me. He continued to slam into me, and each thrust sent more heat into me. I was swinging around in his powerful arms, powerless to stop him. As his hot seed entered me, I felt a warm, pulsing, gentle orgasm slide through me. Not the violent one I had just experienced. This one was like floating on a raft down a river. Despite the violence of his thrusts, I was swirling in a calm pool.

His movements slackened. He slid me back down to the bed, and then lay down on top of me. I pulled his broad shoulders down. We kissed, softly. His acrid sweat spread over me, as I felt him soften. I looked over, and David's eyes were boring holes into us. He began to move more quickly in and out of Keiko. His pace was increasing, and I could see by his movements that he was also nearing climax. He was thrusting into her, and he had a vicious sneer on his face, like a man who knew a dark secret. His face said anger, and rage. And excitement.

I moved Mark off of me, and crawled behind David. My legs were wobbly, and I was already feeling sore between them. Though I knew he was going through a mix of emotions, I wanted David to have what we had all experienced.

When I was behind him, I put my hands on his testicles, which were tight against him, and began to gently squeeze and stroke them. He was pushing hard now, giving her everything he had. I could feel them begin to twitch in my hand. I squeezed harder, and I felt them begin to jerk. He let out a loud groan, and he was shaking as he pounded himself into her. Keiko and Mark were kissing, and he was squeezing her breasts. She did not climax, but gave her attention to her husband. David finished in her, and then fell forward onto her.

It surprised me when I saw David turn his face and kiss first Keiko…and then Mark. As good as it had felt to kiss Keiko, it seemed very wrong to see a man kiss another man. I hate to admit I felt shock at seeing it. I hadn't yet learned to shake off those cultural norms. I wobbled over to the bathroom, and felt Mark's wetness dripping down my thighs. I was already aching.

We were all rather quiet after. Everybody seemed emotionally and physically spent. I was embarrassed, and avoided most eye contact. A few polite exchanges followed, but everything felt stilted and awkward. Mark and Keiko took showers, and then left. I was sure David was mad. I kept envisioning his burning eyes. I thought I had gone too far. I avoided him, and took a long shower. I thought that if I stayed in long enough, I could avoid some of his wrath.

I remember looking at my face in the steamy bathroom mirror. I regarded myself. I was a woman who had just done things I would've considered horribly perverted just a month ago. I would've vilified anybody I knew who did these things. Yet, now I had done them. Myself. This was as serious to me as if I had just tried heroin or stabbed somebody in a fight.

I dressed for bed. I was cringing inside, waiting for David to say something. I didn't think this would go well, and assumed our relationship was over. What had I done? Who was I? While it was happening, it had felt good. Dirty, but good. I had experienced a range of pleasures I had never experienced before. I didn't know my body could climax so strongly. I didn't know I could enjoy the touch of others so deeply. But the aftermath. What would I be now? What would my relationship with David be like? Would he consider me a whore? I'm not sure that I didn't consider myself in that way. I felt a heavy dose of guilt. And shame. Had David shouted at me and told me to leave, I don't think I would have disagreed with him, even though this had been his idea.

When I came out of the bathroom, he was already asleep. Thankfully! I quietly slid under the covers. I could smell the sex. I could see several spots on the bedspread, and the sheets were soaked with sweat. I couldn't believe I was lying in the bed where a perverted sex romp had just occurred. I didn't sleep for a long time. In my mind, I ran over the events. I saw every moment in glaring detail, as if a spotlight was shining on them. I winced as each event replayed in my mind.

Most of all, I saw David's eyes. Weird, unnatural, burning eyes. I wondered what went through his mind. I wondered when he would confront me with my whorish behavior. I felt I deserved his harsh judgment. I would welcome it.

I was also struck by my own willingness to go ahead with things I never thought I could do. I thought I would have to be talked into anything we tried. I thought it would take a slow, steady, gradual slide into corruption. Yet when faced with it, I jumped in readily. On our first swing, I went all the way with a man I knew nothing about and whom I only said a few words to. I had touched another woman as well, and touch was a euphemism for sex. I had always considered homosexual behavior as wrong, and something to be feared and judged. My religion and my culture told me that these things were as bad as murder or rape. Yet, I had not only kissed and touched a woman, I had *enjoyed it*…a lot. The contrast between her flesh and touch and a man's was overpowering. I felt filthy, on the one hand, yet titillated on the other.

What was wrong with me? Was I a deviant? Was I one step away from hanging around a playground in a trench coat? What had I become? What would my father think?

In the morning, I woke up to David putting a tray on my lap. He had made a hot breakfast for me. Eggs. Pancakes. Juice. A small vase with a daisy in it. Not quite what I had been expecting.

"Good morning, darling. Breakfast for you."

I sat up and he moved the tray to a solid position.

"Good morning, David. Thank you." I couldn't look him in the eyes.

He left for a second and came back with a cup of coffee for himself. He sat next to me and watched me as I ate. I looked at the food, afraid to face him again. I took a couple small bites.

"It's delicious, thank you," I said.

"How do you feel this morning?" he asked.

There it was.

"I'm a little tired," I said, staring at my food.

"Yeah, it took you a while to get to sleep last night."

"I thought you were asleep," I said. *Was he really awake?*

"I was, but I stirred a couple of times. You were tossing and turning a bit."

"Oh, sorry."

"It's okay…it was a big night last night. A lot to think about."

And there it was *again*!

"Yeah. Lots to think about." Now I could feel tension I couldn't avoid. He was looking at me, coffee in hand. I looked over, and he was smiling. "Are you okay?" I asked, clenched and ready for a reaction.

"Yeah, never better. The question is, are *you* okay?" *Really?*

"Honestly?"

"Yeah, of course." His smile was still large as I turned to face him.

"I'm worried about how you're going to react to what we did last night." I could feel a pounding in my head. My thoughts were racing.

"Me?" he asked. "You're worried about me?"

"Yeah." And I was.

"I'm just great. This wasn't my first time, Rachel, in case you hadn't noticed."

I felt bold enough to press a little. "Your eyes, though…they were a bit scary last night."

"They were?"

"Yeah, your eyes were burning into me."

"They were?"

"Yes."

"Oh, sorry. It was incredibly sexual. I was immensely turned on."

"It didn't bother you when Mark and I…"

"Of course not." He took a drink of his coffee, and looked at me as if we were discussing the latest movie.

"But your eyes seemed like you were furious."

"Well, that didn't stop you..." He laughed a little.

"It almost did...I thought about stopping at one point..."

"Oh, well, glad you didn't. No, I was probably just focused on what was happening. I try to see everything...burn it into my memory." He sipped his coffee.

"Seriously? So it didn't bother you to see Mark inside me? See us...you know..."

"Fucking?"

"Yeah, fucking, I guess..."

"Not at all. I mean, I was inside Keiko at the time, as I remember it."

"Yeah."

"I mean, are you okay with everything that happened?"

"You mean the sex..."

"Yeah, of course..."

"I guess. I mean, I'm still grappling with a couple things."

"That's not uncommon. Which parts were the toughest for you?"

"Well, I guess I was surprised by the homosexual parts...maybe a bit uncomfortable."

"Well, nobody is a homosexual here. The correct term is bisexual and I think it's a loose affiliation at best. I don't consider myself bi, really. A little, perhaps."

"What do you mean?" I didn't really understand the fluidity of sexuality.

"A bisexual is someone who equally, more or less, enjoys both sexes. A bisexual person will pursue sex with both males and females. I don't, but I have had sex with both men and women."

"What's the difference?" I was so young...so confused by all this.

"Well, a bisexual man might have a boyfriend or a girlfriend. I don't. I have only had girlfriends. However, sometimes while having sex I might have sexual *contact* with a man. I might do some things with him that are sexual. But after it's over, I'm not going to call him for a date and have sex with him. It's more of an 'in the moment' type of experience."

"It just seems so strange...so perverted...my friends would tell me I'm a freak."

"Don't let other people tell you how to feel, okay?"

"I've never imagined doing these things…"

"What adults do behind closed doors is none of anybody's business. Everybody in this bed was a consenting adult. We touched each other. We pleasured each other. You touched and kissed a woman, and I kissed a man. But we're still a couple. We are still in love, right?"

"I do still love you," though inside I knew there was something *different* today.

"And I love you. So as long as we are doing what we enjoy, why would anybody have a problem with that? Why would you let anybody tell you something you did was ugly or dirty?"

"I was raised with certain beliefs."

"We're all raised with good and bad beliefs. Let me give you an example. My father, God rest his soul, was a horrible racist. He hated anybody who wasn't white. If he had met you, he would've called you names you wouldn't have liked. Darkie. Coon. That's the way I was raised. But that's wrong…and I realized that when I met people of all colors, first in college and then in my job. I realized the way I was raised was wrong…horrible in fact."

"I never knew that…"

"I loved my dad, but he had many faults, and racism was one of them. And if he were still here, he would be fighting me to end a relationship with the woman I love. That old way of thinking is dying. Our country is changing. We're growing more open to new ideas."

"Thankfully."

"Yes, thankfully. And it's the same way with our beliefs on sexuality. Twenty years ago, we'd have been arrested for perversion. Now, we'd probably only be embarrassed if this came out. I hope that in a few more years nobody will think twice about how people have sex and pleasure themselves."

I didn't know if I agreed with him. I was raised in such a conservative household. I had broken every sexual rule we had, I'm sure. Yet I didn't hate it. "Well, that helps."

"That's good!"

"But did you enjoy what happened, David? Are you okay with everything that happened? You don't think less of me?"

"Oh God, of course not, Rachel. I asked for this, remember?

There's nothing that could've happened last night that would've made me think less of you. I enjoyed it all."

"You weren't jealous then?"

"No."

"I have to admit, I was a bit jealous at times. I felt a burning feeling when you were with Keiko. At least part of the time."

"But you also enjoyed it a bit too, right?"

"Yes," I had to admit. "I did."

"That's kinda how it works, Rachel. I know it's hard to understand. When you swing, part of the 'turn-on' is the bit of jealousy in your gut. The sting of seeing your lover with someone else. And yet you're doing the same thing. It's hard to explain. The fact that you didn't get up and slap me or scream or call the police tells me that you had more pleasure than pain, yeah?"

"Yeah, I guess so."

"If you could go back in time, would you stop it from happening?"

I had to think about it. "No, I guess not. Maybe. No, probably not."

"Then you experienced what everybody experiences. Believe me, even old swingers like Mark and Keiko feel that burn, at least to a degree. But you get more comfortable with it over time. And, honestly, that's part of the kink of it…part of the unique pleasure of it."

"You felt jealousy too?"

"Oh God, yeah…seeing another man inside you made me angry… and jealous…and horny…and turned on…all those things at once."

"Imagine if a psychiatrist could talk to us now….what would he think?"

"I saw a psychiatrist one time. Didn't help."

"You did?"

"Oh yeah…a couple of them, actually. When I began to experiment sexually, I was sure I was the worst pervert in the world."

"What did they say…these psychiatrists?"

"They told me I was a sexual deviant. They threw out terms like polyphilia and cuckold and all kinds of labels. I reject those terms. Nobody can define who I am. I do what I want because I enjoy it. If nobody gets hurt and nobody is coerced, then it's all fun and pleasure. Nobody can tell me I'm a degenerate. I hurt nobody, or so I hope anyway."

"What about yourself? Do you hurt yourself?"

"I don't think so. I do things with people who I enjoy. I savor this life. While a few women have had hurt feelings, there was no damage to them…only damage they perceived from our broken relationship. It would be no different than had they caught me cheating on them or if I broke up with them."

And it was true…I was here voluntarily, and everything we did had been okay with me. Still, I couldn't take back these things, and I had a feeling I was breaking some moral code, some social contract, some societal expectation. But I had also enjoyed the sex…immensely. I could feel the ache inside me, both physically and morally.

He continued. "So you've touched a woman sexually now." Even now I can remember that I winced when he mentioned it. I was stinging emotionally at the thought of it. "Are you a raging lesbian now? Are you giving up all men to only lie with women?"

"No, of course not!"

"Exactly. You're a straight woman who, in the middle of sexual activities, touched a woman. That doesn't make you a lesbian. At worst it means you have some bisexuality, and probably only a little bit, since it took you twenty-some years to first touch a woman in a sexual way. And even if you were a bisexual woman, and you wanted to be with women more often, what harm is that? As long as you're both enjoying it, so what?"

"But, David, I have to admit it made me feel weird when I saw you kiss Mark."

"Did it?"

"Yeah, a little bit anyway." A lot actually, I'm sad to say now.

"Did you feel angry? Revulsed?"

"No…just…weird, I guess."

"Well, I'll wager the first time you kissed Keiko it felt weird too, yeah?"

"Well, yeah…"

"The first time you saw your parents kiss it felt weird too, right?"

I had to think back a ways…they were not very affectionate around me. "Yeah, I guess it did."

"So I wouldn't worry about it. Unless you feel revulsion, it's just the newness, I'm sure. Anyway, when we do something like this again, just let me know how you feel. We should always talk about what happens...we're a couple, and we need to talk out how we feel about all these things, so that we don't cross any boundaries we aren't comfortable with...or that we at least take some things slowly."

"Okay, that sounds reasonable."

"Good."

I had a lot on my mind, but I went back to finishing my breakfast. It was mostly cold now, but I was hungrier than I thought.

As I finished up, David spoke again. "So now that you've had time to think about it, do you feel weird having touched Keiko that way?"

"After they left last night, I felt *very* weird about it. This morning, though, I feel much better. It still feels odd to me, but it was also very sensual, I guess."

"Well, that's not so bad then, is it?"

"No, not bad." *And she had been so beautiful. And soft.*

"Good. There's something I need to tell you...about her..."

"Yes?" I turned and looked at him.

"As they were leaving last night, she told me she really enjoyed herself with you, and asked if you might be interested in something...just between you and her."

"David, what do you mean?"

"Well, I think Keiko is openly bisexual. I guess she was asking if you would be interested in something just between you girls."

"You mean sex?"

"Well, I would presume that. She didn't say shopping!" He laughed loudly.

"She wants to have sex with me...just the two of us?"

"Well, yeah, it would seem so. You can say no...it's okay. I know you're new to this, and maybe that's not your cup of tea."

"David, I'm not a lesbian."

"Neither is she."

"David, what have you gotten me into?" I felt a flash of anger. What did they think of me? Maybe now that I had crossed a line, they felt I had no boundaries at all.

"Don't worry, it's okay to say no. There's no pressure. Remember, you only do what you're able to do. I'll tell her you said no."

"Good. Yeah. Tell her I said no. I'm not a lesbian. You tell her." Who was I trying to convince?

"Rachel, relax. Nobody is calling you a lesbian. She just wanted to see if you were up to it. If you're not, no problem."

He took the tray away, and went to the kitchen. I heard him at the sink washing the dishes. My mind was flooded with thoughts, hurtling around in random directions. I could see my father looking at me. Judging me. I could see my mother. What would she think of her baby daughter having sex with a woman? *Oh my God...I touched a woman last night...maybe I am a lesbian! Maybe I've crossed a boundary I wasn't ready for. How can I ever look at my father's face again?*

I was angry with myself. I was angry with David. How could I have gotten myself into this situation? How could I put myself in a situation where I'd be getting propositioned by a woman? Normal people didn't do this stuff...abnormal freaks did these kinds of perverted things. They were the people you couldn't trust your children around. Freakish sexual behavior was ruining society.

And yet, I had touched her. Her soft skin. Her lips. Her breasts. I had touched her womanhood. I het lct her kiss me and lick me. And I had loved it. Her touch was new...a sensation I had never experienced before.

I found myself thinking of her soft touch. Her dark, narrow eyes. Her long, sleek hair. Her small, upturned breasts. Her slender legs. I remembered how warm her kiss made me. How hot! I remembered how soft she had felt. I remember wanting her. Wanting her touch. Wanting her to want me. And those feelings came back in a rush to me. I was sitting in the bed, and she had lain right there...with her small, slender body outstretched. Her slender legs raised. Her soft lips on mine. I could picture her clearly, sprawled out in front of me.

As I sat there thinking about it...about her...I found myself becoming wet again. Just thinking of her beauty and softness was enough to make me sexually excited. I looked at the spot where we had touched and I began to touch myself. First I touched my breasts...breasts she had licked and nuzzled. I touched my wetness, and wished it were her hand on me. I felt myself getting more aroused. I was now sexually on an edge. Before, I hardly ever thought of sex. Now, sex was a large part of my life.

My orgasm sneaked up on me. I was looking at the spot where her body had been, and a sudden rush of blood made my face turn hot and red, and then a warm, slow orgasm washed over me. It felt like rain on a hot summer day. The warmth flowed over me. When it was finished, I saw a patch of wetness on the sheets. I hurried to the bathroom, grabbed a towel, and cleaned it up. I was so embarrassed.

I put on some clothes, and went out to the front room. David was reading a book, one leg over the arm of his chair.

"Hi, honey…did you go back to sleep?"

"Yeah," I lied, "I was a little tired."

"Don't blame you. I'm a little bushed myself."

"David, did you call Keiko yet?"

"No, it's still early. Don't worry…I'll call her later…"

"Wait, I want to talk to you for a bit."

"It's okay, Rachel…I said you don't have to."

"How would you feel if I did?"

"What?" He closed the book. The room felt so quiet.

"How would you feel if I met up with Keiko?"

"Rachel, I said you don't have to already…please, let's change the subject."

"But what if *I* wanted to?"

He put the book down on an end table and regarded me. He looked at me silently, and I could feel his examination of me. "Are you interested in being with her?"

"Maybe."

"Well, maybe isn't the same as a yes or a no."

"I want to know how you would feel if I did something with her."

"I'm not sure what you mean…"

"David, just answer the question, please," I demanded. "If I said yes to Keiko and we had sex, how would you feel about it?"

"I'd be happy for you, as long as you did it for the right reasons… and you enjoyed it."

"Right reasons?"

"You did it because *you* wanted to, and not because you were feeling any pressure from me."

I was happy to hear him speak these words. He was concerned about pressuring me. I wanted a sense of control, and he was giving it to me. "Okay, if I wanted to and I did, you wouldn't be jealous?"

"No." His eyes told me he was serious.

"You would not be jealous if I went alone with her, and together she and I had sex."

"No, I wouldn't…if that's what you wanted."

"It wouldn't go both ways, though."

"What do you mean?"

"If I had sex with Keiko, it wouldn't mean that I thought it was okay if *you* had sex with Keiko without me…or Mark, for that matter. Or anybody else."

"Well, okay. I understand."

"That would be okay with you?" I was insistent now, holding eye contact.

"Yeah, very much so."

"Okay, please call Keiko later and tell her I want to." Those words left my mouth.

How did I get here?

I met her at Harry's, which was a great Upper West Side bistro, back when bistros were first becoming a thing. We met for lunch, so it wasn't too crowded—Harry's on the weekend was usually standing room only. It was now early summer…she was in shorts, and I wore a short skirt. Keiko wore a Beatles t-shirt. Her hair was loose, and flowing over her shoulders. It shimmered even in the dim light of Harry's.

We took a seat by the under-powered air conditioner and ordered. As you can imagine, I was very nervous. While I had had lunch with many girlfriends through the years, I had never had a "date" with a girl, especially one I had already had sex with…or at least sexual experiences with. It was doubly confusing because we had both exchanged men, and I had taken her husband inside me. As a good Christian girl, I felt like a whorish Jezebel, bent on further perversions.

Keiko sensed my nervousness. "You okay, Rachel? You seem a bit…jumpy."

"Well, yeah, I guess I'm a bit nervous."

"Why would you be? We already know each other, honey." I guess she meant the Biblical use of "know."

"Yeah, but this still seems a bit odd to me…"

"Okay, well, set your mind at ease. This is just two girls having lunch. Nothing else has to happen, and we'll move at your speed. The best thing about being with a girl is that we move at a woman's pace."

"Woman's pace?"

"Sure. You know men can't wait to stick it in us. Everything is about them scoring before the night is over. We're always having to slow them down. With a woman, though, there's no time limit…no scorecard. We're having lunch, and just doing whatever feels right. If nothing happens we've lost nothing, and had a great lunch." Her eyes twinkled at me.

And that did help. But what was also making me nervous was Keiko's beauty. She was so slender, and her jet-black hair was lustrous and long, reflecting any light nearby. Her eyes would disappear as she smiled. She was so gorgeous…probably still is. I had to admit I was very excited about doing more with her. At the same time, I had never been with a woman one-on-one, and the only time I had ever touched a woman was last week during our encounter. So this was very new to me, and I couldn't stop my knees from shaking.

"So how do you feel about the life so far, Rachel?" She was looking right at me, sipping her Coke.

"Well, it's a lot at once, but I'd be lying if I said I hadn't enjoyed so much of it so far." I couldn't hold eye contact with her. "Still, my only real encounter was last week…" How does one say, *I enjoyed having sex with you and your husband?*

I was surprised at how matter-of-factly she was able to discuss it. "But you didn't feel guilty after, did you? Sometimes that first one can be an emotional challenge."

"Well, I think I did the next morning…I was worried about how David would feel about me the next morning. But everything seemed fine."

"That's good."

"And I was a bit sore…down there…"

"Oh yeah, that takes some getting used to. When we first started dating, Mark took me to a club, and I had three guys at once. I could barely move the next day." She took a bite of her sandwich.

"Seriously?"

"Yeah."

She seemed so calm about it...so relaxed. I had never met anybody like her. "Well, how did Mark feel about that?"

"Oh, Mark is a cuck, so he got off on it."

"Cuck?"

She lowered her voice. "You know, cuckold."

"What is that? I heard David use that term...I don't understand it."

She spoke softly. "Oh, you don't know? Technically, a cuckold is a guy whose wife is cheating on him. But in the life a cuck is a guy who gets off on watching his woman have other men. I don't know if there's a female equivalent..."

"So Mark enjoyed it?"

"Oh God, yeah...he loves it when I do other men. I think he enjoys it more than anything else. It turns him on immensely."

"I guess David is one also, because he said he enjoyed seeing me and..." *Crap!* I still hadn't got my head around the idea that I was talking to a woman whose husband I had slept with.

"You and Mark?"

My face was burning. "Yeah."

"It's okay, Rachel." She put her hand on mine in a comforting way, though she held it there a bit. "I've seen him with many girls. I guess I'm a female cuck. I like it." She was so relaxed about it. So calm. It was hard for me to imagine the types of things we were talking about.

"You like it?"

"Sure. I like most things. There's very little I won't do. Pain and bondage aren't my first choices, but I've even tried them. Enjoyed it a bit now and then too. How about you?" She took a bite from her kosher pickle, snapping it on purpose.

"Me?"

"Yeah, is there anything you don't like?"

"Well, I don't know...I'm still figuring it out I guess. I haven't done much."

"Well, think about it for a minute. How did you feel when I was with David?" She took another bite of her sandwich...she seemed like she could be talking about the weather.

"Well, I have to admit I was a bit stunned at first."

"Yeah? Were you jealous?"

"Yeah, I felt a bit of that."

"Angry?"

"Probably."

"But then you were able to let it go, right?"

"Yeah, it kinda...I don't know..."

"Made you more excited too, didn't it? Made you hotter to do Mark?" She had no boundaries, I now knew. Just imagine if someone was overhearing our conversation!

"I guess...yeah..."

"Yeah, those feelings of jealousy and anger also make for terrific sex. It's part of the thrill. The fact that you worked through it and enjoyed the night says you'll be fine. Many women can't do what you've already adjusted to. The fact that we're here eating lunch instead of you pulling my hair tells me you're gonna like the life."

"You think so?"

"Sure. The first time I saw Mark with another woman, I cried."

"Really?"

"Yeah. I got over it, though." She smiled broadly.

"So may I ask you something, Keiko?"

"Of course, Rachel. Ask me anything."

"How often have you been with women?"

"Well, this isn't my first time." She winked.

"I'm sorry, that might have been a bad question." Women hate when men ask us how many times we've "done it" or how many men we've slept with, yet here I was asking her the same thing, in a sense.

"No, it's okay. I guess I have to think back. I've probably been with twenty women or so. I haven't kept track."

"Twenty! That's more than I would've thought."

"Is that too many?" She batted her eyes, feigning innocence.

"Oh, that's not what I mean. I guess I'm still grappling with the idea if being with a woman makes me a lesbian or bisexual. I don't quite know what to think about what I am for having these feelings. I don't know what people would call me if they found out. Like my family. What will people say if this gets around?" I scanned around the room, and wondered if anybody could hear what we were speaking about. Nobody seemed to be listening, and there was enough of a hum in the room to cover our soft voices.

"Oh, honey, don't do that to yourself."

"Do what?"

"Don't try to assign labels. Don't let other people describe you. You are just you. I don't let anybody tell me what I am. Lesbian? Bi? I don't let someone else tell me what I am or limit what I can do. If I want a man, I'm with a man. If I want a woman, I'm with a woman. I think we're all somewhere between straight and gay, or whatever. Nobody is one hundred percent straight and nobody is one hundred percent gay. We're all on sliding scales, and they change at times. Four years ago, I would've never thought about being with a woman. Now, I like it. Next year, I might stop. I just do what I want and to Hell with anybody who doesn't like it."

"I wish I were as strong as you."

"You will be, if you first stop caring what others think. Be yourself. *Enjoy* yourself. Do whatever feels comfortable. You're you... you're Rachel. Nobody else should be able to attach a label to you."

"Yeah."

"Now, I said that having just called Mark a cuck, didn't I?" And she started snickering.

"Yeah, I guess you did!"

"So now I'm a hypocrite!" She laughed aloud now. She didn't care that others might hear what she was saying. I loved her confidence. "But you see what I mean, I hope. Don't get caught up with what others will try to say about you. Just enjoy what feels good. Set your own boundaries. Like I do with BDSM."

"BDSM"

"That's all that bondage stuff. I guess it stands for 'bondage and discipline, sadism, and masochism.' I don't really like all that, though I did let a lover handcuff me once. That was about four months ago."

"A lover?"

"Yeah."

"So it wasn't Mark?"

"No." She was getting our check.

"Was this at a club?"

"No." She was paying our check. I noticed her wallet was very full.

"Well, details?"

"Let's walk outside and I'll share."

We grabbed our purses and were out the door. It was so humid outside. Hot New York days can suck the life right out of you, and this was one of those days.

Once outside, she continued. "So sometimes in the life you go beyond swapping. Mark and I can solo sometimes."

"Solo?"

"Yeah, I can have a boyfriend and he can have a girlfriend, or whatever mix of genders we want. We'll go out, do things separately, and then share our experiences after. Kinda like what you and I are doing..."

I hadn't thought about us in this sense, but now that I considered it, I realized I was out with a man's wife.

"Let's walk over to the park, okay?" Keiko asked.

"Okay."

Though hot, the tree-lined walks always felt nice. The shade trees helped, and it seemed to generate enough breeze to make it just cool enough. As we crossed Central Park West to enter it, Keiko grabbed my hand and pulled me across the street. Her hand was so soft and it felt so good to touch her again. It wasn't so long ago David and I had our crazy evening not too far from here.

Once across, we entered the park and walked along the path. I didn't pay attention to where we were going.

"Keiko, I have something I need to discuss with you."

"Sure, Rachel, what's up?"

We were walking slowly, shoulder to shoulder. "I've never been with a woman before...except last week when you and I...I mean..."

"I know, honey." She again took my hand. She didn't let go.

"I mean, I don't know 'how' with just a woman. Last week we had the men there. I don't know how women 'do it' by themselves."

"Oh, that's the best part...the how." She turned her beautiful eyes to me and smiled.

"What?"

"Yeah, honey..." I was beginning to love how she called me 'honey.' "The best part of girl sex is the how. With men, it's always rush rush rush...get it in, get it off...which is okay...I like that urgency. But with a woman, it's totally different. We take our time. We start and stop and start again. It's wonderful. I sometimes enjoy it more than being with a man."

"Really?"

"Yeah. You'll see. We don't have to worry about anything. We can just be ourselves. We take turns. It's a beautiful thing. I'm getting horny just thinking about it," she said with a smile.

"I have to admit I'm still nervous."

"Don't be. Remember that I'm a woman. If you tell me to stop, there won't be any hard feelings. There won't be any judgment. We do exactly what we want and we go as long as we want. You can ask for anything or say no to anything...the only rules are the ones we make." She was still holding my hand, and I loved it. I couldn't care less about what anybody would've thought of us.

"Will you tell Mark about it afterward?"

"Of course...we share everything. You'll tell David, too, right?"

"I don't know."

"Of course you will. He's your man. Believe me, men love the 'girl-girl' thing. He'll want to know every juicy detail. But here's our rule...we only share what we want to share. We're women, and we keep some things secret. So remember when he asks, you only tell him what's in your heart to tell him."

"I hadn't thought of it that way."

"And remember to titillate him...men love the tease...the buildup. Tease him with the story."

"I don't know what you mean." God I had so much to learn!

"Don't come home and say, 'We did this and this and this...' He wants you to build it up. Men are excited by the thought of women together, so tease him. Extend the story. Add any details you want to make him horny. He'll reward you with very hot sex!"

"How will you tell it to Mark?"

"Oh, Mark will sit next to me like a puppy, waiting for me to play out the story for him. So I'll build him up." She took on a sultry, breathy voice, like a whisky-soaked jazz singer. "'First we ate lunch. I was looking into her eyes. I couldn't stop staring at her beautiful face. She looked so sexy in her short skirt.' Like that. He'll be so disappointed if I say, 'We ate lunch, walked in Central Park, and then had sex.' That's not what he wants. He wants the story."

"Were you staring at my face over lunch?"

"Of course, honey. Believe me, I'm so attracted to you." My heart rate picked up, and I know my palm was sweaty against her cool hand.

"You are?"

"Oh yeah. Why do you think I asked to meet you?"

It was so nice to hear a beautiful woman tell me she was attracted to me. What woman doesn't want to be desired? "I'm so attracted to you, Keiko. You're so gorgeous."

"Then why are we walking in the park? Why don't we get out of here and get naked?" Her directness surprised me...and excited me.

"Where should we go? David's home today. Is Mark at home?"

"He is, but don't worry. I have a room at the Plaza."

"The Plaza?"

"Yeah, you don't mind, do you?"

"It's so expensive."

"I want our first time to be special."

"Okay, let's get a taxi."

We hadn't ventured far from the street, and we were back to it in a minute. A quick cab ride and we were at the Plaza, at the southeast edge of Central Park. As we got out, I could feel my whole body shaking. I mentally scolded myself for still being so nervous about everything. Keiko just smiled at me, took me by the hand, and led me to the elevator. I was too drunk with nervous excitement to notice how beautiful the hotel was.

Inside the elevator, she pointed to the mirrors around us. "Look at how beautiful we are, Rachel." I looked in the mirror. I saw our contrasts. My darker skin. My long, curly, twisted, unruly hair. Next to me was a smaller, petite Japanese woman. Her hair was shiny and straight. Her features were regal. As I looked at us, she reached up and touched my cheek. When I turned to face her, she kissed me on the lips...so delicately. As her soft lips touched mine, I felt a shock through my body.

We reached our floor, and she took me directly to the room. She knew where to go. She produced the key from her purse, and opened the door. I hadn't realized we would be in a suite. It had a large open living room with three rooms off to the side, all lavishly appointed; I couldn't believe I was in a suite at the Plaza. This was how rich people lived! I was used to living much more modestly. I hadn't thought about it until

that moment, but Mark was a professional football player, so they were
probably doing quite well.

We put our purses down, took off our shoes, and then Keiko took
my hand. "Let me show you the bedroom." She didn't mince words, this
one! She pulled me to the lavish bedroom. A large four-poster bed with
white duvet and sheets was ahead.

"Do you mind if I shower quickly? It was hot outside."

"No, I don't mind. I need one too." I was suddenly self-conscious
about having been sweating.

"Do you want to take one together?"

Another new experience for me. "Sure."

We moved to the bathroom. A large brass-and-glass shower stall
awaited us there. The bathroom was larger than my bedroom at home.
Keiko started the water. I could only look at her. I was too shy to start
stripping. After she got the water going, she immediately pulled off her
Beatles top then unfastened her bra. Her beautiful breasts had my eyes
riveted. She then realized I hadn't gotten undressed.

"Rachel, you're not still shy around me, are you?" she asked,
sliding down her shorts. Oh, how I wanted to touch and kiss her body.

"Well, a little, I guess…" I made a half-hearted attempt to remove
my top, but my hands were shaking.

She stepped forward to me. Her eyes were digging into mine…her
eyes controlled me. She took my trembling hand, and placed it on her
soft breast. She put her hand behind my neck and pulled my face to hers.
Our mouths met, and her tongue pushed past my lips. Her soft, lightly
damp breast felt so good to touch. I wanted her. I could feel my kiss
getting stronger, and pushing against her lips. I wanted her…badly.

She pulled away. "There's my girl. Now, let me get you out of
these clothes." She started pulling at my top, and I now wanted
everything off. She reached behind me and unfastened my bra. As my
breasts fell out, she took one in her mouth and sucked on it ever so
gently. I pulled her face against it, and she bit me softly. I was instantly
hot and ready. I wanted to be naked with her so badly.

"Let's get in the shower, honey," she said. My skirt and panties
flew off, as if on their own. She was naked also, and stepped into the
shower first.

Once again, I was captivated by her beautiful, soft, milky-white skin. Her dark triangle of hair seemed so light, yet dark against her whiteness. As the water hit her, her nipples hardened. She beckoned me in, and I stepped in next to her. The warm water felt so wonderful against me. Our breasts touched, and the electricity of her skin on mine caused me to shudder. The warm water and her cool skin felt so natural...so clean. I wondered how I could've ever felt weird or dirty about her...and us. I wondered how I could've been hesitant to be with her. Together, we were pure. Together we were soft. Our breasts rubbed against each other. Our eyes stayed focused on each other. Our smiles and giggles felt so natural, like two innocent children running in a field of grass. Like the only two people on the planet, standing under a waterfall and being washed by nature.

Keiko produced the soap, and began to lather my breasts. Then she lathered her own. When both were soapy, she pressed her breasts against mine. The slippery soap created such an incredible sensation. My nipples were harder than I ever imagined they could be. The softness and firmness of her breasts against mine made me dizzy. I had to twist my legs against each other in a desperate attempt to put pressure on my clitoris.

And then she put the soap between my legs. I wondered if she could feel how wet I was down there. She slipped the soap against me. She then used her other hand to slide the soap all over me. I was aching for her to put her fingers in me. I opened myself to her, inviting her in. She licked her lips as she slipped first one, then two fingers inside my opening. I felt the familiar hot waves burning through me. I began to gasp...I thought I would have an immediate orgasm.

"No you don't," she scolded. I looked up...eyes refocusing...I had been so close I had already lost myself in it. "Don't come yet, honey...I want you to come on my mouth."

"God, I want you now, Keiko..." I was panting and shaking. My orgasm hovered just out of reach. I wanted that one so badly.

She rubbed the soap on her own crotch. I was so dizzy with my near climax, but I put my hand between her legs...I wanted to feel her softness. I didn't tease her, though; I immediately put a finger inside her. I felt her gasp against my chest. She took one of my nipples in her mouth as I slid my finger into her. Then I slipped in a second. I felt her push against my hand. She was soaking wet inside...I could feel her slippery juices and I wanted them.

"Let's get into bed," she gasped. We quickly finished washing ourselves, and then grabbed the thick, white towels hanging outside the shower. I was still reeling…lost in another world. As I watched her dry, I saw that beautiful, slender body and I knew I would do anything to please her. I would give her anything she wanted. I would lick and suck and finger any part of her body that would give her pleasure. I wanted her. Badly. So badly it ached.

I felt her hand grab mine and pull me toward the bed. Once there, she slid backward onto it, and pulled me after her. Her eyes were playful yet demanding. Her beautiful breasts swayed just a little. Her soft womanhood was already opened and ready. I knew she was as turned on as I was, and I wanted what we were about to have. As I slid onto the bed, our mouths met. Her soft lips were against mine, and her tongue again entered my mouth. I pulled and sucked on that tongue so desperately, as if I wanted that tongue down my throat. My hands explored her soft skin. Her breasts, her belly, her slender legs.

But before I could reach her womanhood, she pushed on my shoulders. She was trying to lay me down on my back. I wanted to be on her so badly that at first I resisted. But then her insistence made me surrender. I lay back. She kissed from my mouth down to my chin. Then to my neck. Her neck kisses sent tingling goose bumps down my body. I honestly had never been this wet and excited before…even with David. My breasts were throbbing, aching to be touched. But she kissed me slowly. Teasingly. When her lips brushed my nipples, I remember gasping loudly. I pulled her head, and ground her into my breasts. She sucked hard on my nipples…just to the edge of pain, and it drove me insane. But she took her time on them. First one, then the other. Her right hand teased me. She used her nails to gently scratch my stomach. Her lips then replaced her nails, and as she kissed my stomach, her nails scratched along my thighs, and played with the curly hairs between my legs. I opened my legs in anticipation. I was physically burning with tension and desire. I could feel my moisture making my bottom wet. I wanted her to take me so badly, I felt like I would scream.

But she didn't. As she kissed down to my mound, I expected her tongue. I wanted her tongue. I needed her tongue. But I didn't get it. Instead, she kissed down my thigh. Down to my knee. I tried to grab her hair and pull her to me, but she slid just out of reach.

When she reached my knee, I was almost nearing orgasm without her touch. My body was sending waves of warmth through me. I was just about able to grab those waves. So close. But not quite. My breaths were getting desperate. Frustrated pants.

And then she slid up, and all at once she put her mouth on me. The fire between my legs erupted. She forced her tongue into me so suddenly I gasped and jerked. She licked at my wetness, then drove her tongue inside me over and over. She then slid her tongue up to my clitoris. As her tongue touched it, I exploded!

I remember grabbing her hair and shouting out. I ground my hips into her face. Her little tongue furiously pressed against me. Hot fire roared through every nerve ending. Each wave of pleasure hit me like a hammer, and I bucked with every successive undulation. I was pushing my crotch against her mouth with each boiling breaker inside me. A grunting yell left my lips with each throb of pleasure.

And then I was gone again. Out in space. Flying between solar systems. Far away. My body was connected to me by the slimmest of threads. I could almost not feel myself. I was away. Flying. My body was the universe.

When I slowly drifted back, I realized I had let go of her head. She was lessening her pressure, but making sure I received all the pleasure I could get. She timed the movements of her tongue with my twitching, and even to the last it felt like I was flying freely.

When I returned to my body, I looked down to see her smiling eyes looking up at me. Her face looked so beautiful between my legs. I saw my dark thighs, my pubic hair, her nose and sparkling dark eyes.

And now I needed to pleasure her. I rolled up and grabbed her shoulders. I pulled her up to me. I kissed her passionately. I tasted my slippery juices on her mouth, and I knew I wanted to taste hers. We kissed so passionately. I have to say that I had never kissed a man this passionately. I had never lost myself in a kiss like I did with her. It felt like our souls intertwined. Her breasts crushed against me. Her soft thighs slid against mine. I loved the feeling of her delicate, cool skin against me.

But I had to taste her. I had to pleasure her. I pushed her down to her back. She relented to my touch. My force. I took control of her, and she let me.

"Yeah, honey, take me…" she gasped, and I knew she wanted to be had. She wanted me to control her and pleasure her.

One last hard kiss, and I was on her delicate breasts. But I wasn't nice to them. I bit her immediately. She gasped, and yelped, "Yeah, bite me, honey." I chewed on her nipples, and she pushed them up to me. She wanted me to. As much as I wanted to be rough with her, she wanted me to be rougher. I slid down her stomach. I kissed her. I nibbled her sides, and I felt her jerk in my mouth. She was already opening her legs to me. She surrendered to me. I could smell her wetness.

I didn't tease her like she had teased me. I took her. I moved between her legs and I jammed my mouth down onto her. She was so wet! She was swollen and open to me. I had never tasted a woman directly before, but I knew her taste from Mark's body.

I slid my tongue across her, and opened her up with my lips. I pushed my tongue into her opening, and I tasted her tangy, slippery juices. I wished my tongue were a foot long so I could plumb her depths. I forced my tongue against the walls inside her. She was panting now, and her small hands were gripping my hair.

I then slid up to her clitoris. Her breathing quickened. I felt the tension in her body. Her soft shudders moved her in my mouth. As she had done to me, I put constant pressure on her little bud, moving it under my tongue. Her shaking intensified. I kept sliding across her, and I could feel her move with the movement of my tongue. She was building. Her nails dug into my scalp. Her thighs squeezed against my ears. I looked up at her, and her eyes were locked on mine. She moved her hands up to her breasts and began to squeeze. I reached up with my right hand and took her left breast and I squeezed it roughly. Her hand cupped mine, and guided me. She was nearly there, I knew.

She twisted under me, like a snake moving in the grass. But I kept the pressure on. I continued to slide my tongue with pressure over her. Her twitching and twisting made clitoral pressure a challenge, but I was not going to let her move away from me.

And then she mouthed words. "Oh God…Oh God…honey, I'm gonna come on your mouth" and I felt her jerking. She relaxed for just a second, and then she shouted, "Oh fuck, yeah!" and her body began to shake violently. It was all I could do to keep the contact on her, as she was moving so forcefully. Her legs and hips were moving against me, and then away, against me, and then away. I could hear her gasping and mewling. I peeked up at her, and her eyes were completely rolled back. Her back was arched, hard. Her breasts were driving up toward the ceiling. Her mewling cry disappeared into a long exhale.

And then she relaxed. The tension eased. The twisting stopped. She was slackened against me. I slowed my tongue down, and was only softly caressing her orally. I looked up again and she was smiling at me.

"That was so great, honey," she said softly. "Oh God, I came so good!"

I said into her, "That was my first time."

"Well, you're a natural. Come here and kiss me."

I moved up, and our mouths met again. I could still taste myself on her, and I knew she could taste herself on me. Our tongues danced softly, rubbing against each other. Changing mouths. Her soft, delicate skin was against mine. We were both warm, and had a gleam of sweat that mixed together as we held each other. Our arms and legs intertwined.

Keiko pulled the white duvet and sheets over us. We lay there, facing each other, breasts softly touching, kissing lightly. I felt so relaxed. So feminine. Any thoughts I had had before about this being wrong or dirty were gone. It felt so natural to have her there beside me.

I also knew I was developing feelings for her.

We lay there kissing lightly for a few minutes, getting our breath back, and then Keiko asked me, "Do you like toys?"

"Toys?"

"Sex toys, silly."

"I've never used one before."

"Are you interested in trying one? I have a few of them."

It finally hit me that Keiko had already had this room, as she was already checked in and had the key. "How long have you had this room?"

"Well, for a while. Months."

"You rented this room for months?"

"Mark and I keep this room for our…adventures. Our apartment is in the Beresford, and security can be an issue there. Plus, we have to worry about what the newspapers will write about him, you know? He's famous here in New York." She thought for a second. "Plus, I love this hotel…The Beatles stayed here when they first arrived in the US. I love that connection to them. I'm told Paul and Ringo stayed in this room."

I never realized a football player would be famous. I never followed the sport myself. My father was a Knicks fan, but he never watched football. I wasn't a Beatles fan either...I was more into folk music, which spoke to me. Folk was the music of revolution in those days. No longer, unfortunately.

"So you keep toys here too?"

"Sure. Toys aren't for everyone, but if you'd like to play with them, I have a few." She had a devilish sparkle in her eyes.

I thought back to the room at the Trojan and the numerous toys they had there. Nowadays, most women have a vibrator at home. In 1979, though, few did, and they were hard to find even in New York City.

"What do you have?"

With a girlish giggle, she hopped out of bed and went to the closet. She took out an athletic bag. It had a logo: The New York Giants. She brought it back to the bed. She looked like a child opening a present on Christmas morning.

"I like toys myself, but if you don't like any of these it's okay, honey," Keiko reassured.

Out of the bag, she pulled several rubbery dildos of different sizes and colors. She had a plug-in vibrating wand that looked like an old-fashioned massager...maybe those were always sex toys under different names. She also had a dildo that was attached to a harness. It reminded me of the one the girl had strapped on in the Trojan. She held this up and looked at me.

"Later, I would like you to use this on me. Would that be okay?"

"Okay," I agreed. I knew I couldn't say no to Keiko. I wasn't sure, though, that I would know how to use it.

"Good," she smiled. "But first, let me use this vibrator on you."

She didn't wait for an answer. She plugged it into the wall, and it leapt to life in her hands. Instead of putting it on me, she put her mouth on mine and began kissing me. I warmed to her kiss instantly. Her lips were so soft and sweet, and I lay back and let her kiss me, then pulled her face down against mine. We kissed for a few moments, and then I felt her move the vibrator against my belly.

At first I was a bit nervous, so I kept my legs closed. She didn't push. She didn't insist. She simply laid it on top of my mound and continued to kiss me. I loved her kisses, and kissed back. She moved her mouth to my breasts, and began to suckle my nipples. As she did so, I relaxed more, and I felt my legs open just a little, then progressively more as she continued to lick and suck them. They were a bit sore from her love bites earlier, but it felt so good to have her face on them. Soon, I had opened my legs enough to let her slide the vibrator to my opening.

This was a completely new experience for me, and at first it was overwhelming. It was just too much sensation on my already abused womanhood. I pushed her hand away a bit. She held it back a moment, and continued to nuzzle my breasts.

But soon the toy was against me again. This time she put it lower, away from my clitoris. The warm, vibrating toy felt good, and I was becoming wet again from Keiko's kisses and licking. At my opening, it provided enough vibration that I could feel it in my clitoris without it being overpowering. The warmth of it spread through me, and I began to get very wet. I opened my legs more, and she pressed it against my opening with more pressure. Its vibrations moved throughout me.

I didn't realize it at first, but she began to kiss down my belly, and soon her face was at my now swollen womanhood. She stuck her tongue out and put it against my button, and kept the pressure of the vibrator against my opening. Though it was too large to go all the way in, it did create a stretching that was pleasurable. The vibrations moved through my whole pelvic area, even rattling my pelvic bones.

As she pressed her tongue against me, the intense warmth and vibrations and wetness began to create a sensation I had not experienced before. It was a mechanical pleasure that was unlike anything a human body could create, and it moved through me in a unique way. Not worse or better…just different. Overpowering in some ways. Not the same as a human…not warm and fleshy…but still pleasurable.

Soon, I felt the waves hit me. But these weren't warm, coursing waves I was used to. They were sharp, angry waves, and my nerve endings throughout my body all stood on end. The combined vaginal and clitoral pressure were so strong that I was not able to ride the pleasure waves…they rode me.

And then it hit me. It overpowered me. It was a tsunami smashing against me. Instead of the warmth flowing through me, it flowed over me, smashing me against the rocks of my orgasm. It was pleasure, and pain, and force, and solitude. I was overcome by these smashing waves and competing pleasures. I felt myself jerk away from Keiko's tongue and the vibrator. Yet, I continued to orgasm, and soon the sharp breakers turned warm and relaxing...my orgasm went on for a long time after the pressure was gone. I lay there, groaning as the last waves moved through me.

I heard the vibrator turn off. Keiko was smiling at me.

"You okay, honey?" she asked.

"Yeah, give me a second..." I let those final waves wash through me. Finally I could speak again. "That was something I had never felt before."

"Intense, right?"

"Too intense, I think."

"Well, it takes some getting used to. But it's an incredible feeling, yeah?"

"Yeah, incredible."

"So it was too much on your clit?"

"Yeah, I think so...but it felt great when you pressed it lower."

"Yeah, that's how I like it too. The combined pressure is overwhelming."

"Can I do that to you too?" I was already grabbing for the vibrator.

"Sure!" She slid down to her back, with an impish grin and a sparkle in her eyes.

I tried to duplicate what she had done to me, though I had never used this before. I kissed her to relax her and get her ready. When my mouth was on her breasts, her legs were open and ready. She wasn't afraid of it. I pressed the top of the wand to her, and she grunted with pleasure. I continued to nuzzle her breasts and press it against her opening. Her hips began to move and twitch beneath me. I moved down her, and put my tongue against her clitoris.

It was harder than I thought. The vibration of the wand and her bucking, twitching hips made it hard to keep pressure on her little nub. I kept at it though, and I felt her body moving in a rhythm. I knew she was feeling the waves inside her. She seemed to be ready for them, though, and they didn't overpower her as they did me. She set up the rhythm and went with it. Soon, she was groaning...a loud, plaintive groan. I felt her hand on my head again, and then she suddenly made a tight fist.

When her orgasm began, she let out a loud shriek. "Oh fucking God, yes! Yes!" she shrieked. And then I could feel her body shaking and twitching. She bucked her bottom off the bed and into the air. I could keep pressure on with the vibrator, but could not hold on with my tongue. She bucked and pushed against the vibrator, and continue to shake and shout. She then started cussing again. "Oh fucking Jesus, I'm coming! Fuck, it feels so fucking good! Keep pushing it, honey…keep pushing it…" I pushed the wand against her as hard as I could. It was almost inside of her, despite its width and odd shape. She was shaking so hard, and then her hands slammed into the bed and gripped the sheets. Both hands pulled at the bottom sheet…I thought she would rip it.

And then she relaxed, and I pulled away just enough to let her ride the waves down. She slowly, ever so slowly, drifted down from that towering orgasm. I could feel her slowly release tension, and then she was limp. She pushed my hand away.

"That's it, honey…I can't take anymore."

I turned it off. She hooked her hand behind my neck and pulled me to her lips. I kissed her softly, and she took my tongue into her mouth, sucking it slowly.

Though I knew she was exhausted, I wanted to give her more. I pulled up the dildo with the straps and showed it to her. She looked at it, and then at me, and she simply nodded her head. She was too breathless to say anything.

I wasn't sure how it worked, but I saw two leg holes, which I slid my legs into. Keiko helped me with the straps. She was still panting and felt very weak. I was wondering if I should let her get her strength back, but she wasn't slowing me down. She tightened the straps on me, then reached into the bag. She pulled out a bottle of baby oil. She put some oil into her hand, and then rubbed it all over the dildo. It was long and thick, just a bit smaller than David's penis.

I looked down and saw the long, flesh-colored erection sticking out from me. I thought, this is what a man sees. It was highly erotic…the idea sent shockwaves through me. The gender-bending aspect excited me…*really* excited me. And that surprised me. How would I find this exciting? Yet, I did. The role reversal was immensely intriguing.

I knew I was in foreign territory now, a million miles from my "home"—my beliefs and upbringing. Yet, this foreign land was intriguing, and beautiful, and sensual.

I was beginning to like it here.

After she oiled it, she lay down on her back, and opened herself to me. A beautiful woman was lying in front of me with her legs open. I saw her sparkling eyes, her white porcelain skin, her soft breasts, her smooth legs…and her open sex. I took hold of the dildo, and stroked it a couple times. I looked at her, and I felt like I was a man coming to give her my manhood.

I lay down on top of her, and our mouths met. She reached between us and guided it inside of her. I slowly pushed it into her, keeping in mind to be gentle. I felt her slowly accepting it…letting it move inside her and open her. She gasped a couple times, and grunted as it moved deeper into her. I understood that internal pressure and how exciting yet scary it could be. I also knew she was taking it and enjoying it.

And then I was all the way in. The soft rubber balls were against her. And me. I wondered if this was how a man felt, being deep into a woman. If only this dildo could transfer the feeling to me the way a penis would to a man. All these thoughts raced through me as I lay on top of her, giving her my rubber sex.

I began to move my hips into her. She moved in rhythm with me. We found an instinctive rhythm to our strokes. She kissed me passionately, and I kissed her back. I kissed her hard. I raised up on one elbow, and squeezed her breast. I was inside her and having her body. I was taking her.

I pushed up on both hands, and saw her beautiful body beneath me. I began to thrust harder into her. She accepted these thrusts, and began to push back against me. Our eyes met, and she smiled at me.

"Yeah, honey, fuck me with your dick. It feels so good." Her words were hungry.

I don't know why, but that turned me on even more. Maybe I felt like a man at that moment. I was giving her my cock and she was taking it. And I was loving the feeling of giving it to her. I could feel her getting wetter and looser. The more I pushed it into her, the more she was accepting of it.

And she was so beautiful. Soft, smooth skin. Shiny, beautiful eyes. Long hair spread around her. I was seeing her how her husband, Mark, saw her. How David had seen her. She was the woman, and I was the man pushing myself into her. And she spoke more.

"Oh honey, you fuck me so good. Fuck me with that hard dick. I love it."

And I couldn't help myself. I growled back at her. "You want this cock, baby? You want it hard?"

"Yeah, honey, give it to me hard. Fuck me with it."

And I did. I began to push as hard as I could. Now, we women aren't built like men...it took everything I had to thrust forward with my hips the way a man would. But I did. I kept my legs together and used my body weight to drive it all the way in, with as much anger and aggression as I could. She hooked her heels against the back of my thighs and pulled me in with all she had. She was pushing back as hard as I was pushing.

"That's it, honey. Fuck me. Oh God...Oh God, I'm going to come!"

And then she did. I felt her push against me one final time and then she shouted out a loud, mewling cry. Her nails dug into my arms. Her feet kicked against my thighs. She was thrashing below me. The more she thrashed, the harder I pushed into her. Her eyes were slammed shut and she was crying out. I swung my hips into her as roughly as I could manage. It felt animalistic. It felt aggressive.

When her cries became softer, I shortened my movements and softened my strokes. I moved very slowly in and out of her. She finally looked up at me and smiled. Her eyes were shiny.

"That was great, honey. Thank you."

"My pleasure. Do you want more?"

"Can you give me more?" she asked.

"Yeah, but this position is making my arms tired." While some women have the shoulder strength, I didn't. My arms were already burning.

"Okay, let me turn over."

I pulled out, and she rolled over onto her hands and knees. I moved up to her. She opened herself and I slid in. She was loosened up and ready, and I was slick from her.

I began to move in and out of her again. This position was much easier on my arms, but harder on my hips. She helped by pushing back against me. She was very wet and open, and I could see her eyes already get a distant look. I knew it wouldn't take long. She was already talking dirty to me, which excited us both.

"Yeah, fuck my pussy with your big cock, honey. It feels so good when you're in me. I want you to fuck me all the time."

"You love fucking my cock? You like when I'm in you?" I growled, using the deepest voice I could. I wanted to be a man for her.

"Oh yeah, honey. You make my pussy so wet. Keep fucking me, honey. Keep fucking me."

And I did. I kept swinging my hips into her. Though my back and legs were cramping from this exertion, I was so excited I just kept going. I realized how hard it was to be in the man's position, but I also loved it. Dominance. Power. Strength. I loved giving it to her. I loved taking her to the edge of pain and pleasure. I loved being in the man's role. Being a man. My hard dick was slamming inside her. I could feel her softness break under my strength.

As she pushed against me, I took hold of her hips and began to drive even harder into her. I pulled her weight against me, and felt the slapping of her butt against my body. I was picking up power, speed, and technique. I knew I had her. I knew she was mine. I knew she would come again, and that knowledge and power made me incredibly excited.

As I felt her nearing her orgasm, I stuck my thumb in my mouth, and then stuck it into her open anus.

"Oh God, yeah!" she shrieked. Fuck that asshole with your thumb, honey. Fuck it."

I drove my thumb into her. I drove my cock into her. I was giving her all I had.

And then she buried her face in the pillow and shrieked. I felt her jerking and twitching. She was thrashing and shrieking and crying. Her screams into the pillow were loud and angry. She was shouting as if she were trying to scream to someone miles away. Even in the pillow, her voice was loud.

And then she slowed her motions. Relaxed. I matched her pace. I let her enjoy the last trembling shudders of her climax. I loved that I had just done that to her. I felt so powerful...so strong.

She collapsed forward onto the bed. I looked down at the soaking wet dildo between my legs. She looked up at me and smiled. I lay down next to her, both of us panting, eyes to the ceiling.

"That was incredible, Rachel. Thank you."

"You're welcome." We were both out of breath.

"You took me like a man...you're very good at it."

"Thanks. It felt good."

"I know what you mean. It's fun to play the boy sometimes."

"You like it too?"

"Sure. I'm still a woman and like to have it done to me, but it's fun once in a while to switch it up."

I didn't tell her how much I enjoyed playing the dominant role. Perhaps as much as playing the feminine role—in some ways more. I was still wrestling with my own feelings.

"Honey, can I give that to you?"

"I'm really tired. Can we rest a while?"

"Yeah...we have as much time as you need."

She slid into my arms. I didn't even take off the dildo. She nuzzled her head onto my shoulder, and I smelled her perfume, her hair, and our sex. She gently drifted off to sleep in my arms, and I followed her soon after.

"What happened when you woke up?" His breathing was heavy. He felt so full in my hands. He was dripping a large amount of fluid, which I was using to wet his swollen gland.

"I woke up when she started sucking my breasts. She had a finger inside me already."

"Did you like that feeling?"

"Oh yes, I loved it so much. I was dripping wet already."

"Then what did she do?" His eyes were slammed shut, as if he were picturing everything in his mind.

"She went down on me. I didn't think I could come again, because I had come so much already, but I did." David's breathing was more rapid now. His balls were already beginning to lift up. "Then she kissed me, and I tasted my juice on her mouth. I was so turned on I needed to come again."

"Did she make you come again?"

"She put on the strap-on, and then she started fucking me with it. Oh, it felt so good inside me."

"Did that make you come, Rachel?"

"Not yet. I pushed her on her back, and I climbed on top. I rode her, and made myself come on top of her. She looked so beautiful underneath me. She looked me in the eyes, and squeezed my breasts while I was getting close."

"After that, what happened?"

"After I came, she told me she loved me, and we kissed forever. I told her I loved her too." Just then, his penis began jerking in my hand, and I could tell he was going to come. I lowered my face to him, and took him in my mouth. I got there just in time for his burning hot seed. There was so much! I swallowed some, but the rest slid out of my mouth and down his heavy shaft. I pulled on him, trying to prolong his orgasm. I gently squeezed his balls, which continued to twitch for a while.

He slid back down to the pillow, lost in his buzzing orgasm. I lay down next to him, and put my head on his shoulder. I continued to stroke him softly.

"That was incredible, Rachel. Thank you."

"You're welcome. I enjoyed it."

"Did you guys do it more?"

"No, I was too tired after. We fell back asleep again…just for a little while. Then we got up and had dinner at the Plaza restaurant. Then we sat up talking until late."

"About what?"

"Girl stuff."

"Girl stuff?"

"Yes, girl stuff. None of your business, Mr. Nosy. We drank wine and talked and watched a little TV." I didn't tell him that we sat up all night talking about our men. About the life. About our pasts and our futures. I didn't tell him that she held me when I cried about missing my mother. Keiko was many things to me that night. Lover. Wife. Psychiatrist. Friend.

"Then what?"

"I think I nodded off around two a.m., and she must've slept a bit after."

"Did you sleep in the same bed?"

"Yes."

"All night?"

"Yes. When we woke up yesterday, I was tired and sore, but refreshed."

"Did you make love again?"

"No, we ordered room service, and ate in the room. Then I showered and took the subway home to see Dad." I didn't tell him that Keiko scolded me for not seeing enough of my father, whom I hadn't seen much of since I started dating David. I didn't tell him that Keiko told me that my responsibility as his daughter was to make sure Dad was doing better. We had talked all night about our families and our fears, and Keiko's sage counsel woke me up to what I hadn't been doing in my life, because I had been so focused on David.

I had gone home, and found my dad feeling sad and lonely. The house was filthy. He hadn't been taking good care of himself. I cleaned. Washed the dishes. Bought some food at the market, and made him dinner.

But yet the next night here I was with David. I couldn't stay away from him long. I did promise to see Dad more often, now that I was living with David, more or less. I mean, we weren't technically living together…but I spent most nights of the week there.

I cleaned David off with a wet towel, and he was drifting off to sleep, likely dreaming about what Keiko and I had done. I cleaned up and lay down next to him, but I didn't sleep. I thought about my conversations with her.

We had sat up late, talking and drinking. Part of the conversation had me perplexed, and I couldn't shake it from my mind.

At one point, I had asked her, "What types of things have you seen since you've been in the life?"

"I've seen it all. There probably is little I haven't done, though I'm not a big fan of BDSM, as I told you…"

"Like, you've seen Mark with other women? With other men?"

"Yeah, many times."

"How did you feel about him with other men?"

"Yeah, it's a bit strange at first…I think as women we think of men differently, and perhaps naturally can't picture them having sex with other men."

"I felt so strange when I saw David kissing Mark that night. Even though we had all just had sex together, it felt so weird seeing two men kiss. I didn't feel the same when you and I kissed. Is that wrong?"

"Well, I guess it's our societal roles, you know? Why should we feel different about two men kissing than two women? Yet it did strike me as odd when I first saw it. You'll get used to it, honey."

"You're used to it now?"

"Oh sure. I've seen Mark have sex with several men."

"Several?"

"Yeah. I mean, I guess he's like me...he likes just about everything. He has done all the same kinds of things I have done."

"Has he ever met men for sex in the afternoon, like we did today?"

"Sure. Many times. Even with David."

"Really?" I had been afraid of her telling me something like this.

"Yeah...they met at a swing club. David had sex with Mark before I did, though other people were involved." Sadly, I felt ill hearing this.

"But how did you feel about him afterward?"

"Well, I think it took two or three times to get over it. I was less bothered by him having sex with other women than with men, but after seeing it enough I got used to it. You will too."

"I don't know if I'm ready to see David have sex with other men. It seems so unnatural to me still."

"You can't think that way, honey," she scolded. "Why would you put anything on him that you wouldn't want others to think of you? Why should that be any different than what we did here today? If you feel that way, it's a prejudice you should get rid of."

"Yeah, I guess you're right." Those were my words, but I had a lot of socialization to overcome.

"Of course I'm right. If you would judge David, then you should expect him to judge you in return."

"That's true, I know...it's just..."

"Tell you what...when we get back, let's break you of this feeling...this bias. Let's get Mark and David together. Making them do this in front of you will help you get over it. You'll see that it's no different. You'll get over it faster so you don't get surprised in a club or somewhere like that. Better to break that train of thought now."

"Okay," I had said, but honestly I was having a hard time picturing the two of them together sexually. I knew she was right...I knew it was a prejudice in me. I knew I had no right to judge either of them. Yet, it had felt so strange, I just didn't know what it would do to our relationship. Seeing David with Mark could change everything.

David was sleeping next to me, and I couldn't stop struggling with the idea of the man I loved being intimate with another man. I was to watch the prejudice end soon enough.

Two days later, I met with Stella Metz in Midtown. I was shown into her office, which had a great view of Times Square. She sat in her large chair, leaning backward, fingers on her chin. Her gunmetal hair was pulled up and tight.

"I think I need just a couple of more works from you, Rachel," she said, getting right to the point. "Your poems are powerful, and I think they'll do well. Still, they seem a bit locked into politics and civil rights. While I know that's your intention, I think you should try to appeal to a bit broader of an audience."

"How so?" I looked around the room and saw the signed covers that lined her walls. She had so many that there were several stacked, leaning against the wall, waiting to replace older covers.

"Well, I would love to see a few love poems in your collection."

"Oh, I've never been able to write about love, Stella. It's just not me. When I write, I feel my passion burning toward what's going on in the world. The injustice. The pain and suffering. Poverty and inequality. It's our national zeitgeist…and I'm just expressing it, you know?"

"I get that, and that's the part of your work I've fallen in love with. Still, I want you to spend just a couple of weeks thinking about love.

Consider it. Let your heart explore it, if only a little bit. You might find something inside you, something that yearns to be told. We are women, after all…love comes naturally to us." She sounded like a school principal lecturing a girl caught sneaking a cigarette in the parking lot.

"Yeah."

"Love is always in our hearts. Love is all around us. Look at it, and see what comes to you." If only she knew what was going on with my love life at that moment! I don't imagine she would've wanted to hear about love from me any longer.

"Okay, I'll try, Stella."

"Excellent. So, I didn't just bring you here to lecture you on your work. I have good news." She opened a small leather purse and produced a long, black cigarette. She lit it from an ornamental lighter on her desk.

"Really?"

"Yes, really. You'll be so happy to hear that I already have a publisher who is interested in your work." *Did she just say…?* "Random House has a poetry imprint coming out. They're calling it *Leaves of Grass,* after Whitman. They are looking for 'charged' poems…poems with energy and anger…poems that strive for change."

"Oh my goodness!" I felt hot tears in my eyes.

"They have chosen George Hammitt as the editor, and George and I are old friends from our time with Doubleday. I sent him a few of your poems and he loves them." She had a satisfied look on her face. She flicked ashes into the round crystal ashtray, which sat atop a stack of manuscripts.

"He *loves* them?" Those hot tears now ran down my cheeks, and my heart was thumping.

"Yes, young lady…loves them." She pulled a box of tissues from a drawer and pushed them over to me. I took two. "He told me that your collection will be the first one he publishes."

"Oh, the first." My head was spinning!

"It's an honor given to few people…to be the first publication of a new imprint. You should be very proud, young Rachel."

And now the scalding tears flowed like rivers from my eyes. I put my head down and openly sobbed. Published. Me? I had never envisioned it happening, really. Though Stella was one of the top agents in New York, I was a nobody…unpublished…and my collection was tossed together, at best. I knew it was all because of David. He had done this for me. Without someone like Stella Metz, I would've never so much as gotten a sniff from a publisher.

"Stella, I don't know how to thank you," I finally said.

"You can thank me by giving me some love poetry."

"I will. I promise you I'll write something. I'll give it my very best effort."

"That's my girl. Now, don't get too excited…you have to know that poetry usually doesn't sell nearly as well as fiction. Still, George mentioned an advance in the range of twenty thousand or so."

"Advance?"

"Yes, advance on sales…for future royalties."

"Twenty thousand dollars?" That was a lot of money in those days.

"Oh Rachel, you really are innocent, aren't you? Yes, twenty thousand dollars. But that won't come until the pressing. We'll have a release party and you should have the check within a week of that. Assume two to three months from today. Normally, books don't publish until a year or so later, but this imprint wants to publish its first soon. They're competing against a similar imprint from Simon and Shuster." I didn't really understand or care about all this talk of imprints and things, but I knew I needed to get busy. "Also, we'll need a photo for the book jacket, and you'll need to write a bio."

"I don't have much of a bio. I have only been teaching school since college."

"Don't worry, I'll help you with it. Nothing wrong with being a young writer."

"Stella, I'm at a loss for words."

She smiled at me, showing her yellowed teeth. "This is an important moment for a young writer. Your first published work. Everything is much easier after this. But don't get lazy and don't get complacent. Your *best* work should follow."

"Okay, I'll stay busy, that's for sure."

"Great news. Now I have another meeting, so I need to shoo you out. I'll schedule you for a photo soon, and I'll need those love poems within a couple weeks. Can you muster that?"

"Yes, I can and I will."

"Good, now run along, dearie. Give David my best, and tell him I'm still waiting for his photos from Africa."

"Okay, I will. Thank you, Stella." She was already opening a manuscript, and stubbing out the cigarette.

And then I was out the door and in the elevator. Honestly, I could've floated down from her floor, I was so much abuzz with the moment.

Published. Me. First of a new imprint. Named after Whitman. How did I find myself here? This doesn't happen to a girl from Queens.

When I arrived home, I didn't tell my father anything. I wanted this to be a surprise. I pictured a moment of my handing him my published work. I wanted that moment to be a complete surprise to him, though I did break down and tell him later. It was too much to keep back.

Instead, though, I went to my room and called my school. Though we were off for the summer, I thought it only fair that they know first. I resigned my position, wished them well, and then made my father some lunch.

Later, I sat in my room, looking out the window to my quiet street, thinking about all the events of my life over the last few months. I had been a nervous, insecure teacher, unsure of her direction. Now I was exploring my sexuality with beautiful people, and I had a collection of poems soon to be published. My life had made a hard shift, and I would never be the same.

I had also met and fallen in love with David. And Keiko, I had to admit. And I had a crush, at least, on Keiko's husband. My life was now immensely complex, and part of me secretly yearned for the simplicity I would never have again. Not only would my life never be the same again, but also my adventures were only just beginning.

I knew, though, that I was leaving behind the quiet suburban life of Queens. My neighborhood had informed my life up to that point. I had fallen into the structures of my family. I worked. I lived the life of a Christian girl. My life and my job and my potential were centered on the quieter side of residential neighborhoods. That had been my world until a few months ago.

Now I was increasingly drawn to Manhattan. My life was more centered there. The people I knew lived there. I spent most nights there. My agent worked there. I was moving my life across the Queensboro

Bridge, if not all at once.

And I thought of Keiko. I thought of her kisses and soft skin. I thought of her smile and her soft hands. I knew I did indeed love her. The realization that I loved another woman made me feel that my life in Queens would soon end completely. I knew what was before was gone. I had left behind the bridge I had leapt from. It was my past.

And I began to write.

She is color and magic, dancing oceans of time
She is beauty and love, glistening sweat shine
The touch of an angel, with beauty bright
The fist of the devil, power and might

I guess it's important to pause here, and catch up my mentality at this time. Is that the right word? Psyche? My headspace, as you might say now? I've sometimes wondered at how quickly I moved from reticence to enthusiasm for "the life."

How does a good Christian girl find herself in bed doing things she would've never approved of in others? Yes, I said that correctly. Had you told me the night before I met David that you knew somebody who had sex with her boyfriend and another couple, plus who went to swing clubs and participated in escapades with random people (though I think that's a base way of putting it), I would have judged that person harshly. I would have thought that she was a terrible woman. A whore. A slut. I would have probably labeled her with all of those names, and more. I would have thought she had the blackest of hearts.

And, yet, here I was...*that* woman. A young woman who opened herself physically and mentally to both sexes, married and single. And more was on the horizon. Before I was through, I would end up breaking nearly every gender-based societal norm. I freely gave myself to whomever I wanted. And the worst part? I enjoyed it. Yes, that's right. I took great pleasure in my sexual exploration...or decadence...or hedonism…or whatever label you would like to give it.

Yet I was conflicted. Very. While having sex, it almost always felt right. It was almost always the highest pleasure I could have imagined. For a girl who hadn't orgasmed with a man until my first night with David, I reached multiple climaxes with multiple people. And while loving it, I would pay the price afterward, often beating myself up after the fact. Sometimes, I felt like a whore. Impure. Ugly. Sometimes I felt I deserved the judgment I knew was due me if others knew about my activities.

But I began to find ways to unravel the societal bonds wrapped so tightly around me. I began to find ways to justify my actions. I felt the cords of guilt slackening, and in that extra space, I began to lose some of the biases and judgment (including my *self*-judgment). I began to learn to rationalize my feelings. I told myself that love was always good, and that my sexuality was nobody's business. And it wasn't, though it took me some time to convince myself.

Keiko was a great role model for me. More than anybody, she showed me that I could be a woman…a beautiful, cultured woman…and yet live the life. Having lost my mother so early, I had not found many female role models for the life I envisioned. Most women at this time could only be wives and mothers, jumping at the behest of their husbands and children. Keiko, though a wife herself, lived a life free of judgment. She accepted herself, and loved herself. I could see in her the ability to shrug off the callous discernment of others. She knew who she was, and didn't want to be anything else.

So I, too, learned to steel myself. A little at first. Like the first few flaps of a butterfly's wings, still wet from the chrysalis. I stretched these wings. I expanded who I was. I accepted my faults. I began to enjoy the sense that I would be what I wanted to be, no matter who thought ill of me. And I reveled in being different. Unique. I was becoming my own woman. The life was just one aspect of being myself. At times, I would embrace it.

I have used the analogy of a person jumping from a bridge. That reflected my early view, and it reflects a helpless, out-of-control approach. Now, I wanted to be the person walking on a path. Following the path she chose. Facing the demons of Hell. The robbers on the highway. Blake's tigers burning brightly in the forest. Not falling…

strolling, completely in control.

I would fight that unnerving fear, which had held me back in my life. I would embrace myself. After all, I was going to be published soon. I loved David. And Keiko. And perhaps would love Mark. I would accept my new life responsibly, not blaming anybody, and instead letting my life reflect my choices.

Though imperfect in my convictions, I knew this was what I could and should be.

The pace of my life accelerated immensely. What had once been a quiet, mellow, and frightfully boring existence was now an exciting race in the Big Apple. Now that I was no longer teaching, I found myself pouring myself into my work. I wrote a lot. David and I read and talked and visited friends. We strolled in the evenings. We ate at upscale restaurants. We shopped. We discussed literature and art. We were living as I had always dreamed of living.

And we made love.

Minnie Riperton was on the record player (yes, we had records then), and we were all taking our clothes off.

Loving you is easy 'cause you're beautiful.

And we were young. And beautiful. And naked. No taking sides in the bed this time…we were all in it together.

I kissed David, and he began to touch me. I didn't cling to him this time, and instead I moved over to Keiko. She responded to me, and we were soon intertwined. I loved her soft skin. I loved her kisses. I loved how I felt when we touched. I loved the "me" who was with her. When she and I touched, the men would always stop and watch.

But we stopped. We were there for a purpose. We had discussed this moment, and we knew what we wanted. We were in control.

Mark and David were watching us, both of them excited by our touching. Most men are turned on by women touching each other, and I think they were waiting for a show. We knew we had to force the action we wanted and expected that night. At the same time, I loved the feel of her soft lips. Her soft breasts. Her soft thighs. She was white porcelain, unblemished and clean.

Hot summer night. Windows open. Light breeze blowing. Soft sweat. Angelic music.

I leaned back, and Keiko slid up against me. I wrapped my arms around her. She fit against me perfectly. And then we looked at the men. They were waiting for us to do something...waiting for a show. Their eyes were large in anticipation. But we just watched them. And waited.

So they turned and looked at each other. Two handsome, naked men.

One, tall, red haired, and with a recent buzz cut for summer football training camp. Mark was a bit bruised and beat up from the pounding he had taken in training. But he was also magnificently handsome. Largely muscled. The summer weight training had made him even bulkier. He was so tall and athletic and strong.

And my hawk-eyed David. Slender. Wild, dark hair and penetrating eyes. Tanned. Gorgeous. Talented. Lean and graceful. The heart of an artist. An old soul who seemed wise beyond his years. The man who had opened many doors for me.

They were such a pair, those two. Even now, through all these years, I cannot help but look back and remember how perfect their bodies were. Their nakedness was raw, like two tigers in the jungle. Two eagles in an aery. Both manly in every way.

Yet my lover and I wanted to see them expose themselves emotionally. Be open. Lose a sense of that masculine stance. Surrender control. Be accepting. Give their bodies to another. Let someone take from them...while we watched. I wanted to see my man do things I hadn't seen. I wanted to see him pleasure another man as I had pleasured him. I wanted to test my own reaction to something I know they had done before. How would I handle it? I wanted to know. I wanted to cross that line, and leave it behind me. For once, I was taking charge, though, with the help and support of Keiko.

The men's nervous eyes went from us to each other. They flicked back and forth. They looked at each other with sidelong glances. They did the mental math. And there they were...they were faced with it.

I think both men were used to using us, their women, as vehicles to satisfy their bisexual pleasures. With naked women around them, a touch, a feel, a grope, a kiss...they were just cherries and nuts, pardon the expression, on a sundae. They could excuse their actions as "in the heat of the moment." They could pretend they weren't gay or bisexual simply by doing it while having sex with a woman.

But Keiko and I wanted to see how far they would go with us there. How much could they do together, while two women watched them? Both had been with men, and they had been with each other...but not with their women watching them. We were observing them like hoary magistrates.

No one else can make me feel
The colors that you bring...

Part of me was still disbelieving. Part of me was even indignant that my man would kiss, touch, fondle, and even penetrate another man. I was still stuck with preconceived ideas of what manhood was. My father would have never done such a thing. I rarely even saw him shake another man's hand. He would hug me...occasionally. He loved my mother immensely, yet I probably saw them kiss no more than two or three times my entire life.

So the thought of my man having sex with another man caused me discomfort. I think perhaps I went along with Keiko to see if David would say, "No, I can't do anything like this," and storm out of the room. Perhaps at this point in my life I would have applauded him taking an ultra-masculine stance like that. I know how silly that sounds now. It's hard to imagine now that I felt that way then...but I guess I did.

Yet I know also that some part of me was intensely curious. How would two men have sex together? Which roles would they play? Who would take the other into his body? What would it look like?

Keiko broke the silence, "C'mon, boys...put on a show for us girls. We're not doing anything until we see you pleasure each other." I loved that about her...she was not afraid to speak up or out. Though only a couple years older than I, she was much more confident in herself and her sexuality. She was not afraid to say what she meant. She was not afraid of who she was. In fact, she loved herself and her life, and she loved her *enhanced* sexuality. Her confidence gave me confidence.

"David, I want to see you and Mark...together..." I said. Not in the quivering, shy voice that marked my life before. I spoke it confidently. I commanded him. I empowered myself to be powerful. Me, sexually commanding? This was my first step down the path I hoped to tread.

They turned and looked at each other. Mark moved first. He leaned over and kissed David. David kissed back. I had seen them kiss before, but this time it was just them. I felt very odd. At first, it looked unnatural to me, and I still couldn't get my thoughts around it. It looked *unmanly* to me. Feminine almost.

David put his hand up to Mark's face, and pulled his mouth more to his own, and their kisses became stronger. I saw their tongues moving against each other. Their heads moved from side to side. And they kissed. Then David put his hands on Mark's shoulders, and pulled his body against him. And their mouths fought harder.

I was surprised when I felt Keiko begin to shudder a little. She pressed herself against me, and her hands began to move, almost imperceptibly, along my thighs. She was becoming excited. Perhaps this is why she was so insistent that we put them in this situation. Did she love watching Mark with another man?

The men were still kissing, but now I saw Mark reach down to David's crotch. He began stroking him. David, apparently, didn't mind this at all. Mark pulled on it, and as it stood up he changed his hand position, pointing it up to their chins. And still their mouths fought against each other.

David soon moved his hands from Mark's shoulders, and was instead rubbing his palms against Mark's large, muscular chest. I couldn't blame him...I loved Mark's chest. It was massive, and his shoulders were so broad. He was larger than any man I had ever met. Watching David touch his chest, I suddenly felt a bit of movement in my own body. Perhaps I was envious of his touching, feeling those soft, red hairs covering massive muscles. I don't know. But I could feel my womanhood beginning to swell, and I was becoming damp. Feeling Keiko's body against me felt so good. I slid my crotch up against her butt. She didn't turn, but I could feel her push her bottom against me. I needed that pressure, and with a bit of movement I could roll my pelvis to match the movements of her butt. We did this with as little motion as possible; we didn't want to stop what the men were doing.

The kissing was more heated now, and the men were beginning to breathe heavier. David turned his hips up a bit, inviting Mark to provide him more touch, more stimulation. Mark pulled his mouth off of David's, and lowered his lips to David's nipples. He licked first one, then the other, and then back again. After a few quick licks, Mark lowered his face to David's now achingly large cock. To me, David's manhood seemed enormous, but with Mark's large hands and body, it looked more of a regular size.

He lowered his head and took David into his mouth. David opened his legs, and Mark slid down, taking a more comfortable position, with his elbow supporting him. His free hand went to David's swelling balls. He started by licking around his head, and then up and down his shaft. He nuzzled his nose against his balls, and then licked and sucked each one.

When he sucked one of David's balls into his mouth, I felt Keiko gasp and jerk. I decided the men were so focused on each other that I could give her just a bit of help. I moved my head against hers, so I could smell her better. My right hand sneaked around to the front of her and began to massage her breast. She moved even harder against me. She touched my legs more openly now, running her soft, delicate hands up and down them. Her touch was electric. Though her hands were cool, her touch was heat. And I was now beginning to drip moisture onto the bed and her butt.

I saw Mark taking David into his mouth with more passion now. His head was bobbing up and down. His own manhood was rigid and beginning to drip. It was all I could do to keep from crawling over and taking him. I was really beginning to rev up now, and I wanted to be a part of some action. But I held myself back.

But David saw what I saw, and slid over a bit and grabbed Mark's very pink penis. He spread the juice around the head, and began to pull on it. Mark moved his hips closer, but never broke contact. That seemed uncomfortable, so eventually David lay down, and they were both in each other's mouths at the same time.

And every time that we...oooooh

I'm more in love with you...

What a sight it was: two very masculine men, both orally pleasuring the other. Both sucking. Both licking. Both doing things any woman would be glad to do to them, including me. Oh, how I wanted to jump in between them and take those glands and put them in me. I was so excited to see their beautiful bodies. They were both gorgeous men, and I wanted one or both of them inside me in the worst way.

Just as I was reaching the point where I was going to start playing with myself, I felt Keiko slip her hand behind her back, and she touched my now very agitated opening. I was so wet her finger slipped in so easily. Thank God! I was so wired at this point I couldn't have held myself back much longer. I then realized that she was probably just as excited, so I moved my hand down from her breast to her soft mound. She was as wet as I was, so I roughly jammed two fingers into her.

I was panting in her ear already. I was nearing the outer edges of my first orgasm. Keiko sensed that, and slowed her touch. She whispered back to me, "Go slow, honey...I want to see them do more..."

Right. The guys. I was already losing myself in the heat of my impending orgasm that I would've stopped everything for a hot body on top of mine. It took some doing, but I refocused on the men.

Both were still exchanging orally, but I knew Keiko wanted more. Before I knew what was going on, she had slid over the top of me, and reached down to her purse that was on the floor next to the bed. She grabbed a bottle of lotion. When she pulled herself back up, she gently tapped her husband's foot. As he looked up, she showed him the lotion. He nodded, and reached out for it. She put it in his hand.

Keiko resumed her place in front of me, and this time slid two fingers inside me. It must've been hard from her angle, but she did a good job of putting enough pressure inside me to keep me going, though not to orgasm. I put my slick fingers back in her.

Mark moved first. He sat up a bit, and broke contact with David. They made eye contact for a second, and Mark showed him the bottle. David simply nodded, then moved over onto his elbows and knees, facing us. His face was about a foot from Keiko. Mark moved behind him, standing next to the bed. David slid back to him. I saw Mark moving his hand over himself...he was applying oil to his engorged penis. He then took some in his hand and smeared it on David's backside. David shuddered, put his head down, and closed his eyes.

I had never had anal sex before, and with the sizes of these two men I couldn't have imagined it. Yet, here was a very large, well-endowed man preparing to enter the man I loved. You would think I would've been horrified, ready to jump up and start slapping people. But instead I was so excited that I wanted to see Mark enter him more than anything. Keiko picked up the motion of her hand, and I was already feeling those distant waves again.

As he began to penetrate David, both men began to grunt. With each hip movement and grunt from Mark, David would jerk his head up just a bit. He was biting his lip. I imagine he was trying hard to relax and take Mark into him.

I watched them, intent on the grunting and squishing sounds. I was watching my man take a feminine, submissive role, just as I had taken a masculine role with Keiko. He was taking another man into his body. I knew the pain and pleasure that brought. I knew what it was like to take a different role. I wondered if he was enjoying it as much as I had.

And then Mark was in. I could see his hips against David's butt, and I knew that he was completely inside. He paused there…patiently… letting David relax and get used to his size inside him. David breathed heavily, and lowered his head to the bed. He was working to accept the largeness in him.

And then they were moving. Long, slow thrusts. With each push and pull, David would say "Unh!" He was taking a large penis inside him, and he was doing all he could to manage that experience. Mark was gentle at first. Long, leisurely strokes. In and out, in and out. David stayed on his elbows, face down to the bed.

I could smell the musky heat of the anal sex so close to us. I could smell their sweat. The lotion. David's open body. I could hear the squishing. The grunting. It was a whole new set of sensations. I also knew it might be hard for me to deny David anal sex now, having seen him receive the same thing. That was a mountain I had not yet climbed.

Soon Mark was picking up the pace. I looked down between David's legs, and I saw his penis dripping more fluid than I had ever seen before. It looked as if he had already had an orgasm. There was a long stringy glob, and a puddle under the tip. I didn't, at this point, understand enough of the male anatomy. I didn't know what a prostate

185

was, nor that anal sex could stimulate it. As a woman, I often echoed complaints that men didn't know our bodies. Yet...

Though I was still sliding my fingers inside her, Keiko apparently had had enough. She slid her hips to David's face. Though he was concentrating, he took her offered opening. He stuck out his tongue and she rubbed herself onto his face. She must've been closer than I had thought, because she began to climax almost instantly, throwing her head back and shrieking. I pulled around in front of her and put my mouth on her breast. I bit her breast and she ground herself against my face. I sucked and nibbled her through her orgasm. David's face was close to mine, though it was between her legs. His eyes were closed, still concentrating on Mark inside of him.

I thought it was time to get some for me also. I moved over on my knees to Mark. He was so large that I instantly felt very small beside him. I reached behind him and began to squeeze his now tight testicles as his hips swung back and forth. I sucked on his nipple. I caught the full strength of David, open in front of us. I heard the squishing of Mark's penis inside him. I reached under David and began to pull on his wet, dripping manhood. It wasn't hard, it wasn't soft...it was somewhere in between, and dripping a great volume of liquid.

I had my hand on David's dripping length, Mark's tight balls, and I was licking Mark's nipple. I was on my knees next to Mark, bent forward. I was surprised, then, to feel Keiko sliding underneath me. I lifted up, and her face was on me. Her tongue shot into me. I was so worked up, my orgasm came racing toward me, like an avalanche after a skier. I ground my hips down on her, moving her to the spots I wanted.

As I started panting, I felt Mark starting to twitch. I squeezed him tighter, and bit his nipple. He started to say, "Oh, Oh..." just as my own orgasm hit. He and I both exploded at the same time. I never let go of him, and he slammed his final thrusts into David. As he did so, David dripped out even more liquid. My hand was covered in his sticky secretions.

And it was yet another powerful orgasm. The hotness and dirtiness of what was happening played into my brain. The wet insistence of Keiko's tongue inside me. Feeling two men in my hands. Both muscular, beautiful men. It was too much for me. I collapsed onto David's sweaty back, and howled out my orgasm. I was shuddering and shaking, grinding my hips down on poor Keiko. She never stopped though, and slammed her tongue against me. It was so intense I felt myself twitching from every nerve ending in my body.

And then Mark pulled out of David with a wet schlooping sound, and we all collapsed onto the bed. As I looked around in confusion, I saw Mark's seed dripping from David's behind.

I was panting and dizzy. I realized, though, that David hadn't finished. I didn't know how he would feel, having just been had by Mark, and roughly at that. As I moved over to him, I saw Keiko's hand was already on him. He was flaccid, but with a few pulls he began to stiffen. Keiko slid up, and after a quick swipe of her free hand, she cleaned off his slippery gunk. She then lowered her head down to him, and took him into her mouth.

Mark got up, and went to the bathroom. I saw him standing by the sink, and I assumed he was washing himself. The air was still darkly musky, but now it was filling with pants and slurps.

I leaned back on my heels and watched them together. David's hand was on her head, pushing her down onto him. She was on her elbows twisting her hand around him while she swallowed as much of him as she could. I felt a bit put off, at first, as I was the only one in the bed not getting attention. After the initial flush, though, I looked down on Keiko, and was again entranced by her lithe, supple, smooth body.

I moved behind her, and as she felt my presence she lifted up on to her knees. Instead of lying under her, I put my face directly onto her. My nose was to her anus, and my tongue was inside her. She was so incredibly wet and slippery my tongue was soon covered with her juice.

"Lick me all over, Rachel," she panted as I began to tongue her, and then she shoved David back into her mouth. I knew what she meant. I slid my tongue up to her small hole, and tongued it. I felt it relax, and I pushed my tongue inside her. I then slid my tongue down to her raging opening and tongued it. I moved back and forth between them. After a couple movements like this, she broke contact with David, though she continued to stroke him. She was now panting loudly, and pulling on him rapidly. I sensed that she was near her orgasm, so I pushed my tongue as deeply into her as I could, and then tickled it up to her little button.

As I did so, she began crying out, and pushing against me. I pushed my tongue hard against her, licking her slippery juice and sliding my tongue all around her. She was shuddering against me. She jerked and then relaxed, and then fell against David's crotch. When I looked up, David was looking at me and smiling.

"You like that, David?" I cooed at him.

"You know I do. I love to see you eat her pussy."

I saw the bathroom door open, and Mark came back to the bed. "Do you want me to fuck Mark while you fuck her?" I was again cooing. She had told me I should play on his fantasies, so I wanted to give him all I could.

"I want to watch Mark fuck your brains out, Rachel," he said.

Mark moved onto the bed, and I met his lips with my own. I was going to enjoy what David wanted me to do. I couldn't wait to touch his strong muscles. I wanted his massive body on me. I wanted him to hammer me even more than he had last time.

I was all over Mark. I grabbed him and touched him and squeezed his bulging muscles. I felt the sting of watching Keiko pleasure David, and I was going to take it out on her husband.

I was always so enraptured by Mark's power. His frame was so large it was like kissing a gorgeous, red-haired truck. His size and power overwhelmed me. I pushed him back and put my mouth on him as quickly as I could. Though he had just recently finished, he was soon full again. As soon as he was, I lay back and pulled him down on me. I wanted contact…I wanted a man inside me…I wanted to make David watch me again. I was so turned on I felt aflame.

As Mark moved himself into me, I looked over at David. His eyes were burning again. His glare was steel, cutting through both of us. Keiko was sliding onto him, but David moved slowly…he was reluctant to take his eyes off of Mark and me. Keiko was insistent, though, and was soon on top of him. David and I were face to face, though Mark's large forearm was between us. Mark and Keiko were next to each other as well. I looked up and saw this couple pleasuring themselves on David and me.

I was going to show David everything his dark fantasies had brought us to, everything his fantasies craved. I wanted him to feel all the hurt and pain and pleasure he had wanted, and then some.

So I talked to Mark, though I was really talking to David.

"Oh God, Mark, you feel so hot inside me." I wrapped my legs around him, and pulled him to me. "You feel so good. Fuck me, Mark. Fuck me like only you can." I wanted those words to hurt. I had told David I wasn't interested in physical pain. Apparently, I was into emotional pain.

He began to move with more force. His powerful body slammed against me, sending him deeper into me. Each push blurred my vision. I could feel the hammering sending pulses through me. I could feel the tension inside me already.

I peeked again, and saw David watching Mark's crotch pound against my own. "C'mon, Mark baby…fuck me harder than that! Give me all you got!" Though Keiko was riding him, David seemed to hardly notice she was there. His eyes were on our union, and his brain was eating the images, as were his ego and pride.

I should have probably been more careful. Mark began to really pound me. He was so strong that he could've knocked the wind out of me easily. I was a bit afraid to have him truly unleash…he could've really hurt me. Yet I was so excited knowing that I was wounding David that I furthered my banter.

"Oh God, Mark, you're so strong. Fuck me! You're the best…fuck me even harder!"

Soon the loud popping of our crotches was drowning out the other noise. I couldn't hear the music. I could only hear our wet slapping. Mark was giving me such a pounding that I felt I would be bruised and battered. And I wanted that. Badly. I wanted to show my bruises and swelling to David in the morning, and give him what he wanted.

And then it started. As I felt the flame begin to move within me, I looked first at David and then at Keiko. David's face was blanched. Keiko gave me a wry smile. Just as we locked eyes, Keiko's eyes began to lose focus, and I knew she was going to the same place I was. We both reached that place at the same moment.

As I surrendered to the pleasure, I began a loud, wailing cry that seemed to come from somewhere deep inside me. Keiko loosed her mewling cries, and then we both began to shout at the same time. She reached down and put her hand on my thigh.

Though I was tired, I felt myself drifting away…flying like a bird over a mountain. So far away. So far removed from David's Manhattan apartment. I was soaring to a distant place. As I returned, I felt that Mark had climaxed, and he put his seed deeply into me. He collapsed down on to me, and I tasted his hot, sour sweat. He put his mouth on mine, and his kisses returned me to the moment. My eyes were lidded.

When I regained focus, I saw Keiko kissing David aggressively. She was moving her hips up and down on him with a fast tempo. She was trying to bring him to his climax. He was still looking at me. Instinctively, I knew what he wanted.

"Did you like that, David? Did you like seeing Mark come inside me?" I clucked my voice to him.

"Yes, Rachel...I loved it."

"You're a dirty, little cuckold, aren't you?" My eyes burned at him.

He didn't answer, but I saw his eyes begin to drift. I wanted to hurt him more, because I realized now it was the hurt he enjoyed. I pushed Mark off of me, and turned my crotch toward David. I growled at him.

"Look at my pussy, David. Look at Mark dripping out of me..."

He jerked his eyes back into focus and looked at me there. His face flushed...he was almost there. I put a finger inside.

"His come is so hot, David...he came so much in me." Keiko looked over at me and smiled. She knew what I was doing.

As David's eyes again lost focus, I took the finger out of me and pushed it into his mouth. He sucked on it passionately, and then his entire body jerked hard as he climaxed intensely. I heard him grunting with each jerk of his body, "Uhhh...uhhh...uhhh..." but I kept my finger in his mouth. Even as he slackened, I didn't remove it. I wanted him to enjoy the taste of his girlfriend and another man. I knew he did.

La la la la la...la la la la la...la la la la la, la la la lahhh

190

Part IV: Chrysalis

The best day of my professional career was the worst day of my adult life. Stella Metz and George Hammitt threw a great publishing party for me at Random House's New York office. The Lower Manhattan building was a stone's throw from the Battery. David and Keiko were with me that day, but Mark was in the last week of training camp before the football season.

It was a hot August day, and the wind through the opened windows made the balloons and pages flutter. The stifling Manhattan heat made sure we all had beads of sweat and wet spots on our clothes. But I was in heaven. George made a touching tribute to my work, while holding up his glass of expensive champagne.

"I am so proud that Random House is launching the *Leaves of Grass* imprint, as it allowed us to capture the most innovative and exciting poet I have read in some time. I believe Whitman would be proud to see the language of culture, revolution, and love blend together into the collection we are distributing today. Rachel Walker, thank you for sharing your work with us. Cheers!" Everybody raised their glasses, and sipped the rather nice bubbly. We snacked and talked and laughed. I was dizzy with all the attention.

Keiko stayed by my side and held my hand for much of the time. She whispered little encouragements. David was tall and proud standing next to me. Dr. Frank and Dr. Bill were both there, and Dr. Frank beamed with pride. He told me, "I always knew you would write something special, Rachel. I always knew." My friend Clarice even made it, leaving her firstborn with her nanny. She was very pregnant with their second child, and had to sit for most of the party. In addition to my friends, Stella made sure several of her other writers, her fellow agents, and Random House's senior officers were all present. I was surrounded by talent and energy.

One person was absent. My father had called me that morning and told me he couldn't attend. He had a case of the flu, and felt a fever. I told him I would come by after the party. I was hurt and sad that he wasn't there. More than anybody, I wanted to see him. I wanted him to see that his little girl was a woman now. I wanted to feel his hug and see his tears. Just before he hung up he said, "You've done something special, but you'll always be my baby girl."

I was given a box of my books, and in that box was a check for the first half of my advance. Ten thousand dollars on a single piece of paper! It felt so good; that was a lot of money in those days. I signed the first few books and gave them to my guests. I also gave one each to Stella and George. On each of theirs I wrote, "I hope this is the beginning of a long relationship." I meant it too…I wanted to work with those two for as long as I possibly could! I think it was the selfish belief that I somehow deserved to keep writing and having that work published. I'm not sure anymore. But they were great to work with, and they did publish a few of my best works.

We drank champagne and talked and laughed. All the focus was on me and my book. For a girl who had felt outside of society and social circles, I was surrounded by smart, gifted people who were toasting *me*. I was with beautiful people, two of whom I loved physically. I had come so far, so fast. I knew David was the catalyst. David put me in this spot. All of this came from him. I loved him more than ever at this moment. Perhaps that was selfish as well, but it was how I felt. And beautiful, sweet Keiko was by my side telling me how proud she was of me. I honestly didn't think the moment could get any better.

But something nagged at me. I knew something was wrong. A

tiny, distant voice inside me told me something was wrong. It was like a shout across a valley, insistent but faint. But it kept shouting, and the echoes brought it to me. It became urgent and demanding.

The tiny voice told me there was something wrong with my father. I ignored it at first…I didn't want to spoil the festivities. I would call him later. My friends had come to see me and share in my moment. But it kept after me. Something in my father's tone had been off. Something needed to be discussed. Wrong…it was all wrong. I couldn't ignore it any longer.

I asked George to use his phone, and he led me to his office in a quiet corner. I dialed home, just wanting to hear my father's voice. I wanted to hear him say he was okay, and then I would return to the party and drink too much.

The phone rang. No answer.

I knew then. It was an immediate knowledge. No more pretending.

I dialed one more time, but knew he wouldn't answer the second time.

I made my way back out to the party. David smiled at me, but his brows furrowed when he saw my face. "You okay, Rachel? What's wrong?" He put his hands on my shoulders, and looked directly into my eyes.

"Something's wrong at home. My father."

"How do you know?" I felt Keiko move next to me.

"I just know. Can we leave soon? I want to go home and check on him."

"Sure, whatever you want." He immediately moved to collect our things.

"Honey, tell me…what's wrong?" Keiko's hand had slipped into mine. She stood very close.

"My father didn't answer the phone. There's a phone right by his bed. I know something's wrong."

"I'll go out front and get a taxi for us." She moved quickly to the door.

I gave quick apologies to everybody, and followed David out to the street. Everybody saw the consternation on my face, so nobody protested.

During the ride, nobody spoke. David and Keiko flanked me, and I held their hands. I began to squeeze as we crossed the Queensboro. When we reached my neighborhood, I felt the hot tears burning my eyes. I knew. In my heart and mind I knew what I would find.

My father was already cold when we arrived. I saw his twisted and anguished form on his bed. His frozen expression was panic and fear. I should have known…no matter how sick he was, he would've come to see me that day. His "flu" was the beginning of the massive heart attack that took his life that day. I should have been there for him. In many ways, I never forgave myself for not being there in his last hours. My father, a man who gave everything for me, died alone.

I t took months for the shroud to lift. That merciless black pall smothered me. I was crushed under the weight of it. The Fates laughed as Atropos cut my father's thread, measured far too short by Lachesis. We mortals live in the ash and ruin of their weaving, don't we? My father was fifty-five when he died. And I now had no family.

I wouldn't talk to anybody, not even David. I sat alone in our house in Queens, and fully realized my solitude. The immensity of it hit me like a freight train. When my mother had died, I still had my father, and I still had our home. I still had all the trappings of our family. My father's presence and calm had reassured me. His strength had protected me. He and I had built a new life. Though I had missed a female influence in my life, especially as I grew into puberty, my father was granite strength and calm. A foundation I could always depend on.

But then my new life and loves had taken hold of me. Entirely. All at once. I had flown into their arms. Satisfied my lust on their bodies. Found solace in our shared sweat and heavy breaths. I let passion and desire control nearly every waking moment.

In doing so, I had left my father alone. The house had dirty dishes. The laundry wasn't done. I had left my father to die alone in a bed with dirty sheets. What kind of daughter was I? I blamed myself. I had let my loins lead me away from my only remaining family. My father hardly saw me once I met David. Despite my promises, I was rarely there. Had I been home, I would've seen my father's ill condition, surely. How could I have missed that his health was deteriorating? I would have insisted he go to the hospital, and perhaps he would be alive.

In the refrigerator, there was almost no food. The freezer was stuffed with frozen dinners. My father was forced to eat poor food, and sit at home alone without anybody there to care for him. I was all he had, and when I ran to my lovers he sat alone, eating crappy food and having little contact with others. His death was just a matter of time.

To this day, I haven't overcome the guilt. I abandoned the father who stood by me, and I did so to pleasure myself. I did so to do things sexually he would've never approved of. What kind of woman does this? I was sleeping with my boyfriend and another married couple regularly. I had sex with strangers in swing clubs. I was living in sin. I was ignoring what my parents had taught me.

My father's funeral had two attendees. One of them was our pastor. I had not told anybody about it, especially not David, Keiko, or Mark. I didn't want to deal with other people, and I felt having them there would have been unseemly. I stood there in my black dress and cried rivers as the pastor read his passages. As my father was lowered, I knelt by the grave and watched the box enter the earth. I threw flowers on his casket and then sat and cried as they covered him. Reverend Johnson had to drive me home.

Two days after his funeral, a buyer approached me about his business, which was now my business, though I knew little about it. I might have put it out for bids and gained a much better price, but I was lost and over my head. I took his offer, signed the papers in my kimono, and was glad to be done with it. I didn't even deposit the check for some time.

I refused to answer the phone. We didn't have answering machines in those days. I refused to answer the door when David or Keiko came by, though they did several times. When I heard them knocking and calling out to me, I sat motionless and waited for them to leave. I was beyond consolation. I began to think I didn't deserve to live myself. I began to think about the type of person I was and the type of person I was becoming. I didn't like what I found. No, that's not strong enough. I *hated* the person I was. The thought of ending my life ran through me several times.

After a few weeks of sitting alone, I found myself one day dressed in a stained sweatshirt, an oversized pair of shorts, and socks with holes in the toes. I looked in the mirror and didn't recognize the face staring back at me. My hair was knotted. My eyes were sagging. I was blanched and drawn. I looked like a horror show. I was a goblin living in the home of my dead parents.

That image of myself made something in me snap, like a guitar string strung too tightly. I think it was a coping mechanism that kicked off inside me. Survival instinct, perhaps? Overnight, I became obsessive. I decided I needed to clean the house. It began simply by doing the laundry. Then I swept. Then I mopped. Then I cleaned out the refrigerator. I washed my father's clothes, though I knew he would never need them again. I mopped and dusted the attic. I cleaned the windows. I ironed the drapes. Before I knew it, I was scrubbing the corners with a toothbrush. I had to make this house clean.

I think now it was me I was cleaning, not the house. This cleaning was a cathartic experience for me. I had to clean the filth of the house to clean the filth I felt inside of me.

When I finally had done all I knew how to do, weeks later, I picked up the phone and called Keiko.

"Hello?"

"Hi, Keiko, it's Rachel." I was surprised at how tired my voice sounded.

"Oh my God, Rachel. Are you okay? We've all been so worried. I came by a few times. I've called and called…"

"I know, I'm sorry…"

"Are you okay, honey? Where are you?"

"I'm at my father's house, in Queens."

"Have you called David? He has been worried to death."

"No, not yet. I called you first. I'll call him next."

"Can I come over?"

"I'm not sure if I'm ready yet. Maybe in a few more days."

"Okay, honey…whatever you want. Can I do anything for you?"

"Actually, that's why I called. I need your help."

"Sure, honey…anything…what can I do?"

"I need a good real estate agent. I want to sell this house." I was looking around at the house as I said this. So many memories. The Christmas tree in the corner of the living room. The pencil marks on the wall showing my growth. All there.

"Of course, I know several. The market is slow right now, so it might take some time."

"I know…I'm in no hurry. I just can't stay in here any longer."

"Yeah, no problem. You should do well when it finally sells. It's larger than many in that area. Are you going to move in with David?"

"No. I don't think I'm ready to do that. I think I want to buy my own place. Maybe the Upper West Side."

"Okay, honey, I'll tell him. It's pricey there, but if you find something, it's a great location." She paused. "So how about us, honey? Is everything okay?"

"Okay?"

"You know…"

"I can't even think about that now, Keiko. Please give me some time."

"Of course…whatever you want." Her voice sounded plaintive, but I had nothing to offer her.

"Okay, we'll talk later."

"Bye, honey."

I hung up the phone.

David stood on my doorstep for some time, knocking softly at first, but progressively heavier. I had seen him, and hoped he would go away. He didn't.

"I know you're in there, Rachel. I spoke to Keiko. Open up... please." His deep voice boomed, and I was worried the neighbors would get interested.

I opened the door. I was a mess...I hadn't showered; I was wearing those same sweats, and my hair was everywhere. He stepped in and put his arms around me.

"Where have you been, Rachel? I've been coming by and calling. Where were you?"

"I've been here."

"The whole time?" He seemed stunned.

"Yes, the whole time."

"Why didn't you answer the phone? Why didn't you answer the door?" His hands were on my shoulders. I was looking down. I didn't have a face to show him

"I needed some time alone, David. I needed to be by myself."

"Rachel, it has been almost six weeks!"

"I know. I'm sorry. You wouldn't understand."

Now he seemed hurt. "Why wouldn't I?"

"This is deeply personal, David. I've lost my family. All of them. I'm all alone. My family has been everything to me."

"You're not alone, Rachel. I love you."

"My mother and father were all I had most of my life. Now they're both gone. This house…this house is where we all lived."

"I'm so sorry they're gone, Rachel. But you can't be mad at yourself over this."

"Can't I? Can't I, David? I promised to visit my father often. But how many times did I? I saw you and Mark and Keiko all the time. I had time to have sex with all of you. Regularly. Yet I couldn't come by and take care of him. If I had taken care of him, maybe he wouldn't have died. He was living on TV dinners and junk food. He was too young to die like that."

"Oh God, Rachel. You're blaming yourself for his death? Because you weren't cooking for him?"

"He was my father! It was my job." My voice had risen too much, and he could sense my anger.

"Calm down, Rachel. He was a full-grown man. He could take care of himself. Don't do this to yourself. Don't, okay?"

"David, I need you to leave. I need some time alone. I need to think things through."

"Keiko told me you're selling this house."

"Yeah, I am. I have too many memories here. Ghosts."

"She told me you didn't want to, but I'd like you to move in with me."

I was surprised, but not too much. "No, David, I'm not ready for that." It might seem like a small thing now, but moving in with someone in those days was a big deal.

"Well, you are free to do whatever you want…"

"Thank you," I interrupted.

"…but think about it, okay?"

"I will." I was lying, though later I would.

He tried to kiss me, but my face dropped. He kissed me on my hair. I had never seen his body language show defeat, but he showed it now. I didn't care. I wasn't in a place to think about him. He turned to the door, and grabbed the knob. Over his shoulder, he spoke softly.

"I'm leaving tomorrow. Three weeks."

"Where are you going?"

"Moscow. We're doing a story and shoot. Then I'll fly up to Saint Petersburg and do some solo work on the palaces there. I'm starting to work on another book." He turned back, waiting for my response. I didn't have anything to offer.

"Have a good trip, David." My words were without affect.

He didn't say another word. He walked out, and closed the door behind him. For a moment I wanted to follow him. I wanted to go after him and hold him again. But I was too wrapped up in myself. I had nothing emotionally to give him.

I knew I was being exceptionally selfish. I knew I was chasing away people who loved me. I knew all of this, but I couldn't stop my self-destruction. I was paying penance. I was punishing myself for my crimes.

Keiko's real estate agent helped me get the property listed. I decided to stay in it until I sold it. Living there until it sold would be my last contact with that house. When sold, I would donate all the furniture, and besides a few old photo albums I would get rid of anything that would remind me of my days living there.

The next Sunday, I slept in. I was sleeping more and more, but this day I slept until the afternoon. I got up and made myself some eggs. I sat on the sofa, and turned on the television.

I hadn't watched the TV since I had been there. I honestly had lost track of which day it was. Football came on, so I knew it had to be Sunday. I was about to turn it off when the announcer came back from his commercial break and told me, "Welcome back to the Meadowlands of New Jersey, where the Tampa Bay Buccaneers are facing the New York Giants."

I sat on the sofa slowly eating my eggs. I didn't understand football, but I was curious if I would see Mark. First, though, I noticed the horrible orange of the Tampa Bay team. What were they thinking? They looked more like Halloween costumes than football uniforms.

Then I saw Mark make an important play. I saw the quarterback throw the ball to a tall, muscular receiver. I knew right away it was Mark from his movements. A member of the Tampa team attempted to tackle him. Mark shoved him off with his left arm, and ran down the sideline. He kept running, though several men were in pursuit.

The announcer went wild! "That's Freeman on the catch. Oh! He shoves the defender out of the way. He's running loose! 50...40...30... nobody will catch him! Touchdown, New York Giants!" As Mark ran into the end zone, he threw the ball hard onto the field, and then was mobbed by his teammates.

And I was ecstatic! Not because he was someone I slept with or anything like that. He was a friend who had just done something amazing. I didn't understand it, but obviously this was a stunning feat of athleticism. I could see how powerful his strides were, and he looked so immense and muscular, even next to others his own size.

I jumped up and shouted when he scored! I spilled my eggs, but I didn't care. I was so happy for Mark. I jumped around the living room and hooted. I wondered if Keiko was at the game. I wondered if they would celebrate after. I wondered how it felt to see a game like that. I watched replay after replay, and they showed the catch and touchdown from several angles.

It's interesting that a football game was what brought me back around, but that's what did it. A game I didn't understand gave me a quickening in my soul. I started thinking about David, and Mark, and Keiko. I started to think about the love we shared. I started thinking about the life and the experiences we had together. I started to miss them, especially David.

I watched the rest of the game, and shouted every time Mark's name was called. It was a close game...that team in orange put up a good fight, despite their dreadful attire. In the end, the Giants prevailed. And when they won, I felt fully awake and engaged.

I went upstairs and took a long, cleansing shower. I let the water flow over me and refresh my soul. I fixed my hair and put on makeup. I wasn't going anywhere...I just wanted to feel beautiful again. I went out to the front porch, and for the first time in a while I was outside. I sat on the porch on my father's old chair, and felt the cool October breeze on me. I breathed in that sweet air, and let it enter my spirit. I wanted to be a part of the world again, and I wanted life to go on in me and around me and through me.

After sitting a bit, I went for a short walk around the neighborhood. These were streets where I rode my bicycle as a little girl. I had played jump rope at my neighbor's house. I had sat under that tree and read poems to fill my heart. All of this neighborhood was who I was. And it filled me with life to be in it. Though I would leave this neighborhood soon and not return, it had left its mark on me, and revitalized me once again. It wasn't the last time it would do this for me.

The next day, I called Keiko, and told her I had watched Mark play.

"Oh that was such a great game, wasn't it? I was in the stands. I yelled so loudly when Mark scored that touchdown." I could still hear a bit of hoarseness in her voice.

"It was so exciting, Keiko. I don't know how you stand it—knowing it's your husband doing that."

"I've kinda gotten used to it, but that touchdown was fantastic. We have a very tough game next week. They play the 49ers. Should be another close game. It'll be another home game, so I'll be there."

"What do you do when he's on the road?"

"I go to some of his games on the road, but only a few. Hey, do you want to go with me to the game this weekend? I know Mark would love to see you again."

I didn't expect the offer. "Oh, it would be too much trouble…"

"Nonsense. I mean, I know many girls don't like football. I didn't watch it until I met Mark. But they're fun even when you don't understand the game. Lots of yelling and cheering. C'mon…why don't you come with me?"

"But I don't have a ticket…" I protested faintly.

"I can get you a ticket easily. So will you come?"

"Okay, if it's no problem."

"Great! I'll come by and get you around ten o'clock Sunday morning. You'll see…we'll have a blast. And I'd love to have someone to talk to during the game. The other players' wives are cunts…I avoid them."

"Okay, see you then."

Two days later, I had a buyer for the home, and we would close rather quickly. I was already seeing apartments on the Upper West Side.

And the game was wonderful fun. The Giants destroyed the 49ers, and the stadium was absolutely rocking. It sounded like a hurricane! It had turned suddenly cold, so Keiko and I snuggled together under a blanket she brought, while taking shots from a little whisky flask. Mark made several catches, and when his name was called on the public address system we would scream. I still don't understand football, but that was one of the best days of my life.

By the time David returned from Russia, I was moving into my new apartment, just three blocks down from Central Park on 72nd. I called him and told him all that I had gone through. I told him I loved him, and we cried together on the phone. We agreed to meet at the subway station on the edge of the park, and then I would walk him back and show him my new place.

As I walked down 72nd Street, passing the porte cochere of the Dakota, I saw a long black car pull up just ahead of me. Stepping out was a slender man with light hair and glasses, and with him was a smaller Asian woman. I didn't register them until I was directly in front of them. I spoke despite my shyness.

"Hi, John and Yoko," I said. "Love your music."

"Thanks, love," John said, and then they were through the portico into the building.

I was so happy to have seen them. I knew they lived close by, but just assumed they'd travel with an army of security. Seeing them out on the street like that made me think I would see them often. I told myself to carry a pad of paper so I could ask for an autograph when I saw them again.

But I never did see them again. Just a year later, an attention-seeking lunatic would shoot John, right in that same spot.

hough I continued to spend many nights at David's place, I insisted on staying in my own apartment a few nights a week. I think it was important to me to maintain my sense of identity and self. Though I loved him and did hope for marriage someday, I also knew that our relationship was fraught with peril. How would a bond like this work with children? How could you maintain a regular (whatever that is) life when you sleep with other people? I knew I wanted children. I knew I wanted a home and a normal life for those children. Right now, that dream seemed light-years away. Once again, a tiny voice was shouting at me across a distant valley. I did not want to hear it, so I worked hard at ignoring it.

David began feverishly working on his next book, which would focus on the palaces of Eastern Europe. I was stunned by the pictures he brought home from Russia. I never imagined such opulence was still on display in that country. I assumed the Soviet Empire would have turned them into state office buildings.

"Oh, I would've thought that too, but Russia tries, at times, to show off its history, if only for a cultural lesson…showing the evils of noncommunist systems. They point out that the tsars lived like that while their people starved. It's true, I guess, but I think all of Europe would be guilty of the same.

I marveled at David's discipline. When he began to write, he stayed completely focused on his work. He could write for several hours at a time, and didn't require inspiration. I was the opposite. I needed space and a spark to write. David sledgehammered through his work. I chased it like a feather in the breeze.

We were at David's, working away on a dreary Sunday in November, when I heard the radio commenting on unrest in the Middle East. Iran, of all places. We stopped working, and turned on the news. We heard that our embassy in Tehran was overrun. Then we heard hostages were taken. We saw images of women in black, burning the US flag. Young men climbed over the gates of the embassy and chanted, "Death to America." We didn't say a word. We just sat and listened and watched as the information trickled in. We couldn't believe what we were seeing. Every once in a while, David would swear under his breath.

I remember feeling so violated. America had been attacked, even if on foreign soil. This was new to me. Certainly, we hadn't fared well in Vietnam. We had been slowly losing our sense of invincibility for a while. But this attack really shocked us. We felt so vulnerable. Night after night, we watched women in headscarves and men with beards threatening our destruction. Our hostages were paraded in front of cameras. These next months were horrifying to us. I felt that our future was more uncertain than ever. It felt like 9/11 would later feel, though obviously with much less loss of life. Still, we were shocked and horrified.

As we headed into the holidays, we began to spend more time with Keiko and Mark. Not just sexually, but all together as friends. David and I sat with Keiko for the Giants' final game against the Baltimore Colts. The season had turned disappointing, and they were beaten badly. Mark had been battling an injured ankle, and he was much slower than he had been previously. He didn't have any big plays, and we left the stadium feeling bad for our friend.

All of us spent Christmas together, but there was a feeling that things just weren't as new and exciting as they had been. I felt it strongly. Yet David and I were together constantly, and I did love him so much. I was afraid that all the recent events would make him restless and that he would move on. I worried about the overall state of our relationship, and wondered where we were heading as a couple. I worried also about our communal love with Mark and Keiko. While we continued periodic sessions together, nothing new or interesting was coming out of them. It was becoming a bit routine, and I could sense that this would be trouble for our relationship. David, after all, craved new adventures.

I noticed that I had now fully accepted the life we had. During our first few encounters, everything had seemed rather scary, and every sexual congress was a new exploration and, for me, an emotional hurdle to get over. I guess I became used to that sense of danger and challenge. Now, the four of us would just get together, have some drinks, and get to the bedroom. While the sex was great, and I never left unfulfilled, it was rather, I guess, boring. Instead of falling into a routine with one person I had fallen into a routine with three people.

Keiko and I never had a repeat solo session. We talked about it now and then, but with our schedules it just never materialized. During the football season, she had devoted a lot of attention to visiting Mark at practice and going to his games. I was busy working on my first novel while still writing new poetry.

The good news was that my work poured out of me. David's focus on his own writing gave me the perfect excuse to chase my muse. I was covering a lot of ground. In the past, I had approached my work delicately. David showed me how to sit down and do *something*, rather than just wait for inspiration. He told me once, "Even if you're writing garbage, you can always edit it later and put it into shape." That was a new way to tackle it, as I usually waited and waited and waited for inspiration. Now that I was a professional writer, this new approach was critical to my growth, and it served me well in the years to come.

After we enjoyed a pleasant Christmas, I found us in a cold January wondering what my future would hold. I finally broached the topic with David. As we sat watching the news one night, I turned to him.

"David, what is our next adventure?"

He looked a bit surprised, and turned to me. "Adventure?"

"We've hit a dull patch. Everything was so new before, but now we're like an old married couple. What are we going to do for our next adventure?"

"You mean sexually?"

"Yes, sexually. Honestly, I'm a bit bored. You got me used to new things all the time, and now we're in a rut." Yes, that was me saying this.

"I never thought you wanted more than that. I was afraid to ask you about it, Rachel."

"Why?"

"Well, I really love you, and cherish what we have. But yeah, I have been burning to try something new. I didn't know how to talk to you about it. You had said you wanted to maintain a sense of control, so I didn't want to push you."

"David, why didn't you talk to me?"

"Well, this is the first time I've felt really comfortable with someone...I didn't want to blow it by demanding too much. We have been swinging with Mark and Keiko, so that has kinda held me over, I guess. I know it has been a while."

"I love them both, but I think you and I need to do some things on our own."

"Okay, let's plan something, then. What do you want?"

"Well, I'm sick of this horrible weather. Any chance we could go somewhere warm? Do you know anybody down in Florida?"

"No, but I could make some calls. Maybe get a referral. Yeah, I'll work on that."

"Good. Let's do something soon."

I wondered, for a minute, if I was using sex as a tool to manipulate David. I wanted out of New York's snow, and I wanted to dry out somewhere warm. But I *did* want to try something new, and if David wanted to continue to explore things sexually then the onus was on him to help make that happen. I guess I had the right to expect some small bonuses along the way, such as a nice trip to somewhere sunny.

I got up to fix us both a little lunch. When I was in the kitchen, I flipped open a magazine, and saw a photo-spread that would change our lives forever.

The story was about the burgeoning reggae scene in Jamaica. Following the success of Bob Marley, several other reggae bands were coming out of this island in the Caribbean. A couple of photos showed these beautiful, tall black men playing soccer on the most exquisite beach

I had ever seen. Soft sand, clear water. Their long dreadlocks flowed over their shoulders, and their lean, muscular bodies shone with sweat.

"David?" I called out. "Why don't we try Jamaica?"

Part V: Imago

We sat in a bar sipping drinks. The tropical heat made us both thirsty. It was night, but the waxing moon lit up the beach and water, and this beachside bar was perfect for watching the sparkling waves roll in.

We had spent a beautiful day there in Montego Bay. We had placed our chairs right near the water, and we had lounged in the angry midday sun. Back to our room, we had showered and napped. Now, in the early evening we were back out and enjoying the warmth. The winter blues were already gone, and a couple drinks had given us giddy smiles and easy laughs.

Kingston, though, had been a pit. After landing there, we realized we had chosen the wrong city to stay in. The place reminded me of a war zone. David had quickly found this hotel in Montego Bay, and we moved over. It was a great choice.

The drinks were cheap, and the smell of hemp was strong. I personally didn't like the feeling I got when smoking marijuana, but David purchased a small amount from the hotel bellman, and smoked a bit before we went out. We were relaxed and feeling no pain that evening. We were enjoying the feeling of sand, the sound of the crashing waves, and the briny-iodine smell of the ocean all around us.

We finished our drinks, and walked out onto the beach. My feet loved the feel of the velvety sand. We strolled along, holding our shoes and each other's hands. It was such a lovely feeling. I wanted to be in this moment forever. My heart was filled with love again. This vacation was just what we needed. Maybe we were letting details of our work and world events distract us from what was really important…us.

We had walked for nearly a mile when we heard the sound of music. Both of us picked up the tuned drums and guitars. We followed the sound, and found ourselves approaching a large shack of a building, complete with corrugated metal roofing. It was set alone, far from the hotels and bars, but still near the beach. There were several dreadlocked men standing around outside it. A single light cast an uneven, flickering luminescence, and we were drawn to the glow like moths.

As we approached, the music became louder. We could hear the beating of drums, and the syncopated upstroke rhythms of reggae. The smell of marijuana was thick, and the sour pungent smell burned my nose a bit. The men at the front were smoking large, rolled spliffs, which seemed giant even to these tall men.

One man stood closest to the door. He flashed a big white smile at us as we approached.

"Aya mon! Are ya lost?" He had to speak loud over the music and the roar of voices inside.

"No, we just heard the music," David replied.

"Ah, you like the reggae, mon?" His eyes roamed over me. "This t'ain't a club fah the tourists. Ya be welcome ta come in if ya like." He opened the rickety door for us.

In the dim lights we could see fifty or more people dancing and swaying to the heavy rhythm. On a poorly lit stage, we saw a large band packed tightly. Drummers, guitar players, and singers all vied for space on this cramped little dais. The heat poured out on us, as did the marijuana smoke. Sweat was shining on the bodies of those inside.

David looked at me. "What do you think? You want to hear them play?"

"Sure." As long as David was there, I felt confident. He took my hand and led me inside. We moved through the loosely collected people near the door, many of whom were smoking the pungent ganja of the island. As we worked our way closer to the stage, we found ourselves compressed against the bodies of men and women who were cheering, singing, and dancing. My sundress left my arms and shoulders uncovered, and the sweat of others made my arms slick instantly.

The band was playing a slinky style of reggae...very rhythm-focused and lyrical. I instantly began to move my hips to the music. In this hot little shack, I began to feel the freedom that reggae gives its listener. I let my body move and the rhythm guided those movements. David moved beside me, and we watched the band play as we danced.

Their first two songs kept a smooth, reggae dance tempo. It was easy to sway and dance, and I continued to let my body feel the beat and send its motions in reply. It was a wonderful feeling. I hadn't danced much in my life, but I was feeling it that night.

As we danced, we felt the elbows and hips of others bumping us. We were packed in so tightly that we all moved against each other in a large, sweaty mass. Elbows. Shoulders. Hips. Every movement brought me in contact with another person. David seemed to have lost himself in the same rhythms, and I saw him swaying with his eyes closed. The tuned steel drums added an almost mystical, unearthly feel to the music, and my mind began to flow with their patterns.

At first, I found myself pressed against a woman in an elaborate, bright teal outfit. She was a large woman. Her body and hair were wrapped in matching material. Her outfit reminded me of an Indian sari, but with her hair wrapped high. Bits of straightened hair came out from the edges. She smiled largely at me, and we danced together. I felt like we were sharing the experience together. Though a large woman, she danced lithely.

As we danced more, I felt a large set of hands on my hips, and felt someone moving behind me. I turned and saw a tall, leanly muscular man in dreadlocks behind me. He smiled at me, and then looked back up to the stage. I looked back to the front and continued to dance, figuring he would move his hands away in a bit.

But he didn't. As the band started its next song, I felt him press closer to me, and I felt his hips against mine. This next song was slower, with a more moody tempo, and soon the man's crotch was pressed against me. I could clearly feel the large bulge in his pants. He was grinding his crotch against me.

While a good girl from Queens should have immediately shrieked and slapped, I didn't. In fact, I found it a bit erotic, to be honest. I was far from home, and didn't have to worry about what anybody would think about it. Plus, by this point I had already experienced many sexual encounters of all varieties, so a little dance floor grinding wasn't going to intimidate me.

In fact, as the song moved on, I began to push back against him. I moved my hips back and forth across him, and could feel him thrust harder. He was holding my hips and dry humping me as I wriggled against him. I peeked at David, but he seemed oblivious to it. He was completely focused on the music. After all, so many people were pressed against us, the only thing different was the man's hands on my hips.

As this man and I continued to grind, I felt him move his torso against me, and soon we were pressed tightly to each other. He wrapped his arms around my waist, and squeezed against me. We were both slippery with sweat. I could feel his hot breath against my ear and neck. He nuzzled his chin into my hair.

"I'm Winston," he said into my ear.

"Rachel," I gasped back at him over my shoulder.

I turned to look at David and he still seemed unaware. I had moved just a bit behind him, so it was plausible to me that he didn't notice what was happening. I also wondered if he was pretending not to notice so I would feel free to do what I wanted, like in the shoe store all those long months ago.

Winston moved his hands up to my breasts, and began to squeeze them through my dress, never losing the contact of our bodies. His hands were very large, and he squeezed them softly but firmly. In response, I moved myself back against him, grinding my butt against his crotch even harder. I felt myself surrendering to him. I could feel his rough dreadlocks against my hair, and his lean, sweaty muscles pressed against me felt very erotic. I was very excited, and wanted to surrender to his touch.

So when we began to cross the line together, I just let it happen.

He pulled the front of my dress down enough to expose my left breast completely, and his right hand worked on my nipple. I realized I was exposed in this crowded room, but I didn't care. I reached my hand around behind me, and grabbed his crotch. I felt the largest penis I had ever felt in my life packed tightly into his slacks. It was positively massive. I stroked it in his pants. The music played on and the people danced around us, but I was losing myself to Winston's touch, to his desire.

I felt his breath coming faster as I stroked him. Soon, he was kissing and licking my neck and ear. My eyes had been closed, but I opened them long enough to see David. He was now watching us, and he smiled at me when we made eye contact. That was his way of granting us permission, and that was all I needed.

I now turned completely to face Winston, and I pulled his neck down and kissed him. His long tongue and full lips felt wonderful on me. I grabbed his crotch again, and I pressed and stroked him. He put one hand on my breast, and another reached behind me. He used that hand to pull me against him roughly.

I wanted his manliness. I wanted his rough touch. I wanted his muscular, dusky body all over me. I was his.

He pulled his mouth away for a second. "Let us go, Rachel." His accent pronounced my name so beautifully. I didn't even look at David. He took my hand and led me to the door. When we reached the door, I looked back and David was following us, but at a bit of a distance.

Winston led me outside, and we walked to the beach. He was moving very quickly, and I had to run a few steps now and then to keep up with him, but he was pulling me insistently. As I followed him, still holding his hand, I marveled at his muscular back and very broad shoulders, which were covered by his thick dreadlocks. His body reminded me of Mark's: tall, thick, and muscular. His dark skin seemed even darker in the night.

As we reached the sand, I paused to kick off my shoes. Then I followed him again. As we moved onto the beach, I looked back. I saw David following, still at a distance. He was trying to appear nonchalant, but I knew his eyes were focused on me. On us.

I have to say I had half expected him to chase us down, and to demand that I return. I'm not sure what I would have done, because I was very sexually excited. Still, I could feel a nudging in my soul. Why would he let me run off with this stranger? We're on vacation together. I think a part of me *wanted* him to fight for me. To demand I return. To verbally lash me for daring to touch another man when I should have been with him.

Yet I knew he wouldn't. I therefore had no boundaries, and this was the result.

I followed Winston to the edge of the water. He turned to me.

"I want you in the water." He began to peel off his shirt, which was soaked with sweat and clung to his body. I hesitated for a second, and then dropped my shoes, grabbed the bottom of my dress, and pulled it over my head. As he slid off his pants, I slipped out of my panties. I stood there naked. A quick peek showed me David in the shadows near a palm tree. He didn't move. He stood there watching.

I felt Winston's strong hand grab mine, and he pulled me toward the water. I saw his enormous penis slap against his thigh as he yanked me into the waves. I was intimidated by its size, but I was beyond the point of no return.

The water was jet black in the darkness, and gray at the breakers. I was a bit worried about what might be out there. I think I hesitated just a bit.

"Don' ya stop, Rachel. I and I wan' ya in da water."

His eyes were gorgeous, even in the darkness. He was so tall and muscular. His dreadlocks gave him a fearful appearance, which was enticing to me. I couldn't say no. I followed him out.

The warm water wrapped around me like a blanket. The waves caressed my body. I had always loved the feeling of the water, and I let it take me. We walked until the water was to our knees, and he turned again to look at me. He took in my body with his eyes. I wanted him to look at me. I wanted him to see my body. He stepped into me and kissed me again. I surrendered myself to him as he pushed his tongue into my mouth. His immense manhood pushed against my thigh, and pressed against my mound.

I had this incredible rush of emotions. An epiphany in the water. Right there, with a naked stranger against me. I guess I had always wanted a man to want me...*only me*. I loved David. He was beautiful. Sexy. Amazing. But he didn't want *only me*, or me to want *only him*. He was in the shadows watching me cavort with a man we didn't know. I had this sense that Winston would never do that. Winston would want me all for himself. There was a primal presence to Winston. He would be assertive at all times. He would be strong and demanding. After all, he took me right from under the nose of my boyfriend. Winston would fight for me. If he caught me with another man, he would beat the man and take me home, probably slapping me around in the process. I would be his only. At this moment, that was immensely exciting. I *wanted to be wanted* like that. I wanted to be desired and possessed. That sounds awfully immature, I know. Very high school. Yet I was so young. My heart wanted to belong to just one man, and I suddenly realized that was a void in my life. What I had been missing was now plainly visible to me. Right at that moment, this all came to me. I understood the source of my dissatisfaction of late.

We stepped farther into the water, until it was to his waist and just below my breasts. I peeked back again, and David was still in the same spot. I couldn't see his eyes, but I knew they were riveted on me. I already knew the expression he was wearing. I had seen it before.

Winston ran his hands through my hair.

"Sistah, ya have the light skin, and ya look mixed. What ya be?"

"I'm mixed, black and white."

"Ya beautiful lady, Rachel."

He lowered his mouth to me, and we kissed again. His thick lips wrapped around mine, and his tongue darted in and out. He grabbed my behind, and pulled me against him. I could feel him grow, and it began to push against my abdomen. His hand reached around me and he pushed a finger inside me. I was swollen and ready, so I rasped at him, "I want you in me."

I felt his arms wrap around me, and then he lifted me. I wrapped my legs around him. I reached down to guide him, but was shocked by his size. He felt absolutely enormous, and I wasn't sure I could take that.

"Go slowly," I asked, as I guided the tip into me.

"Ya, sistah…I be gentle wit you."

Though he was powerful and muscular, he was surprisingly gentle. As he eased himself into me, he gauged my reactions. I realized he must have this reaction from every woman he was with. As I opened to him, I could feel myself stretching to take him in. I immediately felt the intense pressure, and it was a joyous feeling. As he sank deeper into me, I could already feel the waves of pleasure taking me. But I wanted this to last.

I could not take it all inside me; it felt like I had reached my physical limit. I concentrated on relaxing, and then I felt him moving. He held my butt, and used that to pull me back and forth, closer to him and then away. With each gentle thrust, I was slowly stretching to take him more. I took his full lips into my mouth, and let the pleasure fill my body.

"Are ya okay, Rachel?" he asked.

"Yeah, it's so good, Winston. It feels so amazing."

And then he began to move with a bit more pace. He pushed just a bit more into me, but as he pumped in deep, I had to put my hand on his chest to let him know to not go deeper. He understood immediately…he was a very careful lover. He kept his strokes to just the right motion so that he wouldn't hurt me.

I couldn't hold back the pleasure any longer. He was so large and powerful, and it was so erotic to be in his manly arms, my orgasm tore through me despite my attempts to hold it back. It was a bone-breaking orgasm. I felt like it was ripping through my body and sending rushes of warmth into every single fiber. My bones, my muscles…even my hair felt electric. Coupled with the tropical waves of the ocean caressing my skin, it was an indescribable feeling. Never had I felt such an erotic rush of pleasure. I threw my head back and shouted out my ecstasy. My face bayed at the moon like a wolf in winter. I was nature and bliss…a wild creature of the night.

Soon, I realized I had lost myself again. I had to fight to return. Here I was, having sex with a man I had only just met, in the water of Montego Bay, in the tropical air of Jamaica. How odd I felt suddenly.

Winston's strokes had slowed. I pulled back to look at him.

"Ya okay den, Rachel?" he asked.

"Yeah, that was great. Go ahead, honey…give me what you want."

"Okay den," was all he said. And then he picked up the pace again. He was pulling me down onto him. The waves churned around me. While the water felt like it was washing away my lubrication, I knew I was making much more. I had opened enough to take him comfortably now, though he still felt massive inside me. I was at the very edge of pleasure and pain…and I liked it.

His thrusts became more demanding. He was forcing himself into me. Already the pleasure was beginning to align within me again. I felt undulations moving through me. The warm water was so soothing…like millions of fingers caressing my skin. I thought he was near his own orgasm, so I told him, "Go ahead, Winston…you can come in me."

"I not be ready for dat, Rachel. Let's move out to da beach."

He slipped out of me, and then I felt how open I was. I slid down to the sand under me, and I was already sore. I knew I would be very uncomfortable tomorrow, but I wanted that soreness.

We waded back to the sand. I realized the dry sand would quickly find its way inside me, so I held him to the wet sand, but far enough away so that the waves wouldn't overwhelm us. I lay down, and he was on top of me. As with Mark, his muscular body felt so good on me. It's an incredibly feminine feeling to have a muscular, masculine man on top of you. I guess Winston was like Mark to me, though his photo negative. Whereas Mark had very white, freckly skin and short red hair, Winston was dark and sleek, with thick dreadlocks, which now hung into my face.

He guided himself into me, and began to move again. The waves tickled my feet, so I wrapped them around him. I hooked my arms around his upper arms, and pulled him to me. He put his mouth on mine and began to thrust again. Those powerful thrusts sent instant burning electricity through my body. My feet held his muscular thighs and tight butt. Every muscle on his body seemed alive. His thickness threatened to break me.

So I was soon having my second, powerful orgasm. My head thrashed around in the wet sand. I shrieked out my joy, and twisted underneath him like a snake. His hips moved, and kept the pressure inside me. The orgasm seemed to go on forever, and I felt hot tears running down the side of my face.

As I descended from the heights of my rapture, I felt him pressing my hip with his hand. I rolled over, and he entered me from behind.

"Please…not too deep, Winston," I begged. I honestly feared he could hurt me in this position.

"I be gentle, sweet Rachel," he said. His accent was very erotic.

He held my hips and began to push himself back into me. I was *definitely* going to be sore the next day, but I wanted more. His strokes sent hot flames through me…and I was still tingling from my last orgasm. It was almost too intense…but I still wanted more.

From his motions, I could tell Winston was getting near to his own orgasm. I was so used to talking to David as he neared his, but for Winston I knew he wanted to concentrate. I could tell exactly what he needed. But I could not hold back my panting and grunts. And they were loud. As his thrusts became more urgent, I grunted and panted with fury. I knew I was near my next orgasm.

"Ah, Rachel, I come soon," he said in his lilting accent.

"Yeah, Winston, come in me," I shouted at him, though not wholly for him. I knew David would be intent on us.

As Winston began to twitch inside me, I felt electricity in my body. Crackling static raced from his thrusts, up to my brain, and down to my toes. I roared along with those jolts, and shouted out again. I felt his hot seed enter me in jets. I jerked and twitched and let the sparks inside me light up my mind. As the last seconds of my orgasm ran through me, I had no strength left. My face flopped down to the sand…I couldn't hold myself up.

Winston's thrusts tapered off, but did not stop on their own. I had to stop him, as I couldn't take any more. I pulled away from him, and rolled onto the sand, just as a warm wave washed across my body. I looked up at his long, muscular body, with his length hanging down in front of him. He looked so beautiful…so perfectly formed in the moonlight, as the water washed around his knees.

He lay down beside me, and I could hear his heavy breathing.

"Thank ya, Rachel darling," he said.

"It was amazing, Winston."

Then the responsibility of the moment hit me in a rush: David in the trees behind me; I was alone with a stranger on the beach. I felt vulnerable all at once.

"I have to get back to my hotel, Winston."

"Why don' ya stay with me tonight, darlin'?" he asked, rolling a bit toward me. "I and I make ya breakfast in de mornin'."

"No, I fly out early in the morning," I lied. "I have to get back."

"Is ya husband waitin' for ya, or should I walk ya back to de hotel?"

I paused. So, he knew the deal. Nothing got by him in that shack. I looked back and saw that David still waited for us near the palm tree.

"He's over there."

"Okay, I walk ya back to 'em."

We dressed, and then walked right to David. David moved as if to sink deeper into the shadows, but I called out to him.

"It's okay, David. Wait there."

As we approached, he stepped out of the shadows to regard us.

"Ya a lucky man, David," Winston said, "she an amazin' girl."

I stepped to David. Winston turned me, gave me a final kiss on my mouth, and walked cockily back to the shack. The music had stopped, and people were spilling out onto the beach.

I looked insecurely at David. He smiled. "You okay?" he asked, probably because of the look on my face.

"Yeah, I'm okay. Did you enjoy the show, David?" I have to admit I had more than a bit of ire in my tone. David didn't hear it.

"It was fantastic, Rachel. I came in the bushes."

"Glad you enjoyed it," I said, again with spite.

David didn't respond, and I was too tired and sore to make a scene right there. We walked back to our hotel in silence.

I suppose I should have talked to him then. I suppose I should have told him of my growing concerns…my disquiet at our lifestyle. Inside, I was still a young woman who dreamed of a family with the man I loved. White picket fence. Station wagon. That may sound overly quaint, but it was how I felt. I certainly had never dreamed of regular group sex.

But I didn't talk to him. I let it burn in me. Inside was a cauldron of anxiety and burgeoning anger. I felt myself seething at him. Why wouldn't he be repulsed by my actions in Jamaica? He took me to a beautiful tropical island, and I made love to another man while he ejaculated into the bushes. While I wasn't a woman who wanted a man to tell me what to do, I felt that a couple should set parameters for themselves and each other. A couple should have some boundaries. What type of family would we have if I were sleeping with random men whenever and wherever I wanted?

And I blamed David, though it was me in the water with Winston. Though he was beautiful, smart, and hardworking, I blamed David for my actions that night…and all other nights. Though he had given me confidence in myself and my work, I blamed him. Though he had given me my start in publishing, virtually handing me success, I blamed him.

Inside my head, David's image was faltering badly. He was no longer the perfect man of my dreams. Instead, he was a weak cuckold who didn't care what I said or did. Unfortunately, I felt a distance from him, and now considered him only temporary…a person who I would move on from when I was ready.

I began to seek out opportunities to be with other men. I began to ask David to take me places where I could have encounters. The Trojan had closed in December of '79, after an article in Playboy magazine mentioned it in a list of sex clubs. Soon, we saw police and photographers on the street waiting to harass people entering. The property was sold, and many of us waited impatiently for a new location.

But now I was out of sorts. I was unbalanced. I know this now—I can clearly see what boiled over inside of me. I wanted to punish David for what I felt inside me. I accused him in my heart for everything I felt, and condemned him with my actions.

I could not contain the feelings I had. Nor did I want to. I began to have episodes that I blanch at today. When they happened, I felt perfectly justified. Now, I don't recognize the person in these vignettes from my life. I was a child stamping her feet because she didn't get her toy.

In February of 1980, I had my first book reading. It was a black-tie event, and I had purchased a long black and indigo dress. In the auditorium we rented, I took the stage with quivering hands and a dry mouth. In the audience were magazine editors, book publishers, reporters from the major newspapers.

I read a selection of my poems. I shared my favorites. I received a standing ovation, and at the after-party we danced and drank and celebrated my success. But inside, I still burned. Inside I was not who I wanted to be. I smiled, shook hands, and accepted the kind praises of people I could only aspire to. Truman Capote kissed my hand. Though he had obviously had too many drinks, he slurred to me, "Your poem *Mother* made me cry, Rachel." I heard his Alabama twang clearly.

But what I really wanted was to hurt. Like a spoiled brat I wanted someone's attention. I guess that's all it was that I wanted. *His* attention.

I found a young, slender, blonde-haired busboy. He couldn't have been more than nineteen. I didn't ask. I made eye contact with him. When he smiled at me I approached him.

"Is there something I can get you, ma'am?" he asked.

"What's your name?" When I spoke, I realized I, too, was a bit drunk.

"Michael."

"Michael, follow me." He didn't say a word as I took his hand. I pulled him out of the banquet room, down a long, narrow hallway. I found a private bathroom.

I pulled him inside and locked the door.

He didn't hesitate for a second, and probably knew what had I wanted all along. Our mouths were on each other instantly. He began to peel off his clothes.

"Help me with my dress," I commanded, turning my back to him. He unzipped me, and I slid out of it. It was Italian, after all, and I wasn't about to let it get dirty.

When he was naked, I finally had a good look at him. He was too slender...more than I would have liked normally, and very white-skinned. Still, his lean body was attractive, and his stomach muscles were tight.

He pushed me up against the sink and lowered himself down to his knees. He pushed his mouth roughly against my sex, forcing a gasp out of me. He was aggressive, and I wanted it that way. He moved his tongue over me, tasting my body. I was hot for him, but not because I wanted him. The anger made my nerves on edge, and I was ready quickly.

I pulled him up and took him in my mouth. He swelled instantly. He was young, so I was careful not to make him too excited. I took him slowly, carefully. I wanted him rigid but not near climax.

I stood up and slid my butt onto the cold, porcelain sink. He stepped up to me. I was ready, so it didn't hurt when he roughly stabbed himself into my sex. I wanted that. I wanted him to take me and possess me, if only for this brief moment.

I put my hand on his very tight butt, and pulled him against me. His youthful body looked pasty in the poor bathroom lighting. But he felt young and hungry, and I encouraged him.

"C'mon, Michael, fuck me."

He pushed himself into me with all he had. His hardness in me woke my body...pulled me away from my cares and my distrust of my life and relationships. While he was in me, I didn't care that I was in love with a cuckold. I didn't care that my man wouldn't claim me or take control of our lives.

As I began my orgasm, Michael climaxed suddenly.

"Uh, oh God!" he grunted, and then a torrent of hot stickiness was inside me. My orgasm faded quickly.

He slid out of me, and I cleaned myself up. As he dressed, Michael had the nerve to ask me, "Was it good for you too?"

"Sure," I lied.

Back out to the party, I saw David, but I didn't go to him. Instead, I found Keiko.

"Hi, honey, where have you been?"

"I just had to use the bathroom." She looked at me knowingly.

That night was the first in a string of random encounters. I know now that I was hurting, wanting David to validate me…validate our love. When he didn't, and in fact seemed to enjoy how things were, the pain in my heart pushed me to act in ways I never could have imagined. I sought validation in the arms of strangers.

One night, David and I ordered Chinese food. I blew the deliveryman for a tip, while David masturbated just feet from us.

On a beautiful spring morning, we took the ferry from Battery Park to see the Statue of Liberty. I met a handsome Turkish man as we neared Ellis Island, and I let him have me in the bushes, with Lady Liberty watching out for us above.

I kept expecting David to finally say, "Enough!" Maybe even call me a whore and beat up my random lovers. Nothing. He would only pleasure himself or take me when we got home. I knew we were on a path that was unsustainable. A crash was on the horizon.

I n March of 1980, the Warehouse opened in the Bronx. The Warehouse was so named as it was, indeed, a converted warehouse. While that sounds cold and ugly, in reality this was a magnificent club, and probably my favorite from this period. Though a bit farther, the distance from Manhattan-proper provided a much larger and more luxurious location. The Warehouse had rooms for all flavors of activities. Though I was not into BDSM, it had a well-stocked Torture Room (that was, after all, its name), including cages, whips of all kinds, candles, and any manner of punishing sex toys. Its sex cubicles were much larger, and there was even an observation platform that allowed people to walk around the top of the rooms and look down onto the activities. No more bunching up at the door to watch. There were also more private rooms, if that was your preference. Everything in Manhattan is about limited space…even the most luxurious apartments are small compared to homes most Americans live in. The Warehouse had space to spare.

David, Mark, Keiko, and I were there the evening it opened, and indeed there was a Middle Eastern man who claimed to be the owner of the place. He greeted us as we arrived. He called himself "The Sheikh." I thought he was a loon myself, and I still think he was more of a front for the real owners, whoever they might be. The man I met didn't seem to have enough sense to put together an operation of this kind.

As we sat in the spacious bar enjoying drinks, Keiko lowered her voice and spoke seriously to me.

"Honey, what's wrong? You've been acting…distant lately. Are you okay?"

"Yeah, I'm okay. Never better. How have I been acting distant?"

"Well, I never see you anymore. You never call. We hardly talk. I miss you, honey." She smiled at me, and I think she had a bit of pain on her face.

"I'm sorry…David and I have been working a lot on our writing. I just hardly have time for anything lately. I'm nearly done with my novel, and I'm putting together another poetry collection. Just so much to do."

She put her hand on mine. "Rachel, it's me. I can see there's something else. When you guys came back from Jamaica, I could sense something different inside you. It's okay if you don't want to talk about it, I guess, but I wish you would."

Was I that obvious? Still, I lied. "Keiko, I promise…nothing's going on. I think my head is just filled with my writing. Plus, I have a deadline looming. I have to finish my novel by the end of April, and Stella is pestering me about my poems. I have a lot to do and I'm behind."

"Okay, honey," she squeezed my hand, "glad to hear it. I have missed you a lot. I hope I can see you sometime. Mark and I are planning a trip to London next month…I love London in the spring. Maybe you and David can go with us? We'd love to spend some time with you guys."

I felt bad that her eyes looked so hopeful, but I wasn't in the mood to travel with anybody. While I did have writing deadlines, I was actually nearly complete. My words were obfuscation. I felt like my life was about to take a different direction very soon. I just didn't know where or how.

"Yeah, I'll definitely talk to him. Would love to spend some time with you. I only saw a bit of London when we went, and I'd love to see more." At the time I felt no guilt for lying to her. I feel bad now, though, looking back. She had been so sweet and kind to me, and I was giving her the cold shoulder in return.

She still looked at me, and perhaps sensed that I wasn't really telling the truth. She gave me a wan smile, and changed the subject. She and I talked more, and I sipped Mai Tais. I think I got a bit tipsy after a few. Keiko wanted to see the entire place, so she led me around on a self-guided tour, fresh drinks in hand.

As we wandered, we found ourselves on the landing overlooking the cubicles below. Whereas once I was rather startled by all the shenanigans that happened at a swing club, I was now seasoned—nothing really surprised me any longer.

Keiko, I think, naturally picked up on my distance as we walked around. Usually, she would hold my hand…like a schoolgirl showing her bestie something. Now there was just a bit of distance between us, and though she stayed by my side she didn't touch me. I think our spark was flickering. Would it go out soon?

I remember looking down and seeing three people in bed together, and remember thinking that it just didn't seem that unique any longer. We had all engaged in sex together numerous times, plus several trips to the Trojan previously. Whereas once it seemed so dirty and taboo, it now seemed routine, mundane even.

Keiko and I walked along the upper landing for a while. We talked, and even snickered now and then at what we saw. When we reached the far side, we saw a much older, paunchy man with a girl, Valerie, whom we knew to be a pro. Though he obviously wasn't doing much for her, she played it up very well, and made him feel like a champ.

"Oh yeah, Frank…give it to me…you're so good!"

I imagined that it was an occupational skill to make your employer feel like he was doing a great job. Observing as we were, we couldn't imagine that his ministrations were pleasuring her much. Still, I wouldn't fault either of them. He obviously wanted a young, beautiful woman to bed. She obviously wanted to be paid for her services. I don't fault anybody who uses a pro, nor do I understand why it is illegal. Still, it was a bit humorous to watch.

As we reached the end, it struck me that Mark and David hadn't been near us for a while. That wasn't unusual, as we all liked to roam around and fill our eyes. As well, this place was much larger than the Trojan, and it seemed you could get lost quite easily. It was a shopping mall of lust, if you like, and lots of shops to roam through.

As we moved back across the landing and back toward the stairs, we took our time and watched bits of a few more encounters. In one room, two women pleasured each other as a man watched them, masturbating himself. I had a wistful moment standing there, watching. In that instant I missed my encounters with Keiko. I looked over to her, hoping to perhaps see the same feeling in her, but she was focused on the two girls. I guess it excited her. Disappointment ran through me when I saw she wasn't thinking the same about me. Maybe our distance was too much to cross.

After a couple of empty rooms, we were just about to the stairs when I saw two men and a woman in the last room. The room was heavily decorated in red and gold. Though I could only see their backs, I knew instantly it was David and Mark. David and Mark were contrasts of each other in many ways. David was tanned and had dark, tousled hair. Mark was broad and heavily muscled, with straight red hair, now growing back out.

There was a slender, blonde white girl, and they were each on either side of her. Mark was kneeling beside her head, and she was taking him in her mouth. My David was hunched over her, pushing himself inside her. Both were silent, though the woman was grunting and breathing heavily. She was enjoying them, and I knew how she felt, having been there many times.

I watched for a while, oddly curious. I watched David and Mark moving in and out of her. When they switched positions, I looked over at Keiko, and she seemed captivated by the scene below, never taking her eyes off them. When I looked back down, Mark was giving her a strong pounding, and her body jerked with each thrust. He was physically so strong that he was scooting her up the bed. David had to reposition a couple times to keep himself in her mouth.

As the woman began to breathe more forcefully and her eyes began to lose focus, David put his face down on her large, heavy breasts, and then reached his arm to put pressure on her clitoris. That worked, and she almost immediately began to moan…a deep, rasping moan. Mark kept hitting his hips against her hard, and I knew she was flying in her orgasm.

I'll never know what changed inside of me in that moment. I'll never understand why I behaved as I did. I had seen similar things numerous times. I had seen David have sex with other women, and I'd had sex with numerous men…more men than David had women. Lately, I had been sleeping with random people, all while David watched or even when he was not around.

Yet at that moment I felt I was done with it all. Finished. I was no longer getting what I had been getting, if that makes sense. I was no longer feeling the desire to be there. The desire was gone. No more sweaty palms. No more quickening heart. In fact, a jealous rage boiled up inside me.

Perhaps that rage had been there all along, just below the surface. Perhaps I had never put my mind around the things we did. Was that it? While I enjoyed our numerous encounters, and I always had the most intense orgasms, was I really never happy? Or was that my mind playing tricks on me, and justifying my next action. I'll never know.

I took the last drink of Mai Tai, and then hurled the empty glass down into the cubicle where they made love. It smashed next to Mark, though I was aiming for David. Glass flew everywhere. Shocked faces looked up at me from all around.

"Go ahead, fuck her, you bastard! Fuck that whore! Why don't you fuck Mark when you're finished?" I had shrieked these words, and my surprising volume made my own ears ring.

I felt Keiko grab my arm, but I ripped it from her. I didn't even look at her as I stormed down the stairs. All eyes were on me, even as I moved to other rooms. When I reached the front door, I took my wrap from the peg, threw open the door, and then kicked it closed behind me.

The dramatics weren't necessary…I would've never been allowed back just for throwing the glass. Still, I felt immensely empowered at that moment. I felt like I had just turned a new corner.

A corner…or hit a wall? Slammed headfirst into the wall, more like it. I don't know what you call it. I knew something had to change. I knew I had taken the last drink from the chalice of the life. I had seized control of something in that very moment. Sometimes little things can be big things, if you understand what I mean. Something as small as smashing a glass was a pivot-point on which my life turned. Or spun. Turn implies a deliberate direction, which I did not have at this point.

Or perhaps more precisely, I had just jumped off another bridge, and was plunging into another unknown darkness, which would now envelop me. Or would I grow wings and fly? I didn't know.

I walked out to the street and hailed a cab.

Hadn't I been here before? All alone, walled off from everybody else? How many times had I done this? Too often, perhaps. But it was different this time—this I knew with every fiber of my being. I refused to see anybody for about two weeks. I didn't answer the phone. I didn't answer the door. I stayed home, only going out a couple times for food.

I worked.

The weather turned cold, which helped me avoid distractions. I finished my novel, and had nearly completed another collection of poems. I wrote almost the entire day, which is something I can no longer do. I produced some of my best writing. I think the anger and pain poured out of me and into my work. Many still consider this period my very best, but I can't even read these works...all I see is the pain and rage I felt at this time of my life.

When I showed up at Stella's office, she greeted me warmly. She hugged me, and kissed me on the cheek. I was now one of her bestsellers, but I also knew it was more than that.

"I was worried about you, Rachel. David has called me a couple of times, asking if I had seen you. I thought perhaps you left the area."

"No, I'm just keeping to myself."

She must've seen it on my face. "Did David hurt you, honey?" she asked in a lowered voice, stepping closely to me. Her maternal protectiveness wanted to shield me. She stank of cigarettes.

"No, but I think I'm through with him. I probably need to spend some time alone."

"Nothing wrong with that." She put her arm around me, and kissed me on the cheek again.

I showed her my new work, and she spent some time reading it over. She started with the poems.

"For a girl who didn't want to write love poems, you certainly wrote some beauties!" she teased. It was true: despite all the changes going on in the world and the upcoming elections, I had turned my poetic drive to focus on love and relationships, if only for now.

"I can really feel the passion in these words..." she continued. "I really think there are some gems in here. Your best, perhaps. I think we can move this. I'll call George and let him know I have more. We spoke recently, and he was hoping to get more from you."

"Thanks, Stella." At this point, I knew I couldn't hide my inner sadness. She regarded me with a sidelong look, and then looked at my other bundle.

"Tell me about this novel you wrote. I didn't expect that. What drove you to write a novel?" She opened the package and took out my manuscript. I'd had it typed professionally, and was very proud of my presentation.

"It's a bit of a dark love story. A young woman falls for a man who is...different...in need of love but unable to appreciate it." Again, her eyes shot up to mine. "It's not autobiographical," I lied. It was definitely based on my life, though I changed enough to avoid any hurt feelings.

"How does it end?"

"It's not a happy ending, but she finds herself in the final equation."

She read the first couple pages as we sat in her office, then put the bundle down on her desk. We faced each other again.

"I'll have to read over the novel, Rachel. I usually take a couple of months to review work like that, and I send it to a couple of readers. It might be a bit."

"It's okay, Stella, take your time. I just had to get these words out of my heart and mind so I could move on to other things."

"I understand, honey. Most great art comes from pain." She gave me a knowing look. "I'll let you know as soon as I can. Are you still at the same number?"

"Yes, for now. If I move, I'll give you forwarding information."

We talked for a bit more, and before I left she showed me the framed cover of my first collection on her wall. I felt so proud to be on that wall next to the literary legends she represented. She also gave me my latest royalty check, which was greatly appreciated. It was enough to last me the entire year, and that gave me a strong sense of comfort... something in short supply lately.

I left her office, and walked. I hadn't been out for a while, and the day had turned sunny, if a bit breezy. It felt good to be outside. Manhattan is made for walking, and my heels hitting the pavement energized me. I stopped for a quick lunch at a diner, and then walked more. I window-shopped a bit, but honestly my mind was distant.

As I walked down 5th Avenue, I found myself near a familiar storefront. It was Mandy's, though they were taking down the sign as I arrived. I spoke to the two men doing the work.

"When will Mandy's reopen?" I asked.

"It won't. Out of business. Going to be a Levi's store, I've heard."

I stood outside the empty storefront. I could see my reflection in the glass. I regarded myself carefully. It had not been that long ago that I first entered this store, and yet so much had happened...a lifetime of events had transpired between visits here. I looked at my face. I looked into my eyes. A whole new woman stared back at me. A better woman? No, not necessarily. Or perhaps I was, just based on which side of things you were considering.

I was definitely more grown up. I had gone from a shy, awkward girl to a professional author and independent woman. I had moved from the home of my now deceased parents into my own place on the gorgeous Upper West Side. I was soon to publish some of my best work. My life was almost unrecognizable. The young girl who danced into Mandy's that night last year would not even understand the woman I was today.

So what would the butterfly tell the caterpillar, if it could? I think it would say, "You are blessed with never-ending sunrises. Those sunrises are for you to enjoy. Stop wasting time regarding the butterfly, as much as it is your future self. While that is you, it is also not you. You are a hundred thousand events along the path to that change; you are not merely endpoints. You must make the most of the journey. While a caterpillar, enjoy every crawling step you make, and every leaf you eat. Wonder in amazement at the transformation at bay within yourself. You are kinetic capability, and as such you are a wonderment of nature. When you transfigure, revel even in your painful reshaping. Feel every inch of that agonizing growth, for it too is a part of you. As you pull yourself out of your chrysalis, shake off the moisture and sleep vigorously. Spread those new wings and absorb the warmth and sunshine with them. Stretch them. Move them. And then fly with them. Let loose your spirit and fly as hard and as far and as fast as you can. You earned that right. You deserve to experience that flight in all its fury. Fly with all you have, because that is what you were meant to do. There is no other purpose to you, after all, than to do what you do the very best way you know how. Anything less and you might as well have stayed a caterpillar.

I took a cab to the Upper West Side.

When I arrived at my building, I saw David standing near my doorman. They had been talking, but when I approached he turned to face me. He stood tall and square-shouldered. He watched me approach. His hands were stuffed in the pockets of his black overcoat, and he seemed a bit nervous. Cool veneer gone.

"Hi, Rachel. I hope you don't mind. You haven't been answering. I was hoping to catch you out and about."

Despite all of my conflicted feelings from the last few months, especially those in the last two weeks, I was happy to see his face. My mind told me that I was moving on with my life, but my heart wasn't so sure.

"It's okay, David. How are you?" I smiled. He put his arms around me, and kissed me on the cheek. I pulled away before he got too comfortable there.

"I'm okay…I've been missing you…more than I can say. I wanted to talk to you…a little bit at least."

"So talk." I felt a sense of power, but I also had to avoid eye contact, lest I fall into his charcoal eyes. I was going to be strong, no matter the cost. My wings were unfurled and on display. I moved them in the sunshine.

"I wanted to tell you that I understand your feelings exactly. I know this life isn't for everybody. It's rare that someone can put up with all that goes on. I am so sorry if what I did hurt you. I never wanted that."

"I know, David, and you warned me upfront. I'm sorry I lost control as I did. That was uncalled for. I guess I finally reached my breaking point with it all…and it happened suddenly."

"No, it's perfectly understandable." I made eye contact with him, and quickly felt myself softening. Oh my God, he was a beautiful man. The wind was sending his hair into his black eyes, and I think he looked more desirable to me than ever. "I just want you to know that if you don't want to be with me, that's okay…but I hope we can remain friends."

"I'd like that, David," I said, though it was a lie.

How could I see him as a friend, after all? If I saw him by himself, I knew I'd find myself falling for him again. It was all I could do now, while the wounds were still fresh, to keep from jumping into his muscular arms and begging him to take me back.

And if I saw him with another? How could I face that eventuality? See him with a beautiful young woman? See him kiss her and hug her? See them develop a new life together? How about seeing Mark and Keiko? It would be too much. I knew it was completely unrealistic. Both options were impossible. I had to cut the cord and have a life away from him…from them…from the life.

So I stood there, facing him, working my calmest façade and most neutral demeanor. I felt the wind whipping my hair, and flushing my cheeks. I tried to look as frank as possible, even though I was the least sincere person in New York. I measured my smile. I held my posture. I was playing the part of iron, when I was really a marshmallow.

"There's one more thing, Rachel. If you have a second more," he said, looking into my eyes.

"Sure, David. What is it?" I made the mistake of turning my face up to him completely. And there was that face. That manly, chiseled, perfect face. Those eyes. The warmth. He still needed a shave. I could smell his cologne and his outdoors aroma. My heart started fluttering again.

"I'm leaving for Costa Rica tomorrow. I'm spending nearly a month down there. I'm doing some deep-jungle trekking, and working with a crew for a big spread on the regional birds."

"Oh, that's nice...how exciting!" Honestly, I couldn't picture myself being deep in the jungle—give me a hotel with white linen sheets any day. "Have a safe trip, David." I tried to be cheery, but I could feel the cracks in my expression. I'll wager he probably could too.

He was fidgeting in his overcoat pocket, and then he pulled out a small black box. Velvet-covered box.

My heart began slamming in my chest. Tears burned in my eyes immediately, and then ran down my cheeks like a river. Calm, neutral demeanor gone in an instant.

"I know this isn't how it should happen. And I don't want you to answer me right now, Rachel. I want you to know that I love you and want you in my life...always." He opened it, and showed me a beautiful diamond that glittered in the sunshine. A thousand sparkling rays of sunlight. "I know things are not what you would want in a relationship. I know I'm not the type of man you ever expected to be with. I know you don't approve of the life and that it doesn't fit your heart. Yet think about the love we have shared. The good times and the tears. Rachel, think about the future we could have together."

I started to protest, but my stolid appearance was shattered, and I was a weeping girl. I wanted to tell him...I *had* to tell him...but I couldn't do it. The words weren't forming. I could only cry. He stopped me.

"Please...don't say anything. Just take this ring. You can sell it... throw it away...give it to a friend...whatever. Or just keep it. When I return from Costa Rica, I'll call you. If your heart hasn't changed, then we're still friends and this never happened." He pulled my hand up, opened it, and pushed the still-open box into the palm of my hand. A tear splashed onto it. "But if there's still love for me inside you, maybe you can keep it alive. Maybe we can rebuild what we had. I'm willing to work on things, Rachel. I'm willing to compromise. I don't know how much, but I'll do what I can. These feelings I have had...I never felt I could change them until I met you. I never *wanted* to change until I met you."

I was still staring dumbly at the ring. After a pause, I looked up to him, blinking out the tears. I couldn't say anything.

"Okay, I'd better run," he said. He quickly bent over to kiss my cheek, but I turned my face to him and kissed him on the lips. He winked at me and then walked up the street to the subway station. I stood there and watched him walk away.

Brent, my doorman, woke me from my spell. "You okay, Miss Rachel?"

"Yeah, I'm fine." I looked at my hand and I was still holding the box, palm up.

"Can I get the elevator for you?" He was already pulling open the door for me.

"No, I got it. Thanks." I turned and walked into the building.

I think every girl dreams of her proposal. I think I had visions of mine with horses, castles, and a cast of thousands all cheering. Or maybe under the Eiffel Tower, or on a gondola in Venice. Marching bands. I didn't expect to be handed a ring out on a windy, cool day in Manhattan.

And, yet, it was David. From the moment I had set eyes on him he had captured my heart. He was brilliant. He was dedicated to his work. He was gorgeous. He was a gentleman. Yet he was a man who'd had sex with men and women in every possible combination, across the world. That's untenable, right? How can a marriage survive like that?

Still, I had enjoyed so much of it. I had explored things sexually I would have never imagined. I had been places I had never thought possible. David had been the catalyst to my writing career, which was now changing my life and allowing me to share my art with the world.

And he had been there for me when I lost my father. He was as much my family as anybody else on the planet, as were Keiko and Mark.

What would I do about Keiko? I had not yet even begun to tackle my relationship with her and Mark. That was a further complexity that, as a young woman, I didn't feel equipped to handle.

I took the elevator up to my floor, entered my apartment, and sat down at the kitchen table. I opened the box again, and sat staring at the ring.

Whatever course my life would take would be determined by the next decision I made.

I fluttered my wings, and considered their ability to hold me in flight. Was I ready? Should I jump and see if they would lift me to the heavens?

The End